PRICE   Price, Tirzah.

Pride and
premeditation.

$17.99   05/21   21

DATE

Jane Austen Murder Mystery

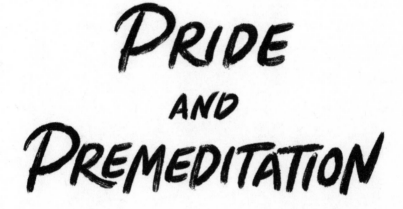

PRIDE
AND
PREMEDITATION

A JANE AUSTEN MURDER MYSTERY

PRIDE AND PREMEDITATION

A JANE AUSTEN MURDER MYSTERY

TIRZAH PRICE

An Imprint of HarperCollinsPublishers

HarperTeen is an imprint of HarperCollins Publishers.

Pride and Premeditation
Copyright © 2020 by HarperCollins Publishers

www.epicreads.com

Library of Congress Cataloging-in-Publication Data

Names: Price, Tirzah, author.
Title: Pride and premeditation / Tirzah Price.
Description: First edition. | New York : HarperTeen, [2020] | Series: Jane Austen murder mysteries ; 1 | Audience: Ages 14 up. | Audience: Grades 10-12. | Summary: Seventeen-year-old aspiring lawyer Lizzie Bennet seeks to solve a murder before her rival Mr. Darcy beats her to it.
Identifiers: LCCN 2020039334 | ISBN 978-0-06-288980-5 (hardcover) — ISBN 978-0-06-311644-3 (special edition)
Subjects: CYAC: Lawyers—Fiction. | Murder—Fiction. | Characters in literature—Fiction. | Mystery and detective stories.
Classification: LCC PZ7.1.P75294 Pr 2021 | DDC [Fic]—dc23
LC record available at https://lccn.loc.gov/2020039334

Typography by Corina Lupp

21 22 23 24 25   PC/LSCH   10 9 8 7 6 5 4 3 2 1

❖

First Edition

To all the obstinate, headstrong girls forging new paths.

"There is a stubbornness about me that never can bear to be frightened at the will of others. My courage always rises at every attempt to intimidate me."

—*Pride and Prejudice*
by Jane Austen

"Instinct is a marvelous thing. . . . It can neither be explained nor ignored."

—*The Mysterious Affair at Styles*
by Agatha Christie

ONE

*In Which Our Heroine Is Wronged,
and Acquires a New Lead*

IT IS A TRUTH universally acknowledged that a brilliant idea, conceived and executed by a clever young woman, must be claimed by a man.

Elizabeth Bennet stood in the offices of the optimistically named law firm of Longbourn & Sons and fixed her father's junior partner, Mr. Collins, with her fiercest glare. However, Mr. Collins just ignored her as he regaled the firm's employees with the details of *her* escapades as though they were his own.

"I knew from the very moment Mrs. Davis pleaded her case with us that something was not quite right about her story. Her husband accused of embezzlement, and she, a clerk's wife, dressed like a baroness?" He let out a loud, abrasive laugh that made Lizzie's head ache.

Mr. Collins was too preoccupied with his own importance to pay attention to something as "trivial" as the state of a woman's clothes! If Lizzie were to demand he close his eyes and name the color of her own spencer, she doubted that he'd be able to. (A fine emerald brocade, let the record show. Her older sister, Jane, had once said the jacket's color made Lizzie's eyes look bright.)

Lizzie's father, Mr. Bennet, listened to Mr. Collins's account with the patience of a man who had a lot of experience in enduring long-windedness. "And what happened next?"

"I made the appropriate inquiries, but still had my suspicions. I called upon Mrs. Davis three days later to question her some more. At one point, she became so flustered that she excused herself, allowing me time to, ah, glance upon the writing desk. I hoped that I might find some stray sum sheet, or letter . . ."

Mr. Collins fumbled, and Lizzie raised her eyebrows. "Is that so?" she asked.

No one paid Lizzie any attention, and Mr. Collins continued. "In fact, I found a rather intimate note, signed 'J.A.' I found that highly suspicious, so I questioned the neighbors and learned that Mrs. Davis stepped out at the same time every Tuesday and Thursday afternoon. She often didn't return for hours. I followed her the next day, and that's when I discovered the identity of J.A.—John Alston, her husband's boss!"

Lizzie's dear friend Charlotte Lucas gasped audibly from

her desk. As Longbourn's secretary, she was privy to many scandalous details of the firm's various cases, but they were rarely as salacious as this. It'd been precisely Lizzie's reaction when *she'd* discovered that Mrs. Davis had been having an affair with the very man who'd accused her husband, James, of embezzlement.

"It was all a deviously clever setup! And now I turn the case over to you, sir, as barrister, to prove our client's innocence and demand justice." With great ceremony, Mr. Collins handed over the letters Lizzie had pilfered from Mrs. Davis's writing desk and gave a slight bow to his audience.

Longbourn & Sons was not a very large firm—it consisted of her father, boorish and barely twenty-year-old Collins, three other solicitors, two clerks, and Charlotte, the secretary. None-theless, Lizzie seethed as she watched Collins publicly claim credit for evidence that she herself had discovered.

"I am going to wring. His. Neck," she muttered, just loudly enough for Charlotte to cast a concerned glance in her direction.

"The important thing is that an innocent man will soon be free," Charlotte said.

"I suppose."

"Lizzie, you know that in all likelihood . . ."

Charlotte trailed off, knowing that she was dredging up something Lizzie knew all too well: She could not argue Mr. Davis's case herself, no matter how much she longed to be called to the bar. It was no matter—even if the courts would allow for a woman barrister, first she would have to convince her father that such a calling was appropriate for his beloved seventeen-year-old daughter.

"I know," Lizzie said. "But that doesn't mean he had any right to steal my work!"

Collins accepted handshakes and claps on the shoulder from the other solicitors and clerks while Mr. Bennet studied the letters. Gradually, the room quieted again as they waited for Mr. Bennet to pronounce his judgment.

"This is good, Collins, very good. I will speak to the magistrate straightaway." He paused heavily, then added, "Of course, our client is not innocent."

"Yes, he is. I've just told you, sir." Collins smiled at Mr. Bennet in a condescending manner that Lizzie positively loathed.

Lizzie's greatest strength was the quickness of her mind, but her greatest weakness, according to her mother, was the quickness of her tongue.

"Our client is *Mrs.* Davis," she proclaimed loudly, unable to stand it any longer. "And *she* is most certainly guilty."

Truly, the amount of patience Lizzie had to exert in this office was immeasurable.

Collins should have been embarrassed by his fumble, but he didn't appear to be. In fact, he didn't even turn to acknowledge the young woman who corrected him. "Mr. Davis, Mrs. Davis, who cares. I should think that Mr. Davis would be so indebted to us for securing his release from prison that he'd be willing to pay us a small fortune."

"Don't count on it. The nature of marriage is mysterious, and besides, Mr. Davis may not have the funds." Mr. Bennet sighed.

"Papa, James Davis is the younger nephew of a baronet," Lizzie interjected. "By marriage, but . . . perhaps he will be grateful to the firm for keeping his relative's name out of the mud."

Lizzie let the suggestion dangle, enjoying the way that Collins's eyes bulged with shock. "How do you know that?"

"Mrs. Davis told me herself. Did she not mention that when you called?" Lizzie let her stare dig into Collins, hoping for some veil of regret or shame, but finding none, she turned back to her father and said, "It's quite marvelous, the things one hears when visiting Miss Lucas."

"Visiting Miss Lucas" was the code phrase that Lizzie and her father used when Lizzie helped out around the office. Longbourn & Sons, though well established and of good reputation, was not a flourishing business. Between Mr. Bennet's preference for studying the law rather than practicing it and his bumbling junior partner, the firm struggled, even with Lizzie's assistance behind the scenes.

"Very good," Mr. Bennet said. "Step into my office, if you please, Elizabeth."

Lizzie was all too glad to sweep past an irritated Collins and into her father's office. It was frightfully messy and her favorite room in all the world. It always smelled of ink and paper and rich pipe tobacco, which her mother strictly forbade her father from enjoying at home. The surface of the great oak desk was covered in books, papers, and a good number of half-empty inkpots. Although the mess itched at Lizzie's inclination for order, she loved everything that this room represented—knowledge, hard work, quick thinking, the pursuit of justice. The cases that unfolded in this room were far more fascinating to her than any drama that occurred in the drawing room.

"Papa," she began once they were seated, "Mr. Collins has been lying again."

"Of course he has. Do you think that I'd believe for an instant Collins would call upon Mrs. Davis? He doesn't have an enterprising bone in his body."

Lizzie smiled. Good, this was going to be easier than she'd thought.

"However, you mustn't goad him in front of the others, Elizabeth. He will be their superior one day, and it does no good to make him look a fool."

The smile slipped from Lizzie's face. This argument again. "Mr. Davis was going to hang, and Mr. Collins would've done nothing to stop it. I only told him because you were out, and the hearing is set for tomorrow."

"Is that the only reason?" her father asked.

6

Lizzie cast her gaze at a smear of ink on the wood of the desk. Her father was likely out of blotting sand again. She had better stop by the stationer on her way home. "No. I heard him say nothing was to be done as I came in—with *my* evidence—and I couldn't help it. Disagreeing with Mr. Collins is entirely too enjoyable."

"It is one thing to be right," Mr. Bennet said, "but it is quite another to always be proclaiming it."

"Anyone with half a brain could see that Mrs. Davis and Mr. Alston set poor Mr. Davis up, likely with the intent to marry once he was out of the way."

"And we know you have far more than half a brain."

"If that's the case, then you should hire me instead of some stranger."

Lizzie had intended to surprise her father, but he looked as if he had been expecting this change in topic. "Ah, you've been speaking to Charlotte?"

"I read the job advertisement myself," Lizzie said. "As your unofficial accountant and assistant, I must advise you that hiring another person is not in the firm's best financial interests right now."

He picked up a stack of contracts that Lizzie herself had proofed and set upon his desk for final approval and signatures. "If Collins is to become a barrister and spend all his time in court, that will leave us short a solicitor. Better to bring some-one on now, before we're shorthanded."

Lizzie ground her teeth so as not to say what she was really thinking: Collins was utterly useless. He was lazy and created more work than he shouldered. Lizzie and her father were constantly tidying up his messes. In her view, his failings as a solicitor—where he was merely expected to attend to legal matters outside of court—did not foretell success as a barrister, where he would be expected to represent clients in a court of law.

For whatever reason, her father refused to see the truth. It was as if he expected that attending an Inn of Court to become a barrister would transform Collins into a different man. Perhaps it was because Mr. Collins was the sole heir to the Bennet family business and much-diminished fortune. Perhaps it was simply because Collins was his cousin's son. Either way, when Collins had arrived on their doorstep with a benefactress and passable letters of recommendation, Lizzie's father took him in like the son he didn't have.

"But if you must hire someone now, why not me?" Lizzie pressed. "I already do much of the work, and I could act as an unpaid apprentice until we're turning a profit again and—"

"Elizabeth," her father interrupted, "I can't go against your mother's wishes where your future is concerned."

Both father and daughter sat up marginally straighter, as if simply mentioning Mrs. Bennet might summon her from thin air. The idea was quite absurd, since Lizzie couldn't remember her mother ever setting foot in Longbourn & Sons. The very act of entering the business might actually bring on one of those dizzy spells she was always on the verge of succumbing to.

"Mama means well," Lizzie said, which was really a generous way of saying Mrs. Bennet didn't know Lizzie at all. "But I don't wish to *marry* a barrister. I wish to be one. And I wish for your support, more than anyone's."

Mr. Bennet gifted Lizzie with one of his small, delighted smiles. Lizzie was certain she was the only one who saw this side of her father: lively and amused at small rebellion.

It was not spoken of, but it was no secret that Lizzie and Mr. Bennet had a special bond. Oh, her older sister, Jane, was lovely and polite and considerate and, if Lizzie were quite honest, the only one of the lot who would never embarrass their father. Her younger sisters, Mary, Lydia, and Kitty, were not interested in anything beyond the drawing room. Lizzie was certain that her father secretly wished she'd been born a boy, and while Lizzie had no complaints about being a young woman, sometimes she wished she weren't a young *lady*.

"It would be an unusual situation," Lizzie acknowledged. "But I'm seventeen now, and if I were your son, you wouldn't hesitate to offer me the position."

Mr. Bennet regarded her for a long moment, and Lizzie hardly breathed in the hope that he was considering her point of view. If he gave in on this one thing, then perhaps, *perhaps* he would allow her to one day train as a barrister. She would show up Collins in every way, if it would convince her father.

"I'm not overlooking your argument," he said finally. "Although your mode of persuasion relies a bit too heavily on pathos."

Lizzie would have laughed if their conversation had a different tone. Her father had been the first one to teach her about Aristotle's methods of persuasion—pathos, ethos, and logos. Pathos was a method of appealing to her father's emotions, which was exactly what she had been attempting to do. The barrister picked up on it, of course.

"Considering I have no authority or experience and cannot use ethos, I assume you would have me rely on logos," she said.

Mr. Bennet chuckled. "If you can convince me that I should hire you using logic and facts, then I shall consider it. Which is a good offer, considering how much your mother will berate me for doing so."

She wasn't sure if he was simply humoring her, but Lizzie began to mount an offense anyway. "I solved the Davis case! Mr. Collins took my work. I am *more* than competent."

"I assigned the case to *Collins*," her father countered. "No, prove to me you are suitable for this job, and leave your contempt for Collins out of it."

Lizzie turned this proposal over in her mind, torn between excitement at an opportunity and resentment that she must work doubly hard to prove herself worthy for something that Collins had merely been handed. She knew she should just accept it—it would be the best offer she would receive—but her instinct to argue kept her from doing so.

As if sensing Lizzie's inner turmoil, Mr. Bennet leaned across his atrociously cluttered desk and added, "I do appreciate you, and your work on contracts is invaluable. And who knows? Perhaps marrying a barrister—one day, in the far future—wouldn't be such a bad fate?"

Lizzie folded her arms across her chest. "I won't marry Mr. Collins."

Even Mr. Bennet looked terrified at the thought. "Oh heavens, no!"

Lizzie stopped at Charlotte's desk on her way out, pausing to adjust her bonnet and pull on her gloves.

"Is he sending you home?" Charlotte asked quietly.

"Not precisely." Lizzie knew that was where her father fully expected her to return. But she'd never convince him to hire her if she simply sat in her room and worked on her needlepoint. "He said that he'd hire me for the position, if I can convince him using *logic*."

"Well, that should be easy enough for you," Charlotte said, unflaggingly supportive.

Lizzie sighed. "The problem is that I've provided him with ample examples of why I am the best candidate. I do most of

Mr. Collins's work, I already know how the firm functions, I read most of the contracts. . . . What more must I do?"

Charlotte cast her gaze about for any lurking clerks and then whispered, "What if you take a peek at the incoming cases, the ones that haven't been assigned yet?" She slid open the drawer where she kept the inquiries for representation, filed by complaint type and sender. She waved Lizzie to come behind her desk and look for herself. "If you could find a few moderately difficult cases, preferably by those who could pay . . ."

"You're very sly," Lizzie said approvingly, and began flicking through letters. "This is why you're such an excellent secretary."

"I hardly think your father hired me for my ability to sneak about," Charlotte said.

"He hired you because he needed someone reliable and organized." Lizzie extracted a letter and scanned it before discarding it. Fidelity cases were so boring. "Now if only he'd extend his daughter the same consideration."

"Don't be so hard on him. I wouldn't work if I didn't have to, and if I had a father such as yours . . ."

"I know," Lizzie said, recognizing the longing in her friend's tone.

Charlotte was the daughter of a successful merchant and a beautiful woman from the West Indies. Their marriage had been quite the scandal at the time, but they passed away when Charlotte was just a baby and she was brought up by her father's business partner, a friend of Mr. Bennet's. She took the job at

Longbourn when she failed to find a husband by the age of twenty-three, and not only was she organized and capable, but she was a great confidante to Lizzie. "But think of this—how marvelous would it be if you and I both worked here?"

Charlotte smiled weakly back. "Quite marvelous. So find your perfect case."

But their plotting was halted by the sound of a male throat clearing behind them. "Miss Elizabeth. Rifling through the files again?"

Lizzie started guiltily and rose from her crouched position near the file drawer. Collins stepped forward and made an admirable effort of looking down at her, which was difficult as Lizzie had a good three inches of height on him. "Mr. Collins," she said flatly. She stared him down and wondered if he felt anything for what he had done earlier—embarrassment? guilt? remorse?

"Shouldn't you be home sewing?" he asked in a flippant tone. His satisfied smirk told Lizzie all she needed to know about his supposed guilt—or lack thereof. "Or perhaps performing other tasks befitting your . . . position?"

When she was very angry, Lizzie found it best to count something—anything in sight—until she calmed down. She picked the gleaming brass buttons on Collins's jacket—one, two, three, four, five, six, seven . . .

Ah, now she could respond.

"And what position would that be?" she asked.

"A lady, and an unmarried one at that."

"I hardly think that my sex or my marital status concerns you."

"Oh, but they might." Collins held Lizzie's gaze for longer than necessary, and Lizzie felt the greatest urge to try out some language she happened to overhear on one of her reconnaissance missions down by the docks. First, he had refused to do his job with Mrs. Davis, then he'd stolen her work without acknowledgment, and now he was implying some kind of budding relationship between them?

In the end, Lizzie chose insult by way of Shakespeare. It felt more dignified. "I do wish that we could become better strangers," she said coldly.

It took Collins a moment to register her jab, and his faux polite expression darkened into open resentment. He reached behind Lizzie and slammed the file drawer shut. "These files are the confidential business of Longbourn and Sons, Miss Elizabeth!"

Lizzie felt her cheeks redden. "My father—"

"Oh yes, let's go speak with your father about how you're meddling with the firm's business yet again."

Oh, he had her there. Mr. Bennet had told her to leave Collins out of her argument, and how would it look if she marched back into his office not five minutes later, complaining that he was getting in her way? Lizzie longed to say something smart to knock the disagreeable smile off his face.

Before she could come up with something clever, the front door of the office was thrown open with a dramatic bang. Lizzie, Collins, and Charlotte all looked in that direction and saw . . . no one. But wait—no. Lizzie looked down. A short boy with the grime of a street urchin but smartly attired in a jacket and cap caught sight of her. He snatched his threadbare hat from his head.

"Beggin' your pardon, misses," he gasped in between massive heaves for breath. "I didn't . . . mean . . . to startle . . ."

"Begone from these premises at once!" Mr. Collins thundered. Lizzie thought darkly it was likely the first time all week he had someone shorter than he to order about. "This is a respectable office of the law!"

"Oh, stand down, Mr. Collins," Lizzie said, hardly able to keep her smile in check. "He's here to see me."

"What business would *you* have with an urchin?"

"Business that doesn't concern you!" Lizzie glared at Collins again before gesturing to invite the boy into the office. "Come along, Fred."

Fred was still panting when Lizzie ushered him to a vacant desk in the corner, so Lizzie guided him to the chair and fetched a glass of water. She had met Fred a few months earlier and so admired his observational skills that she occasionally employed him to report information to her, particularly if any gentlemen were ever led down Bow Street by a Runner. Longbourn & Sons needed all the help they could get rustling up business, and knowing who had been arrested before it reached the society papers was very useful.

Fred drank the water in a series of quick gulps. Lizzie knew she should let him collect himself before pressing him for information, but he had never before intruded past the doors of Longbourn & Sons to seek her out. A rush of excitement flooded Lizzie, the very same rush she'd felt when she had called on Mrs. Davis and uncovered the letter to her lover. Perhaps she didn't need to access Charlotte's drawer of inquiries after all.

Even so, in all her excitement Lizzie never could have imagined that when the boy had caught his breath, he'd look up and say, "Miss, there's been a murder."

TWO

In Which Lizzie Forms a Plan

LIZZIE'S MIND WAS TUMBLING through possibilities. A murder case! This could be just the thing she needed. . . .

"All right, tell me everything."

"A gentleman by the name of Charles Bingley was taken to a magistrate this morning, at quarter to twelve. He was covered in blood."

"The charge?" Lizzie asked.

"Stabbin' his brother-in-law. A bloke by the name of George Hurst, apparently Bingley's sister is his wife. The way Bingley told it, he called on Hurst this morning but didn't wait for Hurst to come down. Went straight into his bedchamber, then he started hollering, and the valet rushed in to discover Hurst's body, and Bingley hunched over it."

Lizzie held up a hand to stop Fred from continuing. "They believe Bingley killed him right then and there? Were there any witnesses?"

"The butler and valet are saying he must have done it, miss, but they didn't witness the murder themselves. It was all chaos at the magistrate's. I did hear Hurst was stabbed with a fine penknife, and they're saying it must be Bingley's. Mr. Bingley claims Hurst was already dead and he tried to revive him, and that's why he was covered in blood. But let me tell you, he made for a frightful sight."

"I can only imagine," Lizzie murmured, but she was already mentally working through the case. "What did the magistrate have to say?"

"He didn't believe Bingley for a second. Ordered him to Newgate and declared there'd need to be a hearing."

"Excellent," Lizzie said, although of course it was not excellent for Mr. Bingley. "And Bingley—do you recognize the name, Fred? I have heard it socially, but what is his business?"

"Shipping," Fred noted. "He owns all of Netherfield Shipping. A fellow in the court said that Hurst worked for Bingley."

Interesting. Perhaps a business deal gone wrong? A family dispute? The facts were scant.

"You did very well, Fred," Lizzie said, and extracted a sixpence from her reticule. She gave it to him and said, "There will be more of that if you can provide me any further details on the case—gossip, even. Anything will help."

"Cheers, miss." Fred exited the office with a grin stretched across his small face.

Lizzie made a hasty departure herself, and once out on the busy street, she turned toward home. Her mother would prefer to hire a carriage to ferry her about town, but Lizzie relished the two-mile walk and the weak spring sunshine warming her face. The offices of Longbourn and the Bennets' home were both in Cheapside, a bustling neighborhood full of shops, merchants, and bankers, where there was always someone Lizzie knew ducking into a coffee shop or stepping out into the street. The atmosphere was overall pleasant and industrious, although it was the sort of neighborhood that the rich chose merely to visit but not to live in. Mr. Bennet would not hear of taking up residence in a quieter, more fashionable neighborhood, although Mrs. Bennet regularly begged him to consider it. The proximity to London's Central Criminal Court and his bookseller was too convenient.

As Lizzie walked the familiar route, she pondered. She got her best thinking done while walking the streets, muddy and messy as they were, and this case was puzzling. The law of the land declared that innocence had to be proven, but Lizzie often found herself needing to be convinced of wrongdoing. She longed to know the context of this case—what was so urgent that Bingley had entered Hurst's bedchamber? Where had Mrs. Hurst been? What was the family relationship like? What was their standing in society?

Lizzie did not balk at these questions. Her father told her to convince him she was worthy of a real job by using logic, but Lizzie knew that if men allowed themselves to be swayed by pure logic, women would be in Parliament! No, Lizzie would have to show not only that it made logical sense for her to fulfill the position but that she was more *capable* than any man.

And what better way to do that than by taking on a murder case?

The Bennets lived on Gracechurch Street, and when Lizzie arrived home she was met at the front door by Jane, who took her bonnet and gloves and asked, "Well? How did it turn out?"

It took Lizzie a dizzying moment to realize that her sister was asking about the Davis case. Lizzie was already well beyond that, but she collected her thoughts and said, "Papa will take my evidence before the judge this afternoon."

"Splendid," Jane said, smiling with satisfaction.

"Although it won't be *my* evidence."

Understanding dawned slowly. "Mr. Collins?"

Lizzie nodded and quickly explained before concluding, "I shouldn't have breathed a single word to him."

"You had no other choice. A man's life was at stake, and Collins was doing what he does best—bungling everything."

Lizzie smiled. "Why, Jane! How very unladylike of you to say so."

"A lady never lies," Jane stated with a faux haughty tone she shared only with her sister, which made Lizzie grin, albeit briefly.

"Papa knows the truth," Lizzie said, then sighed. "And I suppose that should be all that matters. Except, oh, Jane! There's news. A murder!"

"Good Lord!" Jane cried in horror. "Who? Someone we know?"

"No, a Mr. Hurst," Lizzie said, and quickly shared what she knew of the case.

"That's positively horrendous," Jane said. "That poor family."

"Yes, the poor family," Lizzie agreed, feeling a stab of guilt that her first reaction had been excitement, not sorrow. It was rather easy to forget, in the flurry of the moment, that a murder meant more than questions unanswered and a case to be solved and collected upon. It meant grief, funeral arrangements, and lives upended.

So Lizzie tried to temper her tone when she said, "However . . . a case such as this will definitely demand legal advice," and proceeded to tell her sister about their father's agreement to consider Lizzie for the job if she could prove herself capable of the challenge, with the caveat of finding her own case.

"And naturally you decided to find a murder case?" Jane asked, incredulous. "How does one even go about investigating such a matter as this?"

"By collecting information," Lizzie said with a determination that surprised even herself.

She did not wait long to begin her reconnaissance—just until dinner. In true dramatic fashion, Mrs. Bennet had kept to her room for the afternoon, emerging only in time for the family to be seated.

"No Mr. Collins tonight?" she said when she entered the dining room. "Mr. Bennet, are you not passing along my invitations?"

"No, my dear," he replied from the head of the table. "I spend my entire day with the man. I don't need to suffer his presence at home."

"Have you no compassion for your daughters?" Mrs. Bennet gestured broadly. Jane's face was turned down so that no one could see her amused smile, but Lizzie had no such concerns. Mary looked rather bored, and Kitty and Lydia were whispering, ignoring their mother completely.

"Come now. I love my daughters. That's precisely why I do not want to inflict Mr. Collins's presence upon them."

"Oh, he's not all that bad," Mary disputed. "I enjoy watching him trying to puzzle out which fork is which."

Lizzie let out an unladylike snort, drawing her mother's

attention. "You, my dear, should be working to earn his admiration," Mrs. Bennet said.

"With all due respect, Mother, I don't wish to earn Mr. Collins's admiration, nor the admiration of any other man."

"Do you wish to be turned out onto the streets when your father dies?" Mrs. Bennet bellowed, causing Lydia and Kitty to cover their ears and burst into giggles.

"Girls," Mr. Bennet said sternly, but didn't bother looking up to see if Kitty and Lydia paid him any attention.

"Papa, do you plan to die anytime soon?" Lizzie asked.

"Not unless this conversation continues," he replied.

"There you are, Mama. Papa promises not to die if we promise not to speak of any of us marrying Mr. Collins."

"Lizzie can't marry Mr. Collins," Lydia said while chewing, "until Jane marries."

As the oldest, prettiest, and most well-mannered Bennet, Jane was quite the catch, and Mrs. Bennet had set her sights rather high for her eldest daughter. No young man with a fortune less than five thousand a year would be considered. He must own land, maintain a house in town, and preferably be a member of nobility, not to mention handsome. It was quite a lot for one young man to live up to, and Mr. Collins did not stand a chance.

"If I were you, Jane," Lydia continued, "I'd pay more attention to a military officer. Everyone knows that clergy are too poor to marry, barristers are too dull, and merchants too scandalous. But an officer—"

"Papa," Lizzie interrupted, eager to steer the conversation back to sensible manners before the situation was well out of hand, "what do you know of Mr. Bingley?"

Before her father could formulate a response, Mrs. Bennet sat up straighter. "Who is Mr. Bingley? And is Lizzie acquainted with him?"

Not yet, thought Lizzie.

Mr. Bennet's head snapped up, and his gaze pinned her in place. Ah, he knew something. "Elizabeth, this is hardly a conversation to be had at the dinner table."

That confirmed it. After she'd left, he must have gone to court and heard the news!

"Now, he would be an ideal match for Jane," Mrs. Bennet continued. "A young gentleman, recently come of age, involved in commerce, yes, but his uncle's sole heir. Eventually he will inherit that house in Derbyshire. Why, he must earn at least four or five thousand a year! Mr. Bennet, why don't you invite Mr. Bingley to dinner to meet Jane?"

Lizzie eagerly filed away her mother's information as Mr. Bennet replied, "Mr. Bingley is engaged at the moment."

Mrs. Bennet's face fell. "Engaged? To whom?"

"Not to a young lady, but rather his time is engaged for the foreseeable future."

The note of finality in her father's voice told Lizzie he

hoped that Mrs. Bennet would let the issue drop, but the one thing that Lizzie and her mother had in common was their relentless curiosity.

"Where on earth is he?" Mrs. Bennet demanded.

"He's in Newgate Prison." When this news did nothing to dim the excitement in Mrs. Bennet's eyes, he added, "For murder."

The whole table gasped, except Lizzie and Mr. Bennet. Mrs. Bennet slammed her fork down. "You're teasing me!"

Kitty and Lydia begged to know more, and Mary began muttering about sinful excesses. Jane slid Lizzie a look that said, *Well, you've done it now.* Grudgingly, Mr. Bennet provided the barest of details over the second course but admitted he had not heard the full account.

"If only he weren't in prison," Mrs. Bennet lamented, "he would be a perfect match for our Jane."

Jane offered no opinion on the matter, choosing to pay special attention to her tart, but Mr. Bennet asked, "And what if he were a murderer, but not imprisoned? Would he be an acceptable suitor then?"

"He'd still be better than Mr. Collins," Lizzie muttered to Jane, who hid a smile behind her napkin.

Lizzie knew that her mother's single-minded goal of seeing her five daughters married stemmed from her own fear and unhappiness. Mrs. Bennet's father had died suddenly, leaving his family nearly penniless. And while Mrs. Bennet's brother was now respectably settled with his own family, he'd been a mere apprentice in a china shop at the time. Mrs. Bennet had married Mr. Bennet simply because he was the first one to ask, and his future as a barrister seemed bright. She'd been dissatisfied to find her married life consisted not of society parties and vast fortune but of an address in Cheapside, a husband who preferred books to people, five daughters, and not a single son.

Lizzie sympathized with her mother's disappointment, but she didn't understand why being born a girl meant that she couldn't decide her own future. "I think Mr. Bingley's case is interesting," Lizzie said, addressing her indifferent father and ignoring her glaring mother. "Fred said that—"

"Lizzie, I thought you cut ties with those urchins!" her mother interrupted.

"Fred is *hardly* an urchin. He shares his information and makes an honest living of it. But Papa, I keep turning it over in my mind—what could Mr. Bingley's motive possibly be?"

Lizzie was set on acquiring and working through her own case, but she still valued her father's opinion . . . and his instruction. After all, he was the one who had taught her that asking a person's opinion on a matter often yielded a lot more information than simply asking someone what they knew.

"It's impossible to say to what lengths desperation may drive a man, especially when his own family is at stake," was all her father said. Lizzie resisted the urge to scowl. Mr. Bennet would not be helpful.

"A crime of passion?" Jane asked, sending Lizzie a bemused glance.

"I hear that the union between Mr. and Mrs. Hurst was not a happy one." Mrs. Bennet took the opening to gossip. "Just recently, Mrs. Hurst *abandoned* her husband!"

The other Bennet sisters gasped, while Lizzie thought rather irritably that she would like to know where her mother got her information—it was tedious listening to her endless stream of chatter, but it occasionally yielded the most fascinating tidbits. "Why, then it would have to be very foolish of Mr. Bingley to murder Mr. Hurst if such rumors are true," Lizzie thought aloud. "He must've known that he would be the very first suspect."

"One cannot account for all the fools in London," Mr. Bennet observed wryly.

"Mr. Bingley is not foolish," Mrs. Bennet protested. "A foolish man simply cannot be as rich as he is . . . heavens, no. A man like that must be clever, and good mannered, and fashionable. Oh, Mr. Bennet! But what if *you* were able to prove his innocence? He might be so grateful as to marry Jane then!"

"No, thank you, my dear. I suspect Lizzie has already staked a claim on that venture." Mr. Bennet gave her a knowing smile. "Now, I beg of you all, let me finish my meal in peace."

"I shall have no peace," Mrs. Bennet said sadly. "Not when my Jane is lovely and unwed, and my second daughter is determined to be a barrister."

"Don't be absurd, my dear," Mr. Bennet said. "Jane shall have her pick of suitors, and Lizzie will hardly be able to get through the pack of solicitors lining up outside of Newgate to represent Mr. Bingley."

That last comment was made with a pointed look in Lizzie's direction. She chose to ignore both of her parents' words. She would make an excellent barrister. In fact, she'd make an excellent solicitor, too. Any solicitor worth his (or her) salt kept their ears and eyes open, searching out potential clients while the barristers argued in court. But Mr. Bennet was right: Lizzie wouldn't be at all surprised if the prison was swarming with earnest solicitors hoping for an audience with Mr. Bingley and a chance to earn him as a client. . . .

All at once, an idea struck.

"What are you smiling about, Lizzie?" Mrs. Bennet demanded. "Surely not our family's ruin?"

"Surely not," Lizzie agreed.

THREE

*In Which Lizzie Makes an
Unexpected Enemy*

AS FAR AS SCHEMES went, Lizzie's plan to secure Mr. Bingley as the newest client of Longbourn & Sons was not her most far-fetched, but it was perhaps her most daring. It would take impersonation, bribery, and all of Lizzie's wits.

Jane was against it, naturally.

She tried to reason with Lizzie as she made her preparations. "I know you're as clever as any solicitor, but you aren't a solicitor, Lizzie. You're a young lady."

"Why must everyone insist on reminding me?" Lizzie asked as she tied on her widest bonnet. "It's not as if I am able to forget."

Jane gave Lizzie her most serious look. "Lizzie."

"Jane. I will not live my life sitting by the side while there are so many men making a mess of things."

"You're referring to Mr. Collins?"

"Mama thinks that I ought to marry him to secure our future, but why do that when I can secure it just as easily by myself?"

Jane kindly didn't point out that nothing about Lizzie's plan would be easy, but she did promise to cover for Lizzie on the slim chance that Mama went looking for her. And so Lizzie stepped out into the street with a hamper full of pilfered goods from the kitchen and set out for Newgate Prison.

It was not an overly long walk west. She smelled Newgate before she saw it, and the stench made her lift her handkerchief to her nose as she took in the grim stone building, imposing and forlorn for all the bustle of the streets around it. Gallows stood in the open courtyard, a chilling reminder of what might have been Mr. Davis's fate if she hadn't discovered his wife's deception.

She couldn't help but trace where Newgate was connected to London's Central Criminal Court by a stone-enclosed passageway, where prisoners were ferried across to await trial. A brick wall in the shape of a half circle impeded her view into the courtroom windows, and the narrow entrance was beyond her reach. She'd never been inside, although her father had been coaxed into admitting that it was rather fine. Lizzie wanted to see for herself, and this could be the case that finally gained her entry into that building.

With that in mind, Lizzie gathered up her courage and walked past the gallows and toward Newgate's entrance. It took a shilling to convince the man at the gate she was here to see a prisoner, and another to be escorted past the hopeful family members and solicitors seeking out loved ones and clients, into a stale, dusty office where the warden received her. He was a tall, gray man and was quite amused when she demanded to see Charles Bingley. "And who're you?"

Lizzie drew her face into an expression of great disdain—it wasn't very difficult—and said, "His sister. *Miss* Bingley."

The warden studied her for a long moment and Lizzie struggled to keep her composure by counting the bricks above his head. One, two, three, four . . . she got up to seventeen when the warden said expectantly, "There will be a fee."

Lizzie smiled and handed over the last of her shillings. Mr. Bingley had better be worth the trouble, as this was turning out to be quite the expensive venture, and it was not so easy for a young lady to get her hands on coin.

"He's in the statehouse, so it will take a while to fetch him," the warden said, and quickly pocketed the money. "We don't usually let murderers stay in the statehouse, but we don't usually get ones that can afford it."

"Alleged murderer," Lizzie corrected.

The warden gave her one last hard look before setting off.

The wait was long. Lizzie tried to pass the time by mentally practicing what she would say when Mr. Bingley arrived but faltered when she could not imagine his reaction to seeing a strange young woman impersonating his sister. She tried counting the bricks but kept losing track after thirty-five. She began pacing the small office, hoping she might see something of interest, but the desk was locked up tight and the room sparse. Finally she sat again, convinced that she had made a terrible mistake and that the warden was just outside, laughing at her and deciding to lock her up in a cell for her deception. . . .

Lizzie stood the moment the door opened, revealing the warden, a guard, and a rather ruffled-looking young man of about four and twenty. Lizzie noticed his clothing first—he was wearing a fine jacket in a sea-blue linen, covered in garish dark stains that she knew instinctively must be blood. Excitement coursed through her, overriding the pinpricks of horror.

"Brother!" Lizzie cried loudly. "I've come to secure your release from this wretched place!"

She stared at Mr. Bingley, scarcely breathing, praying he'd play along.

The young man's weariness gave way to bewilderment, and Lizzie observed that although he was young, he had fine lines around his eyes that hinted at a tendency to smile. His wavy blond hair was mussed and cravat sloppily tied, but she could tell he came from money by the quality of his clothing and his perfect posture. Luckily for her, proper upbringing prevented him from contradicting her outright. "Don't just stand there," the warden growled. "Your sister paid a fair bit to see you, and she brought food, too."

Bingley's eyes darted to Lizzie's basket, and a smile brightened his face. "Sister!"

Men. So utterly predictable.

"Release him from these shackles," Lizzie demanded.

"I'm sorry, Miss Bingley, but we can't."

"My brother won't harm me," Lizzie declared, hoping that it was true. It was what his sister would say, but Lizzie had yet to judge Bingley's character for herself.

"We've too many people comin' an' goin'," the warden said. "Can't take the chance."

Lizzie didn't wish to press her luck any further. "Fine. May we speak privately?"

Lizzie's mother would positively faint if she knew her daughter was demanding a private audience with one of London's most eligible bachelors, suspected criminal or not. But his sister would not expect to have a chaperone to their conversation, and so the warden obliged.

The moment the door closed behind them, Charles Bingley looked to Lizzie and said, "You're not Caroline, but you play her well. Did you really bring food?"

Lizzie opened the hamper. "Scones, cheese, and strawberry preserves."

"Bless you, Miss . . ."

"Bennet," Lizzie replied, and got to setting out food for Bingley. It was well-known that one must pay for everything in Newgate—food, security, privileges. Bingley was wealthy enough, but she wondered how much he'd spent already and for what.

Bingley helped himself. "To what do I owe the pleasure of this visit, Miss Bennet?"

Lizzie was momentarily disarmed by Bingley's drawing room manners. Either he had no idea how serious the situation was or he was quite guilty and possibly mad.

"Mr. Bingley, I apologize for my deception. It goes against my nature, but it was the only way I knew how to get a chance to speak with you."

Bingley frowned around an enormous bite of scone. "And why on earth would you want to talk to me?"

"I wanted to ask you about what happened yesterday."

Now Bingley's gaze turned shrewd, and Lizzie felt him evaluate her more closely, although his features never wavered from politeness. Lizzie was reminded that although he was young, he was a very successful businessman, and one didn't achieve such things idly.

"I don't know if I should be discussing this," he said finally, dropping his easygoing smile. "Don't get me wrong—George was a scoundrel, a gentleman in appearance only. I can't say I'm upset that Louisa is free of him, but . . ."

"I wouldn't let the magistrate hear you say so," Lizzie advised.

"What are you, a solicitor?"

"Of a sort."

Bingley looked to Lizzie with surprise. It seemed to her that he was taking her in fully for the first time. "And what does that mean, of a sort?"

"My father is a barrister at Longbourn and Sons. Perhaps you've heard of it?"

"The firm without any actual sons?"

"Yes. I work there in a somewhat . . . veiled capacity. When I heard of your case, I was intrigued. Would you care to tell me what happened, in your own words?"

Bingley stared at Lizzie with openmouthed shock. "I thought you were with some sort of, I don't know, ladies' aid association, lending comfort to prisoners. But a solicitor? You are quite the unconventional young lady, Miss Bennet."

"I shall take that as a compliment, sir."

Bingley leaned forward, and Lizzie knew then she had hooked him. In her limited experience, people were all too happy to share when they felt important, and Bingley was no exception. "George was not on good footing; I'm not afraid to admit that. Financially, he didn't have much—although we didn't put it together until after he married Louisa. I did my best, giving him a position in my company, a salary, and . . .

well, I won't bore you with the details. Suffice to say, he did not rise to the occasion."

Lizzie would have dearly loved to be bored with the details, but she kept silent, unwilling to derail Bingley's speech.

"This is rather delicate, but . . . three days ago, Caroline— the one you so cleverly impersonated—called upon Louisa. Louisa was utterly distraught. George had barely come home all week. He was spending most nights at his club, and when he did come home he'd either ignore her or start an argument before running out again. Louisa was certain he planned to leave her, so she returned home with Caroline. I knew there'd be no peace unless I rounded him up, and besides, with my father dead and her husband utterly useless, I'm the only one to speak for Louisa's reputation."

On this front, Lizzie could sympathize. He was young, but responsible for his family. Not just for their financial security, Lizzie suspected, but for how society perceived them.

"I found him at his club, hauled him home, entrusted him to his butler, and told him to sober up, for we'd have many things to discuss in the morning."

Lizzie winced. If this was how he had framed the events to the magistrate, no wonder he had been thrown in prison. He would require a great deal of coaching if he ever went before a judge.

"I went home, and I must confess, this situation kept me up half the night. My sisters and I have been through so much, and nothing has gotten through to him. In the morning, I was prepared to cut him off completely. I've threatened to tighten the reins before, but I've always given in for Louisa's sake. But since she refused to go back to him, I decided that he would either have to repair their relationship or I'd demand a separation. I called upon his residence, but the butler said he hadn't risen yet. At that, I became rather angry. I went straight upstairs and . . . at first, I thought he was still drunk, and I began to yell at him. I reached over to rouse him, and that's when I realized he was covered in blood. I tried to revive him, and got myself . . ." He gestured to the bloodstains on his clothing. "Well, it was no use. He was gone."

"Was his body still warm?" Lizzie asked.

"I beg your pardon?"

"Mr. Hurst, was he warm or cold? If he was cold, then we have a good case that he was dead long before you even arrived."

"He was . . . well, not quite cold but definitely not alive."

Lizzie nodded. "Then he was attacked at some point after you left him the night before, but likely not very long before you called. Did anyone else see him after you brought him home?"

"Banks, the butler, let us in and helped me carry him up the stairs. We took him straight to his bedchamber, and I told Banks to not even bother waking his valet. I thought George deserved to fall asleep fully clothed. Banks let me out, and I went home."

Lord almighty, Bingley was certainly not helping his case any! "Did you see anyone when you returned?" Lizzie asked, hopeful.

"My driver let me out at the door, but I'd told my own butler not to wait up for me, and I didn't call for my valet," Bingley admitted. He looked at Lizzie, and she wondered if he was realizing what she was thinking—that he could have easily turned right around and walked back to his brother-in-law's house. "It doesn't look good, does it?"

"No," Lizzie agreed, because she'd not lied to Bingley when she said that deception was not in her nature. "But the facts of the case still beg a closer examination. There is the matter of confirming the whereabouts of the valet, the butler, Mr. Hurst's entire staff. They all would have had much easier access to him than you, and an entire window of opportunity where someone else could have committed the murder. And . . . well, I'm not convinced that you killed him."

"Because the facts don't line up for you?"

Before yesterday, Lizzie would have said she wasn't convinced because her instincts told her something about this was not quite right. But then she recalled her father's challenge. *I must go about this logically.*

Instead of answering, she stared at Bingley's fine jacket, now hopelessly stained with blood. "I know that this is indelicate, but how many times had Mr. Hurst been stabbed?"

Bingley's face whitened, and the hand reaching for another scone faltered. "I beg your pardon?"

"Once? Twice? More than that?"

He swallowed hard. "I don't know, exactly. There was so much blood. All over him, all over the bed. I couldn't even begin to see. Afterwards, it seemed foolish that I thought he was merely passed out, because even his neck . . . ."

Lizzie shuddered but nodded in satisfaction. "And your jacket . . . it's quite bloodied, but the spots are . . . smeared about. I'd venture a guess that you leaned over Mr. Hurst, shook him, perhaps?"

Bingley nodded. "Why are you asking?"

She took her time answering. "If you had stabbed him, there would be more blood on you, I should think. But the blood is only on the front of your coat."

"How the devil do you figure?"

"I have, on occasion, gone to the market with our cook. Have you ever seen a butcher's apron?" When Bingley shook his head, Lizzie explained. "It is covered in blood, but the patterns of blood are different. When a creature is killed, there is usually a bit more splatter."

Bingley's face went still. "I never thought of that. You're awfully clever, Miss Bennet."

Lizzie smiled at the praise, but her mind was already thinking ahead. "Here's what I propose: We must investigate

Mr. Hurst's murder ourselves. It's the only course of action that will lead to your complete exoneration and lift the tarnish from your good name. If Mr. Hurst was the scoundrel you claim, it shall not be difficult to discover who wanted him dead."

"Discover the true murderer," Bingley repeated. "You know, in all the turmoil, I had rather forgotten there was a killer on the loose."

But Lizzie hadn't. It was rather taxing that the burden of proving innocence fell upon the accused. It didn't seem quite fair when, in her experience, things were hardly ever as they first appeared. But she had solved that Davis case, hadn't she? This was just a step up from that. "Well?" she inquired. "Shall we enter into business together? My first course of action shall be to secure your release. A gentleman such as yourself should not reside here a moment longer."

"You can do that?" he asked eagerly.

"Ah . . . my father certainly can," Lizzie admitted. Between paying Fred for the tip and today's bribery, her reticule was quite light. Besides, she suspected that she could offer the warden the crown jewels and he would still refuse to release Bingley to a woman. "He can be here within the hour, and once you've had time to . . . recover, we can discuss the matter in greater detail."

Bingley considered her proposal, and Lizzie hardly breathed with anticipation. Despite the particular challenges of Bingley's case, she knew she'd presented a convincing argument for

Longbourn & Sons. Also, Bingley had aroused in her a stirring sense of justice and keen curiosity.

"You're very persuasive, Miss Bennet," Bingley admitted. "However, I'm afraid I cannot hire you."

Lizzie had forced herself to prepare for the possibility of this response, but she had not anticipated the crushing disappointment when possibility became reality. Her confident demeanor began to wilt. "It's because I'm a lady, isn't it?"

"Oh, no! You're rather clever, lady or no, but you see, I already— Darcy!"

He already Darcy? Lizzie was confused, until she turned in the direction of Bingley's gaze and realized that Darcy was not an explanation but a person—a very tall young gentleman about Mr. Bingley's age, perhaps a year younger, who was now standing in the doorway.

"Bingley," Mr. Darcy acknowledged. "The warden informed me that Caroline had come to visit you, which I had told her was unnecessary as you will be at home by teatime, but clearly—" The owner of such a brisk, authoritative voice broke off when he took in Lizzie's face and frowned spectacularly. "You're not Caroline."

It should have occurred to Lizzie to be embarrassed at being caught in a lie, but she was far too distracted by this person, this *Darcy*. He was dressed smartly, but not a dandy. His face was somewhat longer than what might be considered attractive, but his slightly crooked nose made his face interesting—like a marble statue where the artist had slipped just the tiniest bit when forming the nose. Lizzie was caught between the urge to stand and curtsy and the desire to stare back defiantly. Mr. Darcy's dark eyes returned her bold look until Lizzie concluded that he was indeed unconventionally handsome, though she herself could not imagine admiring someone with such a forbidding frown.

"This is Miss Bennet," Bingley informed Mr. Darcy. "Of Longbourn and Sons. Miss Bennet, my good friend Mr. Darcy."

"I wasn't aware that any women worked at Longbourn and Sons," Darcy said.

Lizzie smiled politely. "I'm happy to enlighten you."

Darcy's expression didn't alter as he continued. "I'm sorry to disappoint, Miss Bennet, but Mr. Bingley has already engaged legal representation."

"You're a solicitor?" Lizzie demanded.

Here, Darcy hesitated and Lizzie saw his stony demeanor slip when he glanced at Bingley. It was back in place by the time he looked back at her and said, "I am Fitzwilliam Darcy, of Pemberley and Associates."

Oh, he was one of the Pemberley Darcys! Lizzie knew the name. Judging by his youth and indirect response, Lizzie guessed that his standing in the firm—surely his father's—was as secure as her own. "A pleasure," she said, not quite managing to keep the sour tone out of her voice.

"Indeed," Darcy replied flippantly, but when he turned back to Bingley he was all concern. "How are you?"

While Bingley responded, Lizzie did her best not to appear annoyed by this intrusion. So Darcy *was* an explanation after all. It didn't matter how impressive Lizzie's proposition was, not if Bingley had Mr. Darcy of Pemberley & Associates as a close personal friend. Pemberley & Associates was one of the finest, most renowned firms in all of London and, by extension, all of England.

"But Miss Bennet and I have been having the most intriguing conversation, and I say, Darcy, she has some good points about my case." Lizzie looked up just in time to see Darcy cast a disinterested look in her direction. "Perhaps you ought to hear her theories?"

"I detest working alongside someone with whom I am not acquainted," Darcy said.

"Why, Mr. Darcy, were we not introduced just two minutes ago?" Lizzie asked.

He blinked, and Lizzie knew she had caught him off guard. "I am in no humor to give consequence to young ladies who use . . . wiles to gain entrance to Newgate, Miss Bennet."

Lizzie stood to face Darcy, indignant. "I don't need to resort to *wiles* when I have intellect at my disposal!"

He looked momentarily taken aback at Lizzie's response. "My apologies, Miss Bennet," he said, and Lizzie relaxed the slightest bit—until he continued. "Allow me to rephrase. I am in no humor to give consequence to young ladies without common sense."

If Darcy had slapped Lizzie, it wouldn't have been more shocking. "What's the harm in conferring? Would it be so damaging to your pride if it turned out my ideas held merit?"

Ah, *that* achieved a glint of passion in Darcy's eyes. It gave Lizzie great satisfaction to see such an insufferable man ruffled.

"I beg your pardon, Miss Bennet," Darcy said with an uncomfortable laugh. "Naturally, Bingley shall engage the services of whomever he likes and is confident shall handle this case." He turned to Bingley, who was finishing his fourth scone and watching the volley of words between Darcy and Lizzie with wide-eyed fascination. "I have already secured your release on bail with the warden. Will you be leaving with me, or shall you wait for Miss Bennet to . . ."

Bingley looked sheepishly at Lizzie and said, "I'd like to leave, please."

"Just as I thought."

Bingley brushed the crumbs from his hands and said, "Sorry, Miss Bennet. It's just that I know Darcy from when we were at school together, and he's a good friend. Please do call on me at your earliest convenience. I'm indebted to you for your faith in my innocence, and the food, of course."

Darcy cleared his throat, and Bingley added, "You really are quite clever."

Bingley gave her a small bow and shuffled from the room, shackles clanking. Lizzie thought that Darcy would follow him, but instead the other young man paused to look back at her. Lizzie met his gaze full-on, so he'd know she could not be intimidated. He replaced his hat upon his head and his lips quirked into a small, triumphant smile. "Better luck next time, Miss Bennet."

Words scrambled about in her head, but before she could arrange them into a witty response, Darcy swept from the room the same way he'd entered—silently and imperiously.

Lizzie struggled to maintain her composure. Oh, this was worse than standing by as Collins took credit for her work. Darcy seemed like just the sort of man that Lizzie had learned very early on to avoid. They were the first to laugh at her aspirations and the first to overlook her when a conversation turned complex. At best they were dismissive, and at worst they were cruel. It hardly seemed possible that Bingley could be associated with someone of this sort, but it was not something she could have foreseen. Therefore, it was not a personal failure.

No, not a failure. Lizzie took in a deep, calming breath and regretted it as she choked on the Newgate stench. By the time she composed herself, disappointment had strengthened into determination.

Bingley had not dismissed her—he had asked her to call on him. While Lizzie detested idle social visits on principle, this was a chance to prove that she was just as tenacious as Darcy. All she had to do was stand by her original scheme and identify Hurst's true murderer.

Mr. Fitzwilliam Darcy had not seen the last of Elizabeth Bennet.

FOUR

*In Which Lizzie Makes the
Acquaintance of the Bingley Sisters*

JANE WAS JUST AS dismayed as Lizzie to learn the outcome of her visit to Newgate, but for entirely different reasons.

"He asked you to call upon him? Lizzie, that's nearly scandalous—why didn't he ask if *he* could call upon you?"

"Does it matter?" Lizzie asked. "The point is I have another chance to convince him to hire me! Besides, could you imagine Mr. Bingley showing up here? Without Papa's invitation?"

"Mama would keel over," Jane admitted, "but she'd display his calling card for months."

"*Years,*" Lizzie countered, and shook her head. "And this isn't a social call. It'll be business."

"But I thought that Mr. Bingley declined your . . . help. In favor of Mr. Darcy."

Lizzie shuddered at the name. "You know, I am not entirely convinced that he's even qualified—his father is the barrister, not him. He looks barely out of university. For Mr. Bingley's sake, I hope someone at Pemberley is overlooking Darcy's work."

"And *you* are qualified?"

Jane's words were gentle, but they needled nonetheless. "I've been working with Papa for three years now, and reading all his legal texts for a lot longer. I shall prove myself, Jane. There are questions that no one is asking."

"And we can always count on you to ask the questions no one else thinks of," Jane said in a tone that was a cross between amusement and defeat. In the end, she didn't try to stop Lizzie. This was why Jane was such an excellent sister—she was supportive, but she was unafraid to speak the truth, even when it was inconvenient to Lizzie.

But before Lizzie met with Bingley again, she retrieved a small sketchbook from her writing box that had gone unused except for a few feeble attempts at nature sketches in the very front. The sketchbook had been a gift from Mrs. Bennet at her last birthday, a futile attempt to find some feminine pastime that Lizzie might occupy herself with. Lizzie found a stubby pencil and began taking notes on the case so far.

When she was done writing down details that she had learned from Bingley, she had two looming questions:

How far in debt was Hurst?

Whom was he indebted to?

The next day, Lizzie pretended to have a headache so that her mother and sisters went on their round of social visits without her. As soon as they were gone, Lizzie tiptoed out of her room, avoiding the maid, and peeked through her mother's address book—Mrs. Bennet liked to keep track of every residence of importance, whether or not she'd ever called on the inhabitants. The contents of her book revealed that the Bingleys lived in a very fashionable square west of Cheapside. It was a brisk walk there, as Lizzie didn't want to spend the last of her coin on a hired carriage, so she was perspiring lightly and her cheeks were flushed when she arrived at the address. The Bingley town house was a newer construction, yet it had a refined air—just the type of residence her mother would like to imagine one of her daughters living in.

Lizzie was let in by an impassive butler. "Miss Elizabeth Bennet here to see Mr. Bingley," she informed him, hoping she didn't sound too out of breath.

The butler's pause was almost impolite. "Your card, miss?"

Lizzie smiled graciously and produced her calling card from her reticule. "Mr. Bingley is expecting me. This is a matter of business, not a social call."

"Please wait," the butler said, a small frown ruffling his professional composure.

Lizzie let her eyes wander over the receiving hall as the butler disappeared. Even more evidence of the Bingleys' good fortune was found in the richness of the furnishings. Lizzie stepped closer to the lacquered hall table and tapped a fingernail against the fine wood. A genuine Chippendale, she was certain. It fit seamlessly with the maroon entry hall, where every decoration was rich and lovely, from the marble floors to the ornate vases set in small nooks. It was precisely the sort of decor she would have expected from the owner of a worldwide shipping company, even if the tastes did feel rather . . . mature. It seemed as though the Bingley family were trying very hard to appear effortlessly wealthy, not nouveau riche.

Lizzie turned her attention to the calling cards arranged on the hall table, hoping to learn whom the family associated with. She recognized a number of names, including that of a countess. Lizzie didn't see Darcy's card among them, which meant that he was a business associate and not a social acquaintance to the Bingley family . . . or that he was so familiar, he did not even bother with calling cards.

"Miss Bingley and Mrs. Hurst will receive you in the drawing room," the butler said, startling Lizzie. She jumped guiltily.

"Miss Bingley? But I've come to see *Mr.* Bingley."

Vague disapproval flitted across the butler's face. "This way, miss."

Lizzie briefly weighed the benefits of arguing. It wasn't entirely respectable for a young, unmarried lady to call upon the master of the house and not his sisters, but this was business!

Nonetheless, the butler didn't look like the sort to diverge from social graces, and Lizzie was rather curious to get a look at Hurst's poor widow. . . .

She was ushered into a bright drawing room that felt as though it existed in an entirely different decade. It was done up in a rather lovely sky-blue wallpaper and contained feminine furnishings in the neoclassical style. The elegant, straight-legged chairs and low oval settees seemed impossibly delicate and utterly impractical, in Lizzie's opinion. The only advantage to this room was that it didn't feel as stuffy as the hall, and Lizzie appreciated the open airiness to the space.

Miss Bingley and Mrs. Hurst sat on the chaise longue in front of the fire. They shared the same blond, porcelain features, but Lizzie observed that one was red eyed, and she assumed that was Mrs. Hurst. The other young lady, who Lizzie guessed was about seventeen or so, was much more composed, resplendent in a pink-and-gray dress that highlighted her delicate bone structure. Her blue eyes were sharp, a paler and icier version of her brother's, and the butler had barely announced her presence when the younger lady said, "So you're Charles's mysterious visitor."

"I am," Lizzie confirmed, refusing to be intimidated by her haughty look. "I beg your pardon, Miss Bingley, for assuming your identity. Time was of the utmost importance, and I could think of no better way to gain an audience with your brother."

"Darcy said you were forward," Caroline Bingley said with

a bored flick of her gaze up and down Lizzie's gown. Lizzie ventured a glance down and noticed that her hem was stained with mud, an inevitability in spring. This told her two things: Caroline was very proper, and Darcy must indeed be close to the Bingley family if Caroline referred to him with such familiarity.

"In my business, I find it's best not to waste time," Lizzie said.

"Business?" Louisa Hurst asked. "That sounds dreadful."

"I hope not! Not if it may prove your brother's innocence." She remembered a beat later that the deceased was also Louisa's husband. "My condolences, of course, Mrs. Hurst."

Louisa sniffed and dabbed at her eyes with a handkerchief. Her fingernails were bitten to the quick, and a tiny trace of blood streaked her right index finger. It was the only thing that appeared messy about Louisa, who was dressed in a mint-green-and-cream frock. It had a higher neckline than Caroline's dress, and she wore a cream shawl around her shoulders, but it was most definitely *not* mourning attire. Interesting. . . .

"I'm so sorry to bother you in this very . . . troubling time. You must be in shock."

"We are," Caroline said sharply, but her sister merely rolled her eyes, as if the idea were ridiculous to her.

Lizzie stood still, calculating her next move. She had not been asked to sit, but if she wanted to get anything out of Mr. Hurst's widow and sister-in-law, she would not be able to do so by playing by society's rules. She took a seat on a nearby chair, praying it was not ornamental and would hold her weight. Caroline's eyes narrowed at Lizzie's dirty hem.

"I don't believe that your brother committed this crime, and I'd like to prove it."

Suspicious silence made Lizzie hold her breath until Louisa asked, "Why?"

Lizzie had planned for this question and the answer was evasive, with a dash of manipulation. "It isn't right that you should live under the shadow of such a scandalous crime. Murder is quite bad enough." Louisa flinched at the word *murder*, but Caroline did not. "But for the suspect to be your own brother—no. That casts a dark shadow on the entire family."

"That's what I've been saying all along!" Louisa cried, glancing at her younger sister with a look of well-trod frustration. "I'll never marry again, and it's all George's fault."

How very interesting that Louisa's concern wasn't for her dead husband but for her imperiled social prospects. Lizzie dug in. "The only way to clear your brother's good name, and to show the ton that you're merely a victim in all of this, is to discover the true murderer."

"Why, Miss Bennet, you must be some sort of miracle worker if you think that your actions alone might influence society gossip," Caroline said, her tone mocking.

"My father is a barrister," Lizzie said. "I've been his protégée for a number of years and discovered that where men fail to see the truth, a woman may uncover many secrets before tea. I hope that you'll give me the opportunity to ask a few questions and investigate." She looked to Louisa, who was staring at Lizzie as if she were a talking pig. "Did your husband have any enemies, Mrs. Hurst?"

Caroline laughed under her breath, a sound so tiny that Lizzie almost missed it. But she kept her eyes on Louisa, who dismissed her question with the shake of her head. "George was always upsetting some person or the other but he would tell me, 'Don't worry your pretty little head, Louisa! I'll see to it . . . or your brother will.'"

Caroline laughed audibly this time, but when Lizzie looked to her, the other young woman stared back in a way that dared Lizzie to say anything about it. Lizzie worked to keep her expression polite and sympathetic. Caroline was the guard of her family's secrets, then. Lizzie was unlikely to get much out of Louisa with her in the room.

"Mr. Bingley told me that he intended to cut Mr. Hurst off," Lizzie said, trying a new path.

"Our brother did not kill George," Caroline replied. "It was likely some ruffian, shaking him down for money. He had a lot of debts."

"Really?" Lizzie asked, and Caroline flinched. Lizzie felt a surge of triumph at the confirmation. "Did he owe very much?"

Neither woman spoke.

"Hundreds?" Lizzie ventured. When that didn't elicit a response, she added, "Over a thousand?"

"I told him to sell the town house," Louisa squeaked, and Caroline shushed her. But Louisa continued, "I said I could come home, and he could stay at his club until Charles—"

"Did I hear my name?"

Lizzie turned to see Bingley enter the drawing room with a ready smile. A night at home, a proper bath, and good meals had done him a world of good—she had not realized how ashen he had appeared yesterday until she saw him well-fed and clean, with a golden glow. He was dressed in a crisp white shirt and a cerulean silk banyan that brought out the color of his blue-green eyes.

Bingley smiled when he spotted Lizzie. "Miss Bennet, I am very happy to see you. And I see you've met my sisters."

"Yes, I have," Lizzie said, and shook his hand. Up close, she saw that despite his refreshed appearance and cheer, Bingley's face also appeared worried. "I was just telling your sisters about our . . . conversation."

"I hate to worry my family. They've been through enough," he said, so earnestly that Lizzie believed him. And yet it was the second time that he had alluded to his family undergoing "so much."

"More than enough," Caroline snapped.

"No one knew of Mr. Hurst's troubles when Mrs. Hurst married him?" Lizzie asked, hoping that Bingley's good nature would make him forthright.

"No," Bingley said. "And if I had, I would have discouraged the marriage."

Louisa buried her face in her handkerchief and gave out a small hiccup.

"But you . . . helped him. Or tried to help him? For your sister's sake?"

Charles nodded. "I did. I gave him loans at first, and paid off his debts myself. Then I set him up at the office. That was . . . a disaster."

"How so?"

But as Lizzie feared, all three Bingley siblings hesitated at once.

"George didn't have a head for business," Louisa said.

Caroline let out an unladylike snort. "That was the least of his faults."

"Caroline, please," Bingley interceded. "Louisa is very upset—"

"Charles, why is this . . . person here? Isn't Darcy handling the case?"

"He is," Bingley assured his sister, and Lizzie's hopes sank just a little. "And I've told Darcy what Miss Bennet and I discussed—"

"Then let Darcy take care of it. There's no need to bring a stranger into our affairs!"

Lizzie was able to ignore Caroline's jab because Bingley's

words kept twirling in her mind: *I've told Darcy what Miss Bennet and I discussed.* Lizzie had had enough of sharing her ideas with guileful men who then turned about and passed them off as their own.

"Caroline, please," Bingley said. "Miss Bennet did go out of her way to visit me in jail—"

"Don't be foolish, Charles. She sensed an opportunity." Caroline turned to Lizzie and asked, "Were you hopeful that if you solved this crime, my brother would be so grateful he'd marry you?"

The idea of adding Caroline and Louisa to her already overflowing collection of sisters was horrifying. "Absolutely not!" Lizzie objected.

"Hmph!" was Caroline's dismissive response. "You think entirely too well of people, Charles."

At that moment, the butler stepped into the room and announced, "Mr. Darcy."

"Oh, Darcy, thank God!" Caroline cried out, and rose to her feet as the young man entered. "Talk my brother out of confiding in this strange young lady, please!"

Lizzie's gaze jumped to Darcy as he entered the room, looking as serious as he had the day before. Something about his presence made her pulse quicken, and she found she was both annoyed and oddly satisfied to run into Darcy again so soon.

"Ah, Miss Bennet," Darcy said, as if he weren't even surprised. "I wondered if you might be here."

Lizzie's eyes narrowed in suspicion, even though she could practically hear her mother's voice saying she'd give herself wrinkles. "Mr. Darcy. It's flattering to know you've been thinking of me."

This was the dull thing about society—one was always saying what they didn't mean, and if they did say what they meant, it was considered rude.

"Darcy, what news?" Bingley asked as Darcy took the chair next to him. Everyone in the room looked to Darcy, but Lizzie was watching the nervous jiggle of Bingley's right leg.

"I've spoken with the magistrate," Darcy said. "Because murder is a capital offense, the case will be tried in High Court a week from today."

"So soon?" Caroline asked. She sounded offended by the decision.

"The sooner the better," Darcy said. "We don't want to drag this out."

"That doesn't give us a lot of time, then," Lizzie said. Four heads turned to look at her, and she clarified, "To uncover the identity of the real killer."

She was met with puzzled expressions. "Oh, honestly. This is only what I've been trying to say the entire time—if Mr. Bingley is not at fault—"

"He's not," Caroline and Darcy said in unison.

"Then he has been framed. We must prove his innocence."

"That's Darcy's job, not yours," Caroline said.

"No, my job as his solicitor is to advise and collect evidence," Darcy replied. "And to engage a barrister to represent Bingley in court, if it comes to it. I'm no detective."

"But doesn't all legal work require a bit of detecting?" Lizzie countered.

"Not the way I practice."

"Then perhaps you ought to *practice* a bit more."

Darcy's brow furrowed into a dark line. "Bingley, no one believes that you're a murderer. Just stay in until next week, and don't receive any visitors except me"—was it Lizzie's imagination, or did Darcy shoot the tiniest of glances in her direction?—"and I'll assemble some character witnesses. It shouldn't be difficult to discover George's debt collectors. We'll sort this out."

Lizzie fixed Darcy with a condescending look. "Is that how you'll sort it out, then? By insisting, 'Oh no, sir, it couldn't have been my friend, he's far too upstanding to have committed this crime.'"

"He is," Darcy enunciated, as if explaining a simple concept to a child.

"That's not the way the world works," Lizzie said. "Mr. Bingley will be convicted because he's the most obvious suspect."

"Justice will be served," Darcy insisted.

"Not with your help, it won't. Why, it's a wonder you even have a job if you've failed to grasp the injustices of this world."

Lizzie could tell in that instant her words had upset Darcy. His jaw twitched with an unspoken response and he glared at her. She almost yearned to know what he considered an injustice in his fine, privileged life. Was it having to work for a position in his father's firm? Lizzie would gladly work, if only someone would give her a chance. Was it being pursued by eligible young women in want of a fortune? Oh, if only inheritance-seeking suitors were the worst of Lizzie's problems.

"With all due respect, Charles," Darcy said through a clenched jaw, "I see no need for you to accept Miss Bennet's meddling disguised as help. She knows nothing of how these matters work."

"I agree with Darcy," Caroline said.

"Darcy, you know I have the utmost respect for your judgment," Charles began. "But Miss Bennet does have a very interesting point."

"Which is?"

"Which is that someone killed Mr. Hurst," Lizzie cut in. "And don't you want to know who? And why?"

The Bingleys exchanged uncomfortable glances.

"My intention is to minimize the amount of scandal this family is subjected to," Darcy said. "Pursuing the truth of Hurst's habits and whatever else might have led to his demise will only cast a darker shadow on the family."

"That's a rather refined way of saying that you don't care about what really happened," Lizzie shot back.

"Do you purposefully misunderstand everything I say, Miss Bennet?"

"Do you purposefully overlook all inconvenient truths, Mr. Darcy?"

The pair glared at each other, and Lizzie found locking gazes with Darcy proved to be thrilling. His brown eyes were hardened in determination, and Lizzie felt her breath quicken, but she refused to look away first or show any weakness.

"Enough!" Bingley declared, breaking Lizzie and Darcy's intense stare. "Now, it's my name and my life at stake, so I think I ought to say what happens next. Darcy, you're a good friend, and I trust you more than anyone else on earth. Of course you'll be my solicitor. I'm sorry, Miss Bennet."

"The most sensible thing you've said all morning!" Caroline agreed.

Lizzie nodded and tried to shore herself up against the disappointment. "Of course, Mr. Bingley," she said, and cleared her throat. "I understand."

"I won't let you down, Charles," Darcy promised.

"However," Bingley added, and hope blossomed in Lizzie at the sound of that one word, "someone killed George. Who?"

The room was silent, and no answers presented themselves. Lizzie looked at the others, certain that they knew the details of Hurst's nasty habits but due to propriety or shame wouldn't admit them to her.

"Miss Bennet, I speak for my friend because I believe he's too hardheaded to say it himself, but if you find anything illuminating about the case, I'd be ever so grateful. And I'd be happy to compensate you, of course, for your time investigating various leads."

"I don't think that's wise," Darcy said.

Lizzie ignored him and said, "Thank you."

Bingley nudged Darcy when he didn't respond right away, and the young man cleared his throat. "Ahem, yes. Anything helpful you could uncover, Miss Bennet."

It wasn't the answer she was hoping for, but Lizzie knew when to ease up. "Very well. I shall make some discreet inquiries."

As she took her leave, Lizzie would have sworn she heard Caroline remark, "As if that girl could be *discreet*."

FIVE

In Which Lizzie Goes Snooping

LIZZIE'S STRONG DISTASTE FOR Darcy fueled her retreat from the Bingley residence. The nerve! He really was the most unpleasant young man Lizzie had ever met, and Lizzie had met a good many dissatisfying young men, thanks to her mother's efforts to marry her off. She was so annoyed that she nearly put Darcy on the same level as Collins but caught herself at the last moment.

Outside, Lizzie found a bench in a nearby park and drew her small sketchbook and pencil from her reticule. She flipped to where she had written, *How far in debt was Mr. Hurst? Whom was he indebted to?*

She didn't have precise answers, but she suspected he was hundreds, if not thousands, of pounds in the hole—and not to reputable sources, either. She felt dizzy at the sum. And yet,

Caroline had said that some ruffian likely killed Hurst because of debts. If the debt was created through accounts at merchants and dealers about town, then they would have sent bailiffs into the Hurst household to collect the funds and set up residence, not paid someone to have him killed. Hurst couldn't cough up the money he owed if he was dead. What other motive could someone possibly have for wanting him dead?

Lizzie jotted down a few notes and snapped her sketchbook shut. She had to admit one thing—being swept to the side had its advantages. Out of sight was out of mind, which allowed her to embark upon her second impersonation in as many days.

The windows of the Hurst residence on Grosvenor Square were darkened with drawn curtains. It was as if scandal were catching, for even pedestrians crossed the street to avoid the house. Lizzie observed the building from a corner as she gathered her thoughts. This was not like impersonating Caroline at Newgate, where she was unlikely to get caught, or calling upon the Bingleys, where she had been invited. She would be using deception to enter a house when she knew the family was not in residence. If she was caught, there could be serious consequences. The staff might even think her a thief.

But there was no way around it. Bingley had agreed that she could investigate, and if she could solve this mystery, her father would hire her, officially. And logically, how was she supposed to solve a crime without seeing where it happened?

Lizzie gave herself a small shake and stepped into character.

She approached the front door with her head held high, pulled the bell, and extracted the calling card that she'd pilfered from the Bingleys' foyer table on her way out, hoping the sweat on her palms wouldn't soak through her gloves and smudge the ink. It took a very long time before footsteps could be heard. When the door eventually opened a sliver, it revealed not the butler but a timid-looking footman.

Lizzie smiled. *Excellent.*

"Can I help you?" the footman asked, and Lizzie saw his Adam's apple bob. The poor boy had likely never had to answer the front door before, which meant that the butler was either out or indisposed.

"I'm here to call upon Mrs. Hurst." Lizzie presented her stolen calling card. "Mrs. Reed."

"I'm sorry, ma'am," the footman said, "but Mrs. Hurst isn't receiving visitors."

He made no move to take her card, another breach in protocol. She stepped forward to enter and the poor boy stumbled backward. She took another step into the house and said, "Nonsense! I'm one of Louisa's closest friends," which was another lie, as she had no idea who Mrs. Reed was. "Times of tragedy call for support and comfort, don't you agree?"

The footman shifted his gaze around the foyer, as if waiting for backup. "Yes, ma'am."

"Very good, I'm so happy that you agree. I'll just wait in the drawing room, and you tell Louisa to come down when she's presentable."

"But Mrs. Hurst . . . I mean, I don't think . . ."

"You may ring for tea as well." Lizzie took a gamble by walking down the hall and entering a door where she predicted the drawing room would be.

Instead, she found herself in a study, which surprised her for a moment. She peeked over her shoulder to see if the footman had witnessed her faux pas, but the young man had disappeared down a hall, likely to fetch the butler or housekeeper.

She had to be quick.

The air in the room was stale, smelling faintly of old cigar smoke, but the room was immaculate. Her eyes strayed to the bookshelves, which held a small but respectable collection, but she resisted the urge to inspect them. Instead, Lizzie circled around the large desk and carefully sifted through the papers stacked haphazardly off to the side.

They appeared to be a pile of various documents relating to Netherfield Shipping, nothing of great interest—a shipping schedule from the previous month, an inventory of cargo, a note thanking Hurst for his attention to an attached insurance policy. She became excited for a moment, but upon quick glance she saw that the policy was for the business, not for himself or his wife. It made Lizzie wonder if Hurst had life insurance. Perhaps his widow wouldn't be quite so upset if she knew a sum of money was coming her way. Then again, Louisa Hurst hadn't been in mourning dress, so who was to say how upset she really was?

Lizzie tried the desk drawers, but they were mostly empty except for stray bits of paper, writing supplies, and a box of cigars. Keenly aware of time slipping away, Lizzie stepped around the desk with the intention of finding the actual drawing room, but temptation overcame her. She quickly crossed the room to read the spines of books on the half-empty shelf and was surprised to find Shakespeare, Erasmus, and Dryden among a handful of atlases. She picked up a copy of Shakespeare's sonnets and turned it to examine the pages—aha! The edges were uncut. She replaced the book and inspected three or four more at random. All featured uncut pages.

Why purchase new books but not bother to cut open the pages? Books were meant to be read, not used as expensive ornaments! Not only was Lizzie offended by the waste, but she was puzzled. If the Hursts were as destitute as her conversation with the Bingleys hinted at, why keep valuable books on the shelves unread?

Lizzie put everything back in order as she'd found it and slipped out into the hall, keeping an eye out for any of the servants. The next room was the drawing room, and it was obvious from the empty fireplace and drawn curtains that the family was not home. As her eyes adjusted to the dimness, Lizzie noted the room's decorations. Very elegant, in much the same taste as the Bingley house, except that the room was done in a more traditional sage green, with heavy mahogany furnishings and rich velvet drapes.

As Lizzie made herself comfortable on a large chair, she had the unsettling feeling that something was off. The room did not have many objets d'art on the tables or mantel, and there were fewer portraits hanging on the walls than at the Bingley residence. But no, it was more than that . . . in the far corner, beyond the unlit fireplace, there was an odd emptiness to that space.

Lizzie got up and pulled back the curtains with a quick yank, flooding the corner with sunlight. She blinked rapidly, her vision adjusting once more, and looked down. There were scuff marks on the hardwood floor, next to the window. She traced them to the corner, where a writing table stood. The scuff marks ended, matching up neatly with two of the table's legs. Someone had dragged it from the window closer to the corner, and unless she was mistaken, another piece of furniture had lived in that corner until recently.

What had happened to it? She took in the room once more, seeing its emptiness as an indicator of hard times. Had pieces been sold off?

But why sell off drawing room furniture before selling expensive books that were clearly never read? Some of those titles would have fetched twenty shillings.

A tiny rattle startled Lizzie and she turned to find a young woman with dark hair wearing a maid's uniform, not much older than she. She held a tea tray, the source of the rattle. "I'm sorry to startle you, miss. Roger said Mrs. Hurst had a visitor who insisted on coming in."

Lizzie's mind was still on the mystery of the furniture and books, so it took her a moment to reassume her faux identity. She finally managed to say, "Yes, well, I can be very insistent," and tacked on a silly little laugh to cover her nerves.

"Mrs. Hurst isn't receiving," the maid said, staring openly at Lizzie. Lizzie felt as though the maid's brown eyes could see right through her. "I'm afraid you'll have to come back."

"She'll make an exception for her closest friend," Lizzie said, hoping her flippant tone would conceal her bluff.

The maid blinked slowly and a faint smile turned up the corners of her chapped lips. "Begging your pardon, miss, but I've never seen you before in my life."

Bollocks. "You're very clever," Lizzie said, shoulders drooping. "What's your name?"

"Abigail," the maid answered instinctively, then her mouth tightened into a hard line. "And who're *you?*"

Lizzie made the impulsive decision to push ahead. "Abigail, I've been hired by the Bingley family to look into Mr. Hurst's death."

Lizzie watched Abigail process the news with a healthy dose of skepticism on her open face. "*You?* But you're a lady."

"I am, and just think—you didn't suspect me, now did you? Nor did your footman. A lady can worm her way into situations and places that a man simply cannot."

That earned Lizzie another flicker of a smile. "That's the plain truth, miss."

"I'm making inquiries that men might not be able to make. I have a number of questions about Mr. Hurst and his final days."

At that, Abigail's expression went blank, and the tea tray rattled once more. "I think you might want to wait until Mr. Banks returns, miss."

Lizzie shook her head. "I'd like to speak to you, Abigail. Perhaps you have observed something that might give me a clue as to why anyone might want to harm Mr. Hurst."

Abigail was already shaking her head. "I won't gossip, miss. I'd never get another position."

Lizzie didn't want to hurt Abigail's employment prospects, but her fear implied that Abigail knew something worthwhile. "It wouldn't be gossip, Abigail. It would be pertinent information in an ongoing criminal investigation."

"I couldn't go before a magistrate," she said firmly, and then added with a note of resentment, "I thought this was a respectable household."

Lizzie decided to switch tactics. She took the tea tray from Abigail's grasp and set it down on a nearby table. "All right— how about this? I shall ask you a series of questions, and all you must do is shake your head no or nod yes. How does that sound?"

"And then you'll leave?"

"Of course," Lizzie promised.

After a long hesitation, Abigail nodded.

"Did you see Mr. Hurst on the day of his murder?"

A quick shake of her head—Lizzie decided it must be the truth, given that Mr. Bingley told her he'd tracked Hurst down at his club that evening.

"Did you know that Mr. Hurst was, ah, wanting for money?"

Abigail gave a small shrug, which Lizzie suspected meant that the staff had picked up on it, but no one would have openly spoken of such things.

"Did you ever hear Mr. Hurst say anything about bill collectors, or anything of the sort?"

Abigail shook her head once to the side and looked away. Lizzie forced herself to wait, and after an interminable stillness, Abigail looked back at her and said, "Mr. Hurst's pocket watch went missing."

A pocket watch wouldn't even begin to cover all of Hurst's debts, but Lizzie nodded. "When did it go missing?"

"The night he was killed," Abigail said. "After they called the Runners and Bingley was taken away, they asked if anything else was missing or stolen in the house, and the valet said he couldn't find Mr. Hurst's pocket watch. The entire staff was questioned about it."

"So they believe the killer took it?"

"It was a nice watch," Abigail said with a tiny shrug, and then added, "I believe Mr. Bingley gave it to him, when he married Mrs. Hurst."

Lizzie raised her eyebrows. If Bingley had killed his brother-in-law, stealing the watch could have been a symbolic gesture. But if someone else had killed him, someone who was owed money, a pocket watch would be worth only so much. "Thank you, Abigail. That's very useful. Now, what do you think of Mrs. Hurst? Is she a good employer?"

"I've no complaints about her, miss," Abigail said quickly. Almost too quickly.

"Have you any complaints about Mr. Hurst?"

Abigail looked away and shook her head. Lizzie immediately suspected her lack of eye contact indicated a lie but chose to move on. "What do you think of the Bingley family?"

"I shouldn't say, miss. It's not for the help to give opinions on their employer's relations."

Lizzie laughed. "But who would tell? Not me. I'm not supposed to be here myself."

Abigail didn't respond to that, and Lizzie resisted the urge to keep speaking. She was gifted with words, but by far the most useful lesson—and hardest—she'd ever learned was when to let silence speak. She clenched her tongue between her teeth, holding in her words until Abigail said, "Miss Bingley can be sharp."

Lizzie snorted. "Agreed."

"It's not just that," Abigail said cautiously. "Last week, I was bringing in the tea, and it was just the two of them. Mrs. Hurst was crying, so Miss Bingley asked me to pour, and I splashed just a little. She took me to task, miss. Told me if I didn't learn how to pour a proper cup of tea, I'd find myself on the streets without a letter of reference."

Lizzie's eyebrows went up. It was not Caroline's place to reprimand her sister's maid, and yet Lizzie was not surprised she'd taken that liberty. But to threaten dismissal without a reference over some spilled tea? That was rather extreme. "Did you believe that she would do it?"

"I don't underestimate Miss Bingley," Abigail said. "Mrs. Hurst does everything she tells her to do. She convinced Mrs. Hurst to leave. They hadn't even finished their tea when she was ringing her maid to pack her trunks."

Interesting. Had Caroline convinced her sister to leave because the family was fed up with Hurst? Or . . . was there a darker reason? Lizzie thought of Caroline's haughty demeanor and her cagey responses. What did Caroline have to hide?

From Abigail's anxious expression, Lizzie guessed that she had regretted saying as much as she had. Before the girl could refuse her any more help, Lizzie asked, "May I see the bedchamber?"

Abigail gasped. "Miss, no one's gone in there since Mr. Bingley . . ."

Lizzie found that difficult to believe. "No one? Hasn't anyone cleaned up the mess?"

"Mr. Banks did, miss. He said it wasn't right that any of the maids should have to, but we still saw the linens, when he burned them. . . ."

It was almost a shame, really. Lizzie had read a legal text not too long ago that hypothesized crucial evidence could be found in the remnants of a crime. Lizzie wondered if one day, such evidence would be enough to exonerate a man—or condemn him—in a court of law.

"You must understand that it's important for an investigator to have a framework for the crime." This was something her father said often. *You must understand the crime before you can defend it.* "It would be most helpful to see where it took place."

Abigail didn't look entirely convinced, and Lizzie was certain she had pushed the young maid to her limits. "Abigail, you've been ever so helpful. I hope that I can one day return the favor." She removed her own calling card from her reticule and handed it to her. "Perhaps with a letter of reference, in the future. No need to say exactly how I know that you're helpful, only that you were most attentive and discreet."

Abigail's right eyebrow rose, but she snatched up the card. She looked at Lizzie's name for a long time, then said, "This way, miss. Mr. Banks will return soon."

Abigail led her up the staircase to the second level, which contained bedchambers and a more intimate sitting room for Mrs. Hurst to entertain close guests and family. Abigail bypassed three closed doors before arriving at a door at the end of the hallway. She opened it just a crack and then took a large step back. "I can't go in there, miss. It gives me the chills."

Lizzie felt quite the opposite. Her pulse thrummed with excitement, and her mouth was dry in anticipation. For all of her contract work, the witness statements she read, and her unauthorized trips to question suspects, she'd never actually visited a crime scene before. She stepped across the threshold into the room where it happened, careful not to disturb anything.

Like the study downstairs, this room was closed against the daylight, but enough light peeked in between the curtains and from the hall for her eyes to slowly adjust. In the center of the room stood a large bed frame, devoid of a mattress or bedding of any kind. The carpet, which was a fine moss green, had a large, unseemly stain near the bed.

Her mind raced. She tried her best to imagine Hurst, utterly foxed, leaning on his brother-in-law and butler as they dragged him up the stairs and into this room. They would have dumped him onto the bed. It might have been dim, as it was now, but the light would have been different. No sunlight stealing in from between the drapes, only shadows.

She looked over her shoulder to the door, which would have been open. She noted where the candelabras stood, the wax congealed. The fireplace was neatly swept, but Lizzie doubted anyone would have gone to the trouble to light it. The nights were still cool, but not chilly, and the servants might not have bothered if they were unsure that Hurst was even coming home.

As Lizzie took the measure of the large bedchamber, she wondered if it was possible that someone could have been lying in wait. She walked about the room, trying to imagine where the killer could have hidden. The bed was too low for a grown person to hide beneath it and the dressing room too risky— what if the valet had been called? None of the bedchamber's furniture was sufficient for a hiding spot, but she still moved across the room, thinking.

From the doorway, Abigail gasped. Lizzie looked in her direction and then heard what had made Abigail's face turn pale—footsteps on the stairs. Abigail rushed into the room and grabbed Lizzie's elbow with surprising force. "It's Mr. Banks! You must hide," she whispered.

"Where?" Lizzie cast around for a hiding spot, knowing full well that they were all paltry.

"The drapes!" Abigail was already yanking Lizzie to the windows. She pulled the heavy material aside and shoved Lizzie none too gently. Before Lizzie quite realized what was happening, Abigail had drawn the drapes back over her. The sumptuous fabric reached all the way to the floor, concealing her feet, and she was surprised to find that there was quite a bit of room between them and the window, which looked out over the back garden.

"Abigail, what are you doing up here?"

"Mr. Banks! I—I heard a noise."

"You heard a noise?" The butler's disapproval was heavy.

"I'm a bit uneasy, sir. I keep wondering, what if the killer returns?"

Lizzie couldn't help but stare down out the window as she held her breath, hoping not to be discovered. It was a lovely view of the garden, with a beautiful, tall tree whose branches thankfully obscured her from anyone who might happen to be outside.

"Whoever did in Mr. Hurst would have no business with the likes of us," Mr. Banks said, his voice brisk. "Use your sense, girl."

"I suppose you're right." Abigail's voice wavered. "I'm sorry."

In fact, the tree was rather close to the window. Lizzie stared hard at the sturdy branches, trying to judge the distance. It couldn't be more than five feet.

"Do you suppose it really was Mr. Bingley?" Abigail asked.

"It would appear so," Banks said, his voice closer now. Lizzie could have kissed Abigail for asking such leading questions. It saved her the trouble of figuring out how to interview the butler herself.

"It's just so hard to imagine it, sir. He was always so polite. And to think of Mrs. Hurst . . ."

"What's to think about?"

"Well, why would she be staying with her brother if she thought he'd . . ."

Clever girl. That gave Mr. Banks pause, but then he said, "Of course she thinks her own brother is innocent. People of that class stick together, Abigail. But he'll likely hang. The evidence against him is too much."

Lizzie inspected the window's latch as she listened, trying to judge how difficult it might be for someone to gain entry from the outside. That was when she noticed a tiny, dark object caught in the corner of the window frame. She squinted at it and then very carefully reached out to try to pick it up. It was a button, its shank caught in the closed window. She tugged on it, but as she did so, her elbow brushed up against the heavy folds of the drapes. . . .

The fabric was pulled back suddenly, and Lizzie realized a beat too late that she had been noticed. Standing before her in a room now flooded with cheery sunlight stood an elderly yet sturdy-looking man with a disapproving expression, and a shocked Abigail.

The two young women locked gazes, and Lizzie saw the anguish in Abigail's eyes. She made a split-second decision.

"Oh heavens!" she cried out, and yanked the button loose with all her might before throwing her hands up. "Please don't hurt me, sir!"

Mr. Banks looked down with a mixture of bewilderment and distaste. "Young lady, you are trespassing!"

But Lizzie didn't care—she had been successful in yanking the button free. It was now clenched tightly in her fist, and she quickly dropped her arms and affected a look of shame. Mr. Banks took her elbow and propelled her away from the window.

"Well, Abigail, it appears your imagination is not as active as I thought," he said darkly. "Send Roger for a Runner at once!"

Abigail cast Lizzie an apologetic and terrified look before she left, but Lizzie didn't blame her in the least for saving her own skin. However, being marched up Bow Street by a Runner for breaking and entering was the very last thing that Lizzie needed. How on earth would she explain this to her father? Impersonation and trespass would hardly convince him to hire her—he couldn't know about this!

"Please, sir," Lizzie began, "my name is Elizabeth Bennet. Allow me a moment to explain."

"Hurry, Abigail!" Mr. Banks thundered as he dragged Lizzie across the room and out into the hall. She heard distant rustling as the rest of the house caught on to the excitement.

"Mr. Bingley has hired me to look into the crime," Lizzie began to say, and by the darkening of Mr. Banks's expression, she knew she'd said the wrong thing.

"I doubt that. Mr. Bingley is a gentleman and he will answer for his crime, not try to wiggle his way out of it."

"You believe he did it?" she asked.

The butler was so surprised by Lizzie's question that he sputtered, "Who else would have?"

Many people, Lizzie thought. "Did you see Mr. Bingley out that night?"

"Of course, you impertinent—" He cut off when he realized that he was playing right into Lizzie's hands. "Oh, no you don't!"

He marched her down the stairs and to the foyer, where Abigail stood in the open door. "He's coming, sir," she said, careful not to meet Lizzie's gaze.

"Good," Mr. Banks said, and shook Lizzie's arm. "You'll answer for this!"

Lizzie's grip on the button tightened as she tried not to panic. "I always do."

SIX

*In Which Lizzie Gains an
Unexpected(ly Handsome) Ally*

THE RUNNER WHO ARRIVED to escort Lizzie from the Hurst household was not what she expected.

The men she was accustomed to seeing run toward crimes were usually former boxers, quick on their feet but uncomfortably muscular and often bearing the abuse of their former profession across their faces. This Runner was young, first of all—Lizzie would have put him at nineteen or twenty. And *handsome*. She did not blindly judge young men on their looks alone, but one did not live with Kitty and Lydia without picking up on such things.

His dark blond hair was slightly longer than the fashion, and it curled against his forehead in such a way that Lizzie longed to remove her gloves and run her fingers through it. His features, although serious as Mr. Banks leveled charges against Lizzie, were very attractive. He had a strong jaw, and a perfectly shaped nose, and just a small bit of stubble that she was surprised to find alluring, and at one point, he smiled politely at Mr. Banks, and Lizzie caught the flash of a dimple in his right cheek.

It really was too bad that he thought she was a criminal.

When Mr. Banks finished detailing how he'd caught Lizzie snooping about in the house, the young Runner nodded and said, "I'll see to this, Mr. Banks. Thank you for calling."

The butler grudgingly released her, and the Runner offered her his arm as if they were at a ball. But Lizzie was certain the gesture was meant to ensure that he had a good grasp on her in case she decided to flee. While Lizzie was an avid walker and believed in rigorous exercise of both mind and body, she doubted she'd get very far. The young man was fit, and Lizzie felt a hard ridge of muscle below her hand. Lean *and* strong.

She took his arm, and he led her from the house and down the street. The moment they were out of earshot of Banks, Lizzie declared, "For the record, the footman let me in."

"Under false pretenses, I take it?" he lobbed back.

"Well, yes, but otherwise he might not have let me in at all."

He laughed suddenly. "Do you often enter other people's homes on false pretenses, miss?"

"Well . . . ," Lizzie hedged, thinking of the Davis case, "to be perfectly honest, yes. But I'm not a criminal."

"All criminals say that," he replied, and guided her not ungently from the square to a busier street headed east.

"But can all criminals say that they are employed by a reputable law firm?"

Ah, this surprised the Runner. He took his eyes off the street ahead and looked to Lizzie. "You?"

"Oh yes," she said, seizing upon her opportunity. "Are you familiar with Longbourn and Sons?"

"I've heard the name," he said.

"My father is Mr. Bennet, Esquire. He owns the firm. Occasionally I am employed—discreetly, you understand—to look into more delicate matters."

This was a slight exaggeration on the number of hours she spent proofreading and rewriting contracts, but the Runner didn't need to know that. And then, even though it was most improper to do so, Lizzie added, "I'm Miss Elizabeth Bennet."

"Mr. George Wickham. It's a pleasure to make your unexpected acquaintance, Miss Bennet."

Lizzie had him interested now, although he was still propelling her in the general direction of Bow Street. "Likewise. You see, Mr. Wickham, this is all a dreadful misunderstanding. Mr. Bingley has asked me to make inquiries into Mr. Hurst's tragic death, in order to prove his innocence."

"This is quite unusual."

"If you call upon Mr. Bingley, you'll find that he'll vouch for me."

"And how am I supposed to know whether or not Mr. Bingley did it?"

Now it was Lizzie's turn to be surprised. "Come now, Mr. Wickham. That's for a magistrate to decide. If you were accused of a dreadful crime you didn't commit, wouldn't you want others to give you the benefit of the doubt? Wouldn't you want them to be absolutely certain, with proof in hand?"

Lizzie did not expect her words to affect him so much, but something passed across his face that seemed to be true emotion. "Yes, Miss Bennet. I believe that is true justice."

Finally, a man who agreed with her!

"I have grave doubts about Mr. Bingley's involvement in the crime. The facts don't line up, and I aim to discover the truth."

They stopped at a busy corner, the streets clogged with carriages, horses, and the occasional wagon. Many of the vehicles were light, open carriages with high-society ladies and gentlemen out for a pleasure drive or calling on friends. Although Lizzie doubted her mother and sisters would be this far from home, she angled her face away from the street lest she was recognized. Mr. Wickham stared down at her and said, "Miss Bennet, I'm quite glad to have run into you, I think."

"Oh?"

"I too must confess my skepticism. I was one of the first called to the scene of the crime. It felt to me as though everyone was quick to make assumptions. However, I'm just a Runner. Who would believe me?"

"Why shouldn't they believe you?" Lizzie countered. The street traffic was congested, but Lizzie spotted an opening where they could have crossed. Wickham didn't move to take it.

"I'm no gentleman, miss," he said with a smile tinged by embarrassment.

"You seem like one to me." Lizzie realized belatedly that her words could be perceived as flattery, so she hastened to add, "I believe that the quality of someone's character matters more than their family name or their social standing."

"You're very kind." He offered her a smile that made Lizzie feel as though they would agree on a fair number of points, if given the opportunity to explore them—but she must stay focused. The longer they talked, the more opportunity she would have to convince him to let her go. And she would dearly love to get off this busy street!

Lizzie saw another gap in traffic and decided to take the lead. She stepped out, dragging Wickham with her. To cover up her rudeness, she said, "Please, if you are so inclined . . . tell me what you know about the case?"

They narrowly escaped being run over by a shiny black curricle but made it safely to the other side before Wickham found his words. "Not much more than you, I'm afraid. I was patrolling all night, and about to head home when I heard a bit of a commotion in Grosvenor Square. It was early enough for some servants to be up and about, but not quite early enough for deliveries, so I popped down the street to see what was happening."

As they turned down a quieter street of town houses, Lizzie relaxed and was able to absorb Wickham's account. There was nothing better than hearing about cases such as these firsthand, directly from witnesses. She found that every person had a slightly different recollection of a moment in time, and when one gathered each different account, a more interesting story emerged. "And?"

"It was Mr. Hurst's valet, raising the hue and cry. He was shouting that there'd been a murder. Naturally I ran up and identified myself. He took me back to the house, where the butler had Mr. Bingley in Hurst's bedchamber. They were in shock. I stayed with them, and we inspected the bedchamber until a doctor and coroner arrived. Once a large group had been assembled, it was decided that Mr. Hurst had been murdered. Stabbed to death."

He said this quietly, not wanting to attract attention from the few passersby on the street. They were still walking through the finer neighborhoods, but soon they would give way to the busier, more crowded areas of commerce and law. Lizzie had to keep him talking about this case—if she was going to be charged with a crime, she might as well get something out of it!

So she asked, "Were you able to tell how many times he was stabbed?"

If Wickham thought it was an inappropriate question for

a lady to ask, he didn't say. He just replied, "Eleven times. The killing blow was to the neck, to be sure. The amount of blood . . ."

Lizzie clutched Wickham's arm tighter. So her theory about blood splatter had been correct! Logic could prevail!

"It was the butler who accused Mr. Bingley," Wickham continued, unaware of Lizzie's excitement. "The doctor said that many stab wounds could only be a crime of passion. He asked if Mr. Hurst had argued with anyone. Banks pointed at Bingley and sang like a canary."

"But Mr. Bingley told me that the body had grown cold by the time he was discovered, and the blood had begun to congeal."

"He said the same to us," Wickham agreed, "but he had opportunity the evening before, when he brought Hurst home, and Banks testified that Bingley had been in the house."

"But the butler was still awake when Mr. Bingley left, and would have locked up after him. Wouldn't he have noticed if Bingley were covered in blood? And why would Mr. Bingley come back the following morning to *discover* the body?" She emphasized the word to make a point about her skepticism, even as she wondered how the killer might have known where to find Hurst. By all accounts, his movements had been sporadic.

"The coroner and the butler implied that Mr. Bingley must have used some trickery to conceal the crime, and came back in order to appear innocent, but you and I clearly have our doubts."

"Yes, we do," Lizzie agreed, thinking of the snagged button clenched in her fist. It must belong to the killer, but she wasn't prepared to believe that person was Bingley. When Wickham did not say any more on the subject, Lizzie decided to take a risk and show her hand. "I think that someone killed him in the night, after Bingley left, and before he came back the following morning."

Stating this suspicion aloud seemed to give it shape and power in Lizzie's mind, and she stood taller.

Mr. Wickham glanced at her, as if he were sizing her up. "But who?"

Doubt didn't color his question—oh, it felt wonderful to be *believed*.

"I have suspicions." She willed herself not to draw attention to the object still clutched in her hand. "But I cannot disclose my opinions until the investigation has concluded."

This was a polite excuse, of course. Lizzie would not disclose her opinions to the authorities without proof, preferably proof that could not be ripped from her by a man, no matter how attractive and attentive he might be. Suddenly, Lizzie became all too aware of how they stood, close enough to be mistaken as a couple. Mr. Wickham was watching her, and he appeared . . . fascinated.

"I understand, Miss Bennet," he said. "You have your professional duties, and I have mine."

Lizzie wasn't sure if he was humoring her or if he really

felt that way. She decided to take a risk and ask, "Are you really going to take me before the magistrate for breaking and entering?"

Mr. Wickham's eyebrows rose in surprise, but the devilish smile—and the accompanying dimple—did not falter. "I don't believe there would be a valid case against you. Why, you said yourself that a footman let you in and that the Bingleys hired you to look into the case. Is Mrs. Hurst not a Bingley? The most the butler could accuse you of is being in a room where you were not welcome, and, well, that's not against the law. It's just poor manners."

"You aren't teasing me?" she asked, scarcely daring to believe her luck.

"Miss Bennet, if we were to continue our acquaintance, I promise you would know when I was teasing you."

Lizzie felt herself flush, right there on the street as carriages rattled by and a dour-faced matron shuffled past, casting a suspicious glance at the two of them. But once her embarrassment passed, relief flooded in. She would not have to explain to her parents why she was in possession of a criminal record!

"Thank you, Mr. Wickham. You're a good deal more helpful and courteous than most men I've encountered over the course of this case."

He accepted this comment with a slight nod and then said, "May I accompany you home?"

"Oh, I don't live very far—" Lizzie began to say, but Wickham interrupted her.

"Miss Bennet, you just said that I am a gentleman. A gentleman would not leave a young lady to wander the streets alone."

Lizzie found she could not argue. "Fine, but I'm afraid we've got a bit of a walk ahead of us—I live on Gracechurch Street. Do you know it?"

"Cheapside!" he exclaimed. "My own stomping grounds."

Something about being from the same neighborhood made her smile as they continued to make their way east and the streets began to grow more crowded. They stuck out less as they left the finer neighborhoods, and Lizzie found that Mr. Wickham was pleasant company. He inquired after how she had gotten the case, and Lizzie glossed over the truth by saying a mutual friend had connected them.

"It's rather progressive of Mr. Bingley to hire you," he remarked. "I would think that he would do business with a stuffy old firm."

Lizzie sighed. "Oh, he does. His solicitor is a Mr. Darcy of Pemberley and Associates, although Mr. Bingley means for us to both work the case."

As she spoke these words, Wickham's arm stiffened. When she glanced his way, his pleasant expression had hardened somewhat. "What's the matter?"

"You're acquainted with Mr. Darcy?"

"Acquainted would be putting it nicely," Lizzie said. "He's Bingley's close friend, although I am of the opinion that he has no interest in discovering the true murderer. His legal strategy appears to be a passive defense."

"You disagree with it?"

"The best defense," Lizzie declared, "is an offense. I plan to find the real killer."

"I've heard of Darcy," Wickham said, and something Lizzie couldn't quite name strained his voice. Not outright contempt and not quite suspicion.

"What have you heard?"

"Oh, I shouldn't say too much." Wickham sounded nervous, Lizzie realized with a jolt. "Just that the firm's reputation is sterling, except perhaps . . ."

"Perhaps?"

"Perhaps it's not." Wickham shrugged, and Lizzie waited for him to elaborate. After a few prolonged moments, it was clear that he wasn't prepared to say any more. "Promise me you will be careful, Miss Bennet."

"My, how refreshing," Lizzie remarked. "A man who urges me to be careful rather than tells me to stop meddling."

Wickham laughed. "I wouldn't dream of telling you not to pursue your investigation. I have a feeling that I would be met with fierce resistance."

"You'd be correct."

They continued to speak of business, and Lizzie regaled

him with stories from the firm and her successes, but it wasn't long before they arrived on Gracechurch Street. Lizzie glanced toward the illuminated windows of her house and could tell even at this early evening hour that her mother and sisters had returned home. She tried not to show dismay as she stopped Wickham four doors down, before the Myerses' town house.

"Thank you for escorting me home," she said. "And for not taking me to jail."

"I'm obligated to advise you not to enter any more houses uninvited," he said with mock gravity, but she could see his dimple so she knew he was teasing. "I hope you discover the answers you're seeking. If you ever need assistance, please come find me. Messages can be left at the Crooked Cat—do you know of it?"

It was an alehouse not far from her father's firm. Lizzie had never been inside, but she nodded. It might be nice to have a Runner on her side, just in case.

"Good afternoon, Mr. Wickham."

"It was a pleasure, Miss Bennet."

She forced herself to walk away then and to not look back. As she approached the house, she saw the curtains twitch. *Please, please, please be Jane,* she thought.

But she had no such luck. Lydia met her at the door, eyes shining with mischievous excitement. "Who was that?"

"Who?" Lizzie asked, feigning ignorance.

"The young man who escorted you home!"

"I don't know what you're talking about."

"The *man*—"

"Hush!" Lizzie hissed.

Lydia looked victorious, and Lizzie knew that she'd made a mistake by showing her hand. "He's handsome," Lydia teased.

"I suppose," Lizzie allowed, knowing full well Mr. Wickham was quite good-looking.

"What's his name? How'd you make his acquaintance? What does his family do?"

Lizzie felt a headache coming on. "Lydia, what I do in my spare time is none of your concern. He is no one of consequence."

But her attempt at superiority backfired spectacularly when Lydia scowled. "Tell me, or I'll tell Mama a strange man brought you to our door."

Lizzie raised her gaze heavenward. Why did she spend her time pursuing lawbreakers when she lived with a criminal mastermind? Lydia was becoming more and more conniving by the day. "*Fine.* His name is Wickham. He's a Runner, and we're merely consulting on a case."

"Consulting on a case." Lydia sighed, as if it were a promise of marriage. "What's the crime? Theft? Did he steal your breath away?"

Lizzie rolled her eyes and pushed past her sister to the stairs.

"I wouldn't mind if he made off with my heart."

"You would fall in love with the first man who winked at you!" Lizzie tossed back.

"If I am ever kidnapped by a man like him, don't pay the ransom!"

"You've read too many novels!"

Lydia's delighted giggles followed her upstairs. Despite her sensible nature, Lizzie couldn't quite shake the memory of Wickham's easy smile and admiring gaze. How he listened and asked all the right questions. His gentle teasing tone and earnest offer of assistance, should she need it. Their relationship was strictly professional, she told herself.

But she would not object to running into him again.

SEVEN

In Which Lizzie Reconsiders Various
Matters of Friendship and Family

BY SOME MIRACLE, LIZZIE made it upstairs and behind her bedroom door without attracting anyone else's attention. The first thing she did was examine the button she'd plucked from Mr. Hurst's window frame. Her left hand was cramped from clutching it for so long, but when she relaxed her grip she was disappointed.

It was an inch wide and polished, finely made but unremarkable. The shank on the back was torn, and if Lizzie had to guess, it had caught against the windowsill while the person climbed in or out of Mr. Hurst's bedchamber. Other than that, there was nothing to distinguish it from the hundreds of other copper buttons she would find in London. From the size, she guessed it might have come from a piece of outerwear, such as a jacket.

The best she could do was ask Bingley if he owned an article of clothing that held such a button—if he did not, she could eliminate him as a suspect. But it was flimsy, circumstantial evidence. Who was to say that if he had owned this button, he hadn't dumped the jacket?

Lizzie secreted the button in her writing box, the one place her mother and younger sisters wouldn't intrude, and withdrew her sketchbook. She wrote down as much as she could remember—descriptions of Hurst's study, the strange arrangement of the furniture in the drawing room, the scratches in the floor, Abigail's account of the Hursts and Bingleys, and finally her memory of the crime scene. At the very bottom, she wrote and underlined, *Missing pocket watch* and *Caroline persuaded Louisa to leave.*

Lizzie was still thinking about her next move when she woke the next morning. She wrote a quick note to Bingley inquiring after a description of the missing pocket watch and then joined Jane at the breakfast table. Mr. Bennet had left before they even rose, and Mrs. Bennet and the three younger Bennet sisters slept late. Lizzie treasured this time alone with her older sister—and the opportunity to eat as much strawberry preserves as she liked without her mother's criticism.

"The Bingley family is holding back," Lizzie declared. "And I can't figure out why. It seems as though Hurst was in debt, although I don't know to whom. It was bad enough that the Hursts stood to lose their home. But is it enough to have driven them to murder?"

"Losing one's standing in society is hardly motive for killing someone," Jane pointed out.

"Agreed," Lizzie said, "but you haven't met Caroline Bingley or her sister. Besides, Abigail told me that it was Caroline who convinced her sister to leave her husband."

"That's scandalous, but not a crime. I can't say I wouldn't do the same if you or any of our sisters were married to someone like that."

"I would hope that we'd stop Lydia or Kitty from marrying the kind of man we'd later convince them to leave!"

"You can't always know a person's nature by looking at them," Jane wisely pointed out.

"True," Lizzie murmured, and thought of Caroline Bingley. She had seemed uppity and conceited and . . . fearful? "What if someone in the family had other motivations?"

"Such as?" Jane seemed truly startled at the thought.

"I don't know precisely, but Caroline is hiding something." Lizzie tapped her spoon against the shell of her soft-boiled egg rather more violently than she needed to. "It's hard to explain, Jane, but she was dismissive of me, and not just because she thought I was impolite. She's disdainful, to be sure, but she didn't want her brother to tell me *anything* about the family. There are many days when I'd happily let Kitty or Lydia go down for some petty crime, but if it were you or I, don't you think that we'd do anything to help clear our brother's name?"

"You shouldn't be quite so harsh on Lydia and Kitty," Jane admonished her. "But, yes. If you were in trouble, I would throw propriety out the window."

"Exactly. Which makes me suspect that she *wants* her brother to be hanged for the crime."

"Lizzie!" Jane exclaimed. The horror in her voice was endearingly innocent, but Lizzie thought of Mrs. Davis and her plan to implicate her husband so that she could remarry. Who knew what people were capable of?

"Consider it, Jane: What if Caroline wanted to free her sister from a scoundrel of a husband? But what if she also wanted to free herself from her brother's oversight? They've no living parents, so Caroline is beholden to her brother until she marries. This is the perfect solution that gets rid of both men— kill her brother-in-law, and frame her brother!"

"Is Mr. Bingley really that horrible?"

Lizzie considered the question. "I don't think so. In fact, if we had met under better circumstances, I think I might like him. Not like *that*—don't give me that look! But despite his dislike of Hurst, he was truly rattled by his death."

"He sounds quite reasonable, then—so why would Caroline wish to harm him?"

"I don't know!" And yet, Lizzie was determined to play out her theory. "Caroline appears to possess the coldness necessary to execute such a crime. She has means—anyone could acquire a penknife—and she has access. It would not be difficult for her to enter her sister's house and position herself in a secret location in Mr. Hurst's bedchamber in wait. Her sister was safely away, and she knew that her brother would bring Hurst home—"

But Jane interrupted her with words that dashed Lizzie's golden dreams of strutting victorious into the Longbourn & Sons offices: "But you don't have any proof."

"I'll get it. Or I'll get a confession."

"How will you do that?"

Jane's tone was gentle, but it brought about a wave of irritation in Lizzie. Caroline would hardly admit to anything if Lizzie were to present her with the facts of the case. Maybe if she showed her the button? But the button was flimsy and easily denied. Lizzie could try to question Louisa alone, but there was a chance that Louisa didn't even know what her sister had done.

Besides, it would be a very difficult task to turn one sister against another, perhaps more difficult than getting one to confess the truth. She'd never tell Jane because it would horrify her sweet-mannered older sister, but Lizzie would do any number of illegal things to protect her.

"I suppose I shall have to consult Papa." Lizzie sighed,

knowing that asking his advice on the best way to question a suspect might show her hand. Then again, she could see Charlotte.

"I wish you luck," Jane said. "But I'm not convinced. Why resort to murder to escape her brother when she could just do what every other wealthy young lady does—get married!"

Lizzie was about to say that perhaps not every young lady wanted to marry, when she heard Mary's voice. "Who's getting married?"

The two elder Bennets started, and Lizzie chirped, "No one!" as Mary entered the dining room. She was dressed in an old gray frock of Lizzie's that did not fit her well, and her hair was scraped back severely.

"You never tell me anything," she complained. "I know you were talking about someone getting married."

Because you tell Lydia and Kitty everything, and they tell Mama, Lizzie thought sourly, but Jane answered instead. "Just idle talk, not directed at anyone in particular."

"I don't believe you," Mary said, still cross. "I'll just ask Lydia."

"Are they awake?" Lizzie asked, wary of Lydia and her knowledge of Wickham. Mary scowled, but she nodded, always hopeful to win her older sisters' favor.

Lizzie swallowed the last of her tea. "I must go." Heaven help her if she was cornered by Kitty or Lydia begging to know details about Wickham—she'd never leave the house!

"Where?" Mary asked, but Lizzie ignored her.

"Lizzie, what shall I say if Mama asks where you are?" Jane asked.

"I'm sure you'll think of something!" Lizzie called over her shoulder.

"Wait!"

Lizzie turned, fearful her sister would protest her slipping away yet again. But Jane just said, "Remember—drawing room gossip only gets you so far."

It had rained before dawn, turning Gracechurch Street slick with mud. Cheapside always seemed to smell the worst after a rain, but Lizzie didn't mind—outdoor air and the weak sunlight through the clouds rejuvenated her better than the strongest cup of tea could. She gave a wave to their next-door neighbors, the Longs, who were just stepping out.

Lizzie knew that to the Caroline Bingleys and Darcys of the world, living in Cheapside probably seemed humiliating. But Lizzie loved the liveliness of the shopkeepers and merchants who could often be found lining the streets and the cheerful society of bankers and shoppers strolling between storefronts.

Lizzie lingered at the end of her street, scanning the pedestrians for a familiar gray cap atop tightly curled black hair. Fred could usually be found lingering nearby, hopeful for an assignment or waiting with a helpful tip. She didn't spot him this morning, but a little girl with stringy blond flyaways falling out of haphazard plaits caught her gaze and scurried up to Lizzie.

"Anything today, miss?"

Lizzie would prefer to send her message to the Bingleys through Fred, but she couldn't say no to the girl. "Will you tell Fred to find me at the firm?" Lizzie asked. The little girl didn't respond until Lizzie slipped her a halfpenny, and then she nodded once before scampering away. Lizzie saw her grab hold of a passing carriage, hitching a ride before disappearing from sight.

She'd always had a soft spot for the street children. The few times she'd managed to escape from under her mother's thumb as a child, she'd always gone looking for them. They'd been naturally suspicious of her, of course, being well-fed and well-dressed and full of manners, but Lizzie was jealous of the way they ran free through the streets, with no one to scold them about splattering their clothing with mud or shouting too loudly.

They never accepted her, even when she was a child herself, but she learned early on that she had currency with them—food, castoffs from the Bennet household, and, more recently, small bits of money. As she grew older, she began to understand how difficult their lives were, and she wished that she could afford to feed, clothe, and house them all. She didn't understand why they grew more skittish the older she got, until not long after she met Fred he told her no street kid would take a handout. "How d'we know you don't want something in return?" he challenged her, and it slowly dawned on Lizzie that there were other people, not so charitable, who offered the orphans things—and not out of kindness, but to trap them. After that, Lizzie was careful to attach her offerings with a small errand or odd job. At least today that little girl would be able to buy food. It might be her only meal.

When Lizzie arrived at Longbourn & Sons, she pushed the door open, waved at the clerk who sat sentry at the desk near the front, and went straight to Charlotte's desk. She intended to catch her friend up on the events of the past few days but skidded to a stop when she saw that Charlotte was speaking to someone.

No, not just someone. Collins.

Lizzie suppressed a shudder. She went to interrupt—Charlotte would appreciate the distraction—except the sound of Charlotte's soft laugh made Lizzie stop and fully take in the scene.

Collins leaned against Charlotte's desk, an insufferable smile stretched across his face. He laughed, abrasive and full of humor at his own words, and Charlotte's warm chuckle followed. Lizzie's brow furrowed. She'd had a conversation with her just last week about how her father did not pay Charlotte to laugh at Collins's jokes and she was therefore not obliged to humor the humorless. And yet Charlotte was not only laughing with Collins, she was smiling warmly up at him as he leaned forward to whisper something appallingly close to Charlotte's ear. . . .

Lizzie could take no more. She stepped forward and cleared her throat in an exaggerated manner. Collins looked up but relaxed when he saw it was Lizzie. Charlotte merely looked surprised, not at all guilty to be flirting with the enemy.

"Sorry," Lizzie said. "I hate to interrupt what I am sure is a stimulating conversation. But don't you have work to see to, Mr. Collins?"

"I do, Miss Elizabeth," he said almost irritably. "Miss Lucas and I are discussing work. You might not recognize that, given that you're not employed here."

Charlotte cringed at Collins's slight. "Hello, Lizzie. The post has just come, and Mr. Collins was seeing if he had any mail."

"A letter from Mr. Davis!" Collins crowed, waving about a letter, seal unbroken. "Thanking me for my keen senses in uncovering his wife's deception."

Lizzie's eyes darted to the letter in question, and she felt a surge of anger rise in her. She did not need to be praised for her work by the client, but it vexed her that Collins would wave about that letter as if it excused his laziness and utter lack of finesse with even the most basic of contracts. "How very nice," she said sourly. "I do hope that other letter is an offer of employment far from here."

"No," he said, missing Lizzie's sarcasm. "It's a letter from my benefactress! She bids that I keep her updated on my progress in the law, and the general goings-on in town. She doesn't leave Kent, and wishes to hear news."

"My apologies, Mr. Collins." Lizzie was eager to cut him off before he waxed poetic about this benefactress, some elderly widow Lizzie secretly suspected funded Collins's education in London so she wouldn't have to endure his company. "I misread the situation. I thought you were attempting to flatter Miss Lucas when she was in no way interested in your attention."

Collins turned pink, his face resembling an angry badger. It was a rather low blow, but Lizzie knew it would suffice— he hated any implication that he was unwelcome in society. "Thank you, Miss Lucas, for seeing to my mail. I must see to *my* cases," he sputtered before storming off.

Lizzie's smile slid straight off her face when she saw Charlotte's disapproving look. "Was that really necessary?"

"Reminding him of how insufferable he is? Yes, I believe it was," Lizzie replied.

Charlotte sighed as she straightened the writing tools on her desk, putting quill, ink, and penknife back in place. It was a small, disappointed sound that annoyed Lizzie. "Charlotte. Don't tell me you were enjoying his company. It's wholly unfair of him to expect you to break open his correspondence *and* repair his quill."

Charlotte didn't look up right away. "What if I said that I was having a perfectly pleasant conversation?"

Lizzie laughed at Charlotte's joke. "Then I'd ask if you were feeling well."

She realized a beat too late that her friend hadn't been

joking. Charlotte's expression went blank, flattened into a cool mask of indifference. "You can be very judgmental, Lizzie."

Lizzie bristled. Where was this coming from? Charlotte entertained Lizzie's private jokes about Collins and endured long evenings of her complaints that a man so socially and professionally inept should one day inherit her family's firm. Charlotte had never criticized Lizzie for her sharp humor or for pointing out Collins's foibles. He was simply so absurd! What caused this change in attitude? It wasn't as if Charlotte actually enjoyed his company. . . .

"Charlotte? But . . . Mr. Collins? No!"

"Not all of us have the good fortune of having a choice of suitors," Charlotte said stiffly.

Lizzie stepped behind Charlotte's desk and knelt so that she was eye level with her friend. "What on earth are you saying? You are smart and pretty and kind, and you have impeccable manners. You could have your choice of suitors any day."

Charlotte gave her a withering look. "I cannot. You do me no favors by pretending otherwise."

"But of course—"

"Lizzie, you are so naive!"

Charlotte's raised voice drew the attention of a few of the nearby clerks and solicitors until Lizzie's stern glare made them all look away. "Explain it to me, then. Please."

"You're a young lady, even if you don't wish to be," Charlotte explained in a harsh whisper. "I'm poor, and I must work for a living. I have a good name and education and upbringing, but there are some things about myself that I can never change. My complexion, for one."

Lizzie felt terrible for not seeing it sooner. "Your parents? But—"

"No, listen to me, Lizzie," Charlotte said, and Lizzie, unused to Charlotte speaking forcefully, closed her mouth. "There are many good people in the world who are perfectly kind and respectful to my face, but I see them judge me. And I cannot ignore it like you do. There are even fewer people who can look at someone like me and think that I have any prospects."

Lizzie was momentarily speechless. "Charlotte, no one—"

"Lizzie, please do not finish that sentence. You are a wonderful friend to me, and I am forever grateful to your father for giving me a position here. But I am tired of being unmarried and judged, and of working so hard with so little to show for it. I want a home, a husband, and a family. I want a place of my own. Can you understand that?"

Lizzie nodded slowly. She understood all of it—except the part where Charlotte didn't mind receiving attention from Collins. "But surely there is some other young man—"

"Lizzie, I don't wish to speak of this anymore."

"But—"

"I have work to do," Charlotte said, and stood abruptly, gathering files into her arms.

Lizzie watched her friend retreat to the records room, the

sick feeling of having failed Charlotte sinking in her belly. She knew that there were those who thought Charlotte unworthy of respect because of the darker shade of her skin, just as too many shopkeepers assumed Fred was a thief for his own complexion. These were injustices that Lizzie argued against, but she hadn't realized that her sweet-tempered and caring friend was so discouraged about her prospects that she'd settle for *Collins*.

She slowly became aware of the stares from other clerks and solicitors and realized Charlotte would not be returning to her desk anytime soon, at least not while Lizzie lingered. She straightened, went to her father's office, and knocked on the door.

Muffled voices came from within, and Lizzie wondered if he was with a client. She began to slink away when she heard footsteps, and the door opened. Her father appeared, ushering out a wiry young man with a lime-green-striped waistcoat and aggressive sideburns. He smelled powerfully of tobacco snuff, and Lizzie held back a sneeze. He gave Lizzie a cursory glance before turning back to Mr. Bennet and saying, "Thank you, sir. I look forward to hearing from you soon."

"Yes, very soon," her father agreed, and the young man was off. As soon as he was out of earshot, Lizzie looked to her father.

"Who was that? A new client?"

Mr. Bennet looked at her, distraction written across his tired face. "Lizzie. What troubles bring you to my door? Please don't tell me you've found another conspiracy involving one of Collins's clients. One per week should keep me sufficiently busy."

"No new conspiracies," Lizzie said sadly, at least none that she was ready to divulge. "But Papa, who was that?"

"Come in," he said, and Lizzie entered his office. He closed the door after her. "That was Mr. Ashbury. I was interviewing him for the position of solicitor."

Lizzie sat down hard on the seat Mr. Ashbury had just vacated. "But, Papa!"

"He comes very well recommended," her father continued. "Eton educated. A contender, to be sure."

And what about me? Lizzie wanted to ask. Was she not a contender? Lizzie felt silly for thinking that her father would wait patiently until she had solved her next case to offer her the job. He was interviewing other people and hadn't even told her! It felt like a betrayal.

"Is your mind made up, then?" she asked, mouth dry.

"Oh, no. I'm still considering. Now, what can I do for you?"

Don't hire that man, she wanted to say. But she refocused on the task at hand. "I was hoping to ask your advice."

"I'm due in court in an hour, but I think I can squeeze in a few moments for my daughter."

Lizzie wasted no time. "How does one secure a confession from a guilty person?"

Her father paused in replacing the spectacles back on his face. "We are speaking hypothetically, Lizzie?"

"Of course, Papa," she said. This conversation would be entirely hypothetical . . . until Lizzie decided to do something with the information.

"In theory, one would maneuver the questioning to such a point that the truth seems to be the better option than lying," her father said. "One cannot force a confession—not only is it unethical, but they often do not hold up before the magistrate."

"Because they are dishonest?"

"Yes, and because it pits you against the witness. You always want to be working with your witnesses, not against them."

Lizzie did not believe that any circumstance would arise in which she'd find herself working with Caroline Bingley, but she filed away this advice. "And how does one convince a witness that telling the truth is the best option?"

"It would depend upon the circumstances of the crime."

"Say that a witness believes that they are protecting someone they love by withholding the truth," Lizzie suggested.

"That is the most difficult scenario." Her father sighed. "Love is a very powerful motivator. I would advise you—er, anyone—to learn as much as they possibly could about the witness and why they were obstructing the truth. Knowledge is power."

"What if they were motivated by greed?" Lizzie wondered, thinking of her theory that Caroline had manipulated circumstances to free her sister and maneuver herself to control the entire Bingley family fortune.

"Then you must discover what they want, beyond immediate power and money. And what they fear." Her father replaced his spectacles and leaned forward. "All questions can usually be answered by learning as much as you can about your witness."

In other words, Lizzie needed to learn more about Caroline and her motivations. She sighed. It was just as Jane said. She didn't know for certain, and drawing room gossip would only get her so far.

"You're not still pursuing that Bingley case, are you?" her father said, interrupting her train of thought. "I heard that he's employed a solicitor at Pemberley and Associates to take on his case."

"Pemberley? Really?" Lizzie said, feigning surprise.

"Stuffy place," Mr. Bennet grumbled, "but apparently the family has personal connections with the senior barrister."

"Mr. Darcy?"

"I believe so, though I doubt he'd be taking on the case himself. He's elderly, and is rumored to be on his way to retirement. Oh well, a firm that size is likely to have multiple barristers and solicitors, all cogs in a wheel. Now, I must continue my preparations to go before Weatherford."

"Oh, the dour one?" Lizzie asked. She'd never had the pleasure of meeting this particular High Court judge, but she remembered all of her father's stories. Weatherford had proved to be quite the thorn in her father's side over the years, and she suspected that though he complained, Mr. Bennet enjoyed the intellectual challenge. He was the only judge her father seemed to respect.

"One and the same." He removed a few coins from his top drawer. "Now, why don't you go find Charlotte and take her to a coffeehouse for luncheon? Give you ladies a chance to catch up?"

Lizzie accepted the coins numbly, unable to bring herself to tell her father that she'd offended Charlotte, and what was worse was that she wasn't sure how to apologize. "Thank you, Papa."

"Keep out of trouble," was his parting response. Lizzie made no promises.

Sidestepping Collins's empty office, Lizzie went back to Charlotte's desk, hoping for a reconciliation over scones and strawberry preserves. But Charlotte's work area was abandoned. Lizzie stood by, waiting for her friend to come out of the records room, until a clerk asked, "Are you waiting for Miss Lucas, miss?"

Lizzie held in a sigh. Deductive reasoning was truly absent in these offices. "Yes."

"She's gone to luncheon with Mr. Collins," the clerk said, then backed away apologetically at the darkening of Lizzie's expression.

Disbelief blossomed into anger, but it withered quickly at the memory of Charlotte's words. Was Lizzie really as oblivious as her friend had made her out to be? If she was, that did not bode well for her future as a barrister.

Nor for her friendship with Charlotte, who deserved so

much better than bumbling, bragging, boisterous Collins.

Lizzie left the offices and stepped out onto the cobblestones. She swept her gaze up and down the street, looking for Charlotte and Collins. There was no trace of them.

"G'day, miss!"

Lizzie jumped at the sudden appearance of her short acquaintance. "Fred! You're quite stealthy."

"That's what they pay me for," he boasted, brown eyes sparkling with delight. Lizzie smiled, but she stared at Fred, her favorite of the street orphan bunch. Had she ever thoughtlessly said or done anything that was offensive to him? The idea of it made her half-sick with worry and shame.

"Miss?" Fred asked.

"I'm sorry, I'm a bit tired today," Lizzie lied. "Fred, would you be interested in a couple of errands—within the letter of the law, of course?"

"Course, miss." He smiled broadly. "But the illegal ones are more fun."

"I'll pretend I didn't hear that," Lizzie remarked, withdrawing a sixpence her father had just given her. She flipped the coin to Fred, who caught it deftly and stashed it away so quickly, Lizzie wasn't sure where it had gone.

"I need you to deliver two messages for me," she said, making up her mind. She handed Fred the note she had written earlier. "This one to the Bingleys, and I need you to leave word at the Crooked Cat."

EIGHT

In Which Lizzie Enlists Outside Help

THE NEXT DAY, LIZZIE made for Harley Street as soon as she could get away from Mrs. Bennet, insisting that she had made plans with Charlotte. She arrived after a longer walk than she had anticipated, out of breath and rather warm under the midday sun. The Bingleys lived in an elegant new town house on the north end of the street, and when Lizzie had called just days earlier, she hadn't really lingered long enough to get a feel for the neighborhood.

It was much quieter than Cheapside. Cobblestones were carefully placed to keep the fine ladies' feet from the mud, and pedestrians didn't linger. Lizzie found a shaded bench on an adjacent corner that allowed her an unimpeded view of the Bingley residence, hoping to spot Caroline. It would make her job easy if she could observe some nefarious-looking fellows coming to collect payment for an illicit job, but Lizzie suspected that Caroline was sly and careful. Unfortunately, all she saw was an endless slew of society women coming to gossip under the guise of offering condolences.

Of course, if Caroline had really killed her brother-in-law, the wise thing to do would be to stay at home and receive callers, plan a funeral, and act exactly as the sister of a widow would be expected to behave. But according to her father and Lizzie's experience with the Davis case, the perpetrators of crimes rarely acted in their own best interests. Thieves couldn't abide sitting on their riches until the law had moved on—they had to spend that money on fine things, which was how Mrs. Davis had first aroused Lizzie's suspicions. Or they talked, or they went back to their suspicious habits in no time. If Lizzie was right, then with Hurst dead and Bingley effectively under house arrest, Caroline wouldn't resist exercising her freedom.

Every half hour Lizzie got up and took a stroll around the block to shake life into her limbs and try out a new observation position. She hoped that Wickham had received her message requesting he join her surveillance mission. If anything, his presence would break up the boredom of sitting around and avoiding curious glances—there were only so many positions Lizzie could take around the block without attracting the attention of the neighbors. Even the pigeons had grown weary of her presence.

The afternoon passed and the flow of callers slowed to a dribble. The lamplighters were coming down the street and Lizzie was calculating how much longer she ought to stay when a tall figure popped around the corner, looked about, and headed straight for her. Wickham's smiling face appeared through the shadows. "Miss Bennet," he said in greeting, "how is your investigation going?"

"Rather dull," she said, stamping her feet awake. "And now rather chilly."

Wickham laughed. "Now, Miss Bennet. I would've thought you were made of sterner stuff. It's the nature of the work, I'm afraid."

Lizzie found herself warming up to his good humor, despite her anxiety. "To be sure. It's just, I'm not sure how much longer I can be out, so if something is going to happen, it better be soon. Has there been any more activity at the Hurst house?"

"Not a bit, I'm afraid. You've given the butler quite a scare—the house has been shut up tighter than Newgate since your visit."

Lizzie declined to mention that Newgate wasn't quite as secure as he might believe. "There have been ladies coming and going all day long," she told him. "But none of the household has left."

"Do we think that she's likely to leave via the front door, or is there any chance she'll skulk about the servants' entrance?"

Lizzie felt a quickening of her pulse at Wickham's use of the word *we*—was this what it felt like to be in partnership with someone? "I don't know, honestly. I can't imagine her using the back door, and if she doesn't believe that anyone is on to her, I suppose she'll go about as she always does. I've been watching the front, as I'm only one person."

"Good thing I'm here, then," Wickham said with a grin. "I'll loop around to the alley and watch the back, in case she makes a break for it. I'll come out at the top of the lane and whistle if I see her leave."

"All right, but only for a half hour longer," Lizzie agreed, and Wickham loped off before she could tell him to take care. She watched him go, trying to corral her feelings of excitement that Wickham had shown up.

Be sensible, she told herself. Now was not the time to be distracted by Wickham.

But Wickham proved to be correct—not a quarter of an hour had passed before she heard a low, melodic whistle, and she looked up to see Wickham waiting at the street corner, his posture ready for action. Lizzie picked up her skirts and trotted toward him.

He was in the process of hailing a cab as Lizzie drew near. "She climbed into that carriage," he exclaimed, pointing down the block.

Lizzie didn't need to be told to hurry—she leapt into the cab before it made a complete stop, startling the driver. "Follow that carriage," Wickham called to him, jumping in after Lizzie.

"You were right," Lizzie declared as they lurched into motion. "If I'd been alone, I'd have missed her altogether."

"It was just luck," Wickham insisted. "You were the one who suspected she might make a move."

"Depending on where she goes, we may have to drop back a distance," she said to Wickham, who was at the other window trying to see ahead. "She can't spot us."

But Lizzie needn't have worried. The approaching dusk made it difficult to see Caroline's carriage, but she had to give credit to their driver—he kept apace as they drove through the streets. Their chase led them to Sutton Street, which was moderately busy even at this time of evening. Wickham called out to the driver to let them out down a ways from where Caroline had stopped in front of a handsome stone building, rather too big to be someone's residence. Lizzie and Wickham watched as Caroline emerged from her carriage, spoke a few words to the driver, and then went inside. Lizzie noted that she was dressed in a light-colored evening gown, which puzzled her even more— where was she headed?

They emerged from their cab, and when it became apparent that Wickham wasn't going to pay the driver, Lizzie reached into her reticule. Wickham looked up and down the street, and when Lizzie began to march up to the building, he placed a hand on her elbow. "Wait."

"I don't want to lose her," Lizzie protested, but Wickham's warm touch was distracting. It wasn't proper, the way he touched her, and yet she could not bring herself to draw away.

"She's gone inside. I doubt that she'll get away from you now, Miss Bennet." Mr. Wickham drew her back and said, "Let's watch."

Another carriage pulled up to the building that Caroline had disappeared into, and more finely dressed ladies emerged, along with a gentleman. "It's a public assembly," Lizzie realized, and as soon as she spoke the words, she could hear the faint strains of music in the air. Public assembly halls held dances multiple times per week, and if Mrs. Bennet had her way, she would drag her daughters to one every night. They were a convenient way to socialize with other respectable people.

"I would have taken her for the sort of young lady who went to Almack's, myself," Wickham mused.

"Agreed," Lizzie murmured, although she had never been to Almack's. Only the richest, most exclusive members of the ton went there. And by the state of the guests' clothing and their carriages—some hired—she guessed that this public assembly was a step down the social ladder for Caroline, meant for the middle class.

"I suppose she can't show her face in finer places, not with her brother up for murder," Wickham pointed out.

"True." Lizzie heaved a sigh. "We won't be able to follow her in."

"Why not?"

Lizzie held back an incredulous laugh. "I'm not properly attired, never mind we don't have a subscription!"

Public assemblies sold subscriptions at the start of each season, and you had to either have one or be a guest of a subscription holder in order to enter. Lizzie felt her frustration well up—she loathed when her work was impeded by trifling social norms.

"You look lovely, Miss Bennet," he said so earnestly that Lizzie felt her face grow warm, even though her day gown of brown-and-blue muslin was not at all appropriate for an evening dance. "Leave the matter of our admission to me."

He disappeared down the street, and Lizzie lost sight of him in the arrival of two new carriages. She loitered nervously on the corner for five and then ten minutes. She received a few curious looks and moved closer to the venue in the hope that she could pass for a young lady who'd simply stepped out for some fresh air. Just when she began to worry that Wickham had abandoned her, he approached her in the opposite direction from where he'd disappeared. He was, inexplicably, wearing a finer coat than the one he'd been wearing just twenty minutes earlier, and his cravat was freshly tied. "Miss Bennet, would you do me the honor of accompanying me?"

"Where did you get that?" she demanded. "And how will they let us in?"

"I can be very convincing when I need to be," he said, but refused to say any more.

Lizzie was afraid they would be turned away at the door, but it was just a dress ball, not a fancy ball. She passed through the doors with only a slight raise of eyebrows at her plainer clothing. Once inside the crowded hall, Lizzie saw her initial judgment of the event confirmed. This particular public assembly was one of the cheaper ones, with quite a variation in dress. The ladies in attendance were likely lower middle class, like her. She relaxed slightly, even though the atmosphere was more raucous than polite society usually allowed. How intriguing that Caroline would end up here.

"Let's walk about, but slowly," Lizzie said. "I don't want Caroline to spot us, but we need to learn why she's here."

The room itself was plainer than the assembly halls that Mrs. Bennet insisted on attending, but spacious enough. The walls weren't papered, but large wall hangings that had seen better days helped to absorb the swell of music and chatter. Crude benches and chairs were scattered about along the edges of the room, and they were already occupied with pink-faced, gossiping matrons.

Mrs. Bennet would be right at home here, although Lizzie knew that her mother would deem the company not highborn enough for her daughters. The one saving grace to the hall was that the main room was tall, with a line of windows near the ceiling that let in the evening air but not the curious gazes of outsiders. The dancing had already begun, and a good number of couples were engaged in a Scotch reel. Lizzie scanned the crowd but didn't see Caroline anywhere.

They navigated the room, and Lizzie's pulse raced the entire time, nervous that the crowd would part and Caroline's gaze would land on them and the ruse would be up. But the room was packed and noisy, and Lizzie realized that even if Caroline spotted them, she'd have to fight through the crowds to get to Lizzie. . . .

"There," Lizzie said suddenly, and stepped behind a cluster of older women, mothers and chaperones most likely. Wickham stumbled after her, causing one woman to cast a reprimanding look in their direction.

"My apologies," Lizzie said, trying not to seem as if she were craning for a look at Caroline. "I feel quite faint."

The women turned from disapproving to concerned in an instant. "Fetch her a chair," a silver-haired matron instructed Wickham, and he released her arm to do as he was told. Lizzie did an admirable job of playing at being overwhelmed and distracted as she fended off the women's inquiries while trying to keep an eye on Caroline.

"Where's your chaperone?" one woman asked, and Lizzie pretended she was so overcome that she hadn't heard the question.

Wickham arrived with a chair, and Lizzie was promptly guided into it, but she lost her vantage point on Caroline.

Bollocks. Even worse, the women shooed Wickham away. "Plenty of young ladies to dance with here," the silver-haired one chided. "Let her have a rest."

Well, this was inconvenient! *Watch her,* Lizzie mouthed to Wickham over the woman's shoulder, and then submitted to the attentions of the older ladies. "Thank you for your concern," she said. "I only need a moment to recover."

"Some of the young men here can be rather persistent," the silver-haired woman observed, and Lizzie caught a whiff of disapproval in her tone.

"My companion is the utmost gentleman," Lizzie rushed to assure her.

The woman made a tiny sound of doubt but did not press Lizzie. Instead, a cup of tea was ordered, and Lizzie and the woman made each other's acquaintance. Her savior was Mrs. Matthews, and she insisted that Lizzie sit until her tea was gone and her nerves settled. Lizzie knew that there would be no dissuading her otherwise, so she sipped at the weak tea and surveyed the room.

But then the master of ceremonies called a cotillion, and Lizzie saw Caroline step to the dance floor, a red-haired young man as her partner. Who was *this*? An accomplice? Lizzie tried to become as unobtrusive as possible in her seat, but all it would take was for Caroline's gaze to sweep in her direction . . .

Except, she realized rather quickly, Caroline was far too focused on her partner to pay the onlookers any attention. They came together, stepped apart, and passed each other, but their eyes sought each other out on every turn. And it wasn't simply the young man who was infatuated with Caroline—their attentions were equally intense and full of longing.

Caroline was as in love with this young man as he was with her.

Lizzie felt like jumping up from her seat and shouting in victory. She'd known there was something Caroline was hiding. A secret beau, someone who, judging by the venue and the man's state of dress, was no match for Caroline in wealth and social stature. Perhaps her brother opposed the relationship? Bingley seemed easygoing, but one never knew the lengths to which a person would go when inheritances and finances were at risk.

"Don't worry, dear," Mrs. Matthews said. "There will be more dances, more partners."

"I'm sure of it," Lizzie said, and realizing the resource she had at her disposal, she continued, "I was rather eager, I confess. It is my first dance at this particular assembly."

"I gathered as much," the woman continued. "I hadn't seen you here before."

"You attend often?"

"As often as I can. My youngest daughter," she said, nodding at a pretty, petite brunette dancing merrily. "And my husband enjoys the company at the billiards table."

"It seems like a rather lively group. But I wonder, since you are familiar with the company, perhaps you could satisfy my curiosity? The young lady dancing, in the pearl frock—are you acquainted?"

"I'm afraid not," Mrs. Matthews responded. "Although she is a regular fixture at these balls. Her sister, who is married, often accompanies her. I haven't seen her tonight, although I could arrange an introduction."

"Oh, please don't trouble yourself," Lizzie said nervously. "I am simply curious, as I thought I saw her at another assembly last week. It would have been Friday night?"

"It likely wasn't the same lady." The matron cast her a knowing look and added, "That young lady is here every dress and fancy ball, as is her suitor. He asks her to dance twice, and if the evening is slow, three times. He then neglects to ask any other young lady to dance. A wedding should not be too far off."

"I wish them much happiness," Lizzie said, her thoughts racing. "And you're certain they were here Friday? The entire evening?"

Mrs. Matthews gave her a strange look. "I'm sure of it. She wore an emerald gown that had all of the young ladies whispering, and they danced the final reel together."

Lizzie gave her a weak smile. "She looks just like the young lady I saw last week. I must be mistaken."

If Caroline was here the night Hurst was killed, it was highly unlikely that she had left the assembly and traveled halfway across town to slip into his locked house undetected (and in an emerald ball gown!), to wait for the opportunity to murder her brother-in-law. Perhaps her lover could have, motivated by freedom and fortune . . . but Lizzie felt doubt rise in her throat. The timing just didn't match up, and Papa always said that the harder one had to reach, the more unlikely the circumstance.

She had to swallow the facts: perhaps Caroline hadn't killed George Hurst.

The dance ended, and the room applauded. Lizzie was so preoccupied by her own thoughts that she didn't immediately notice Caroline and her partner had wound up near to where she was sitting. There was no way for her to stand and retreat without attracting attention, so Lizzie turned her head to look off to the side of the room, hoping that she would pass notice. The master of ceremonies called out another dance, the instruments began to play, and out of the corner of her eye she saw dancers return once more to the floor. She let out a tiny sigh of relief and glanced back to the dance floor.

And straight into Caroline Bingley's furious gaze.

"Miss Bennet," Caroline said in a tone cold enough to produce ice in summer. "Take a turn about the room with me."

She didn't wait for Lizzie's response before grabbing her arm and jerking her out of her seat, leaving behind a rather baffled Mrs. Matthews. Caroline's hand was a sharp clamp on Lizzie as she propelled her through the crowded hall, through a door Lizzie hadn't noticed before, leading out to a quieter room of cards and refreshments, and then through another door into a shadowy hall.

"You followed me!" Caroline accused.

"I beg your pardon, but I'm investigating," Lizzie said, striving to remain calm.

"Investigate *elsewhere*."

"I don't mean to offend, but I must go where my questions lead."

Two bright pink spots had flared upon Caroline's ivory skin. "Your questions about George's death led you to follow me here? My social life had nothing to do with his murder."

But Lizzie needed to be certain that this secret suitor wasn't the only thing Caroline was hiding. "Who is the young man?"

"None of your concern."

"He's handsome," Lizzie said, although she'd not gotten a decent look at his face, only an impression of red hair and a plain jacket and waistcoat. "I hear he's a frequent dance partner of yours."

"Don't be absurd."

"Does Mrs. Hurst approve? And Mr. Bingley?"

"I don't wish to marry Henry!" Caroline's voice shook with emotion. "He's an inappropriate match."

Hurt flared in Lizzie, even though they weren't discussing her. "Because he doesn't possess a vast fortune?"

"Only someone who didn't possess a fortune would be so crude as to speak of it," Caroline volleyed back.

"I'm not rich, it's true. But that doesn't make me, or any other person lacking in wealth, less worthy of respect."

"You're not worthy of my respect because you're rude and prying. Whom I dance with and where I do it is my business!"

Lizzie's instincts told her two things: First, Caroline was lying about not wishing to marry Henry. Lizzie had seen the way she looked at him. Second, she was still holding something back.

"You're keeping a good many secrets, Caroline. It's a wonder that you can keep them all straight."

"You nose about in a great many lives, *Elizabeth*," Caroline countered. "It's a wonder you have any friends at all."

Lizzie wouldn't normally allow herself to be offended by such words, but Caroline's insult landed close to her heart. She pushed her thoughts of Charlotte aside. Lizzie would not be able to outtalk Caroline, she realized. She made a split-second decision to bargain instead. "My job is to prove your brother's innocence. I have to consider anything I uncover relevant to the murder investigation, and relay that information."

Caroline glowered, but she followed Lizzie's meaning nicely. "What do you want?"

One question, that was all Lizzie would get out of Caroline. She knew better than to waste it by inquiring whether she knew who had killed Hurst. Instead, she asked, "Why did you convince Louisa to leave her husband? Yes, I know, he was terrible. But it would have given Mr. Hurst legal ground for divorce and ruined your family."

Beneath Caroline's contempt, Lizzie detected a hint of

panic. Lizzie pressed her advantage. "There are already whispers that your sister left him before the murder. If we can find out who the real murderer is, perhaps we can recast the story to put your sister in a better light. . . ."

Caroline scowled. "You're not nearly as clever as you think, Miss Bennet."

As if Lizzie needed any reminders of her own shortcomings. But she didn't take the bait.

Finally, Caroline relented. "George was too sly for his own good, and not nearly smart enough to stay out of trouble. I overheard Charles and Darcy speaking of how best to cut him off ages ago, but the only reason Charles wouldn't go through with it was Louisa. I thought if Louisa were home, then Charles could do whatever he needed to—appeal the courts, cut him off completely—and George would be out of our lives for good."

"Was there any particular reason why your brother would cut him off? Aside from the debts, I mean?"

"It may be simpler to list all of the reasons why he might not be cut off," Caroline said, leaving Lizzie no doubt as to whom she blamed for their predicament. "Ask Darcy if you want the details. All I know is that George must have gotten into very deep trouble because I could only get one new ball gown this past season."

Lizzie's skin prickled at the mention of Darcy, but she forced herself to focus. If Caroline's wardrobe was suffering, then it confirmed that Bingley tried to cover Hurst's expenses out of his own pocket. Unfortunately, it also gave Bingley yet another motive. Sensing Caroline's volatile patience with this line of questioning coming to an end, Lizzie asked, "Who do you think killed your brother-in-law?"

"I wouldn't have the first clue, and furthermore I don't care," Caroline said with great indifference, then patted her hair and looked beyond Lizzie to the card room. "Don't follow me again, Miss Bennet. In fact, do us both a favor and stay out of my way."

With that, Caroline whisked away with all the grace of a venomous snake. Lizzie waited a few minutes to gather herself, not relishing the prospect of inserting herself back into the assembly hall to find Wickham. Where had he gone? Had he seen her disappear with Caroline? She hoped so, and that prompted her to venture out from the shadowy hall, looking for his tall, trim figure in that borrowed coat. But to her disappointment, he was not lurking nearby to keep an eye on her.

Not that she needed him to keep an eye on her. But it would have been reassuring to know that he was about, focused on their mission.

As she passed through the card room and into the assembly hall, she heard a man laugh—abrasive and sickeningly familiar. Lizzie went rigid as she looked left and right for the source of the sound, and then—there! At a card table on the edge of the room, she caught sight of a profile she knew all too well.

Collins.

If Caroline spotting her at this assembly had been bad, then being discovered here, unchaperoned, by Collins would be disastrous. He would surely embarrass her, but worse, he'd have no qualms about reporting her whereabouts to her father. And while she could lie to Mrs. Bennet and say she was having dinner with Charlotte this evening, she knew that Mr. Bennet would figure her out—and he couldn't know about her tactics until after she solved the case and convinced him to give her the job!

Without looking to see where she was going, Lizzie made an ungraceful lunge toward cover. She meant to hide behind one of the pillars that ringed the ballroom but bumped into a tall, dark-haired woman who was already there, watching the dancers with a sphinxlike gaze.

"I beg your pardon," Lizzie gasped.

"Not at all," came the response. The woman had a long, rather large aquiline nose and heavy eyebrows. Judging by the fine lines around her eyes and the single striking gray streak to her dark hair, Lizzie guessed her to be in her early forties. Like Caroline, she was dressed just a shade more finely than the others in attendance. "Are you all right?" the older woman asked, her tone polite but without the same concern the gaggle of matrons had shown her earlier.

"My apologies," Lizzie said. "I seem to have lost my companion."

The other woman did not rush to assist as Mrs. Matthews

had. Instead, she arched a single brow. "Should I fetch someone to collect you?"

"No, thank you. I shall collect myself, then . . ." What should she do next? "Er . . . find my companion and leave."

"Very well," the other woman said. "Although I should point out that a young lady will never find a husband if she's in the habit of retiring early."

Unlike Mrs. Bennet, the stranger relayed this warning with a mocking tone, as if she were making fun of convention instead of Lizzie. It made Lizzie regard her with a slight smile. "There shall be other dances."

The woman did not smile back. "There are always other dances, but rarely second chances."

Lizzie wasn't quite sure what she was supposed to say to that. Luckily, she was not obliged to respond, as the woman looked back at the dancers and said, "It's all a beautiful facade for what these balls truly represent."

"And what is that?"

"A market."

Lizzie wasn't sure if she'd heard her correctly. "A market?"

"A marriage market. All the young ladies want good, secure matches and a step up the social ladder. All the young men want a pretty wife to add to their fortunes. Their parents scheme along the sidelines."

Lizzie did not disagree with this stranger's point of view, but she was shocked to hear her speak so openly.

"Women get the worst of it," the older woman continued. "Gentlemen get to choose from a roomful of beautiful ladies. But ladies have no choice. The only power they have is in their refusal, and if they refuse too often, they stop receiving invitations."

This, Lizzie could agree with. She thought of Collins at the card table, pursuing Charlotte one moment and attending a public assembly the next. Was it a betrayal of his interest in her friend or simply what young men did? "I agree with you, madam, but what else are we supposed to do?"

The woman smiled, and it felt like a secret between them. "Refuse to participate in this sham altogether. But only one in a hundred ladies will do that. Perhaps not even that. One in a thousand."

Lizzie's instinct for argument compelled her to respond. "Until there are more opportunities for young ladies, most will continue down the paths set out before them."

"And in the meantime?" the woman asked.

"Forge new paths. It is easier to be brave, perhaps, when one has examples of bravery to follow." She could scarcely believe there was a society woman willing to have this sort of conversation without scandalized gasps. If all public assemblies harbored such company as this one, Lizzie might be more inclined to participate.

The woman regarded her with cool satisfaction, but before Lizzie could engage any further, she spotted a blond head in the crowd. "Oh, I believe I see my companion. I'm sorry, I must depart. Thank you. . . ."

But the strange woman didn't introduce herself. Instead, she inclined her head and turned away, disappearing into the crowd. Lizzie watched her go, perplexed and amused. How very strange.

"Miss Bennet!" Wickham appeared at her side. "There you are. I couldn't find you for the longest time! Caroline has left the ball early, which caused a great deal of speculation amongst the other young ladies, as she's only danced one reel with that redheaded bloke. I couldn't follow her without you, but if we hurry . . ."

"It's all right, Mr. Wickham," Lizzie murmured, feeling quite exhausted all of a sudden. "I believe I got what I came for."

NINE

In Which Lizzie Picks Up a Tail

THE FOLLOWING MORNING FOUND Lizzie restless and uncertain about the case. She'd lost a day to her investigation by loitering on Harley Street, and it yielded only more questions. She had only four days until Mr. Bingley's hearing and nothing in hand but a button. To make matters worse, her mother had reached the limits of her patience regarding Lizzie's absences and insisted that all of the Bennet ladies spend the day together. Lizzie was forced to sit in the drawing room, continually jabbing herself with an embroidery needle, while enduring Mary's mediocre attempts at the piano.

If she didn't get the job at Longbourn, she would wither away from boredom.

Mary's fumblings were good for one thing: covering Lizzie's

whispers as she briefly sketched out the previous night's activities to Jane.

"You're certain that Caroline was telling the truth?"

"She'd have no reason to lie about their sudden lack of money." Lizzie gazed at Jane's perfect stitches, depicting a rather charming scene of marigolds and fronds. Her own bit of muslin was supposed to bear a strawberry patch, but as per usual, her red silk thread had gotten hopelessly tangled. "Besides, witnesses can place her at the dance the night of the murder. So I must conclude that she's merely an unbearable person."

Mary's song ended abruptly, and the end of Lizzie's sentence caught the attention of her other sisters. "Who is an unbearable person?" Lydia asked, eager for gossip.

"No one," Lizzie said.

"Elizabeth, it's impolite to whisper to Jane if you're not going to include the rest of your sisters in the conversation," her mother chided.

Jane smiled slightly, no help whatsoever. "Do tell us," Kitty begged.

"I was speaking of Mr. Collins," Lizzie lied, although the sentiment itself was no lie. But bringing up their father's junior partner reminded Lizzie of Charlotte. Lizzie hadn't been able to bring herself to tell Jane of Collins's flirtatious exchange with Charlotte or of Lizzie and Charlotte's subsequent falling-out.

"Elizabeth! You must stop belittling Mr. Collins."

"Yes, it's quite dull," Lydia agreed. "I'd much rather speak of other more interesting, more handsome young men."

Lizzie distrusted the sly tone in Lydia's voice. Mary began to play once more, but Mrs. Bennet said, "We've had quite enough for one morning, dear," and Mary stopped with a small pout.

"We must strive to be kind to Mr. Collins," Mrs. Bennet continued. "If he must inherit your father's estate, then we should bring him into the family accordingly. Don't make that face, Lizzie. We must all do our duties. I did, although at the time I thought that Mr. Bennet might apply himself a bit more. Let that be a lesson to you all."

"I don't think that Mr. Collins wishes to marry any of us, Mama," Lizzie cut in. She couldn't bear it when her mother criticized her father.

Mrs. Bennet became alarmed. "Why? What have you heard?"

Lizzie bit down on her tongue, but it was too late. She hadn't meant to reveal to her mother that Collins's attention might have wandered elsewhere. "Nothing, Mama."

It was almost the truth. Lizzie hadn't heard anything—just seen him. But why else would he be at a public assembly, if not in search of a wife?

"This is all your father's fault for refusing to invite Collins to dinner so that he can become properly acquainted with you all!"

"Lizzie is at the firm so often, he should marry her," Kitty said.

"As if I'd have him," Lizzie replied.

Mrs. Bennet tsk-tsked. "You'll have any gentleman who asks. You should be so fortunate. . . ."

Lizzie looked down at her tangled embroidery so that her mother and sisters wouldn't see her stormy look. She thought of the nameless woman the night before. Gentlemen get to choose, but the only power ladies have is in their refusal. Lizzie would refuse Collins and her mother. She would, if tested.

"If you're not at the firm to woo Mr. Collins, then how are you spending your time outside of the house?" Mrs. Bennet asked, suddenly suspicious. "Jane, you told me she was visiting Miss Lucas and Mr. Collins."

"I don't think Mr. Collins is the gentleman—" Lydia began, but Lizzie interrupted her harshly.

"I've been helping Papa. And visiting Charlotte. The firm is very busy."

"If business was what preoccupied Mr. Bennet for such long hours, we all should have new gowns this season, but have I been able to call the dressmaker? No, I have not."

Lizzie slid her glance to Jane, who smiled a weak apology. Thankfully, a tirade about dresses and the mercurial nature of fashions was enough to shift the attentions of Mrs. Bennet and the younger Bennet sisters, at least until the maid came in with a letter on a tray.

"Miss Elizabeth," she said, and presented the folded paper to Lizzie. Lizzie felt the weight of five pairs of eyes on her, and she turned it over and took in the return address and seal—it was from Pemberley. Her pulse quickened as she broke the seal.

The quarto sheet contained only a short note:

Dear Miss Bennet,

Please excuse the liberties I've taken in responding on Mr. Bingley's behalf, but I must remind you that as his solicitor, all correspondence regarding his case must be addressed to me. Regarding your question about the pocket watch, I believe you are misguided. Mr. Banks informs me that the watch had gone missing two days before the murder, and Mrs. Hurst suspects her husband sold it himself and pretended it had been stolen. Bingley reports that it was gold, mother-of-pearl inlay, with both a minute and second hand—it would have fetched a good sum.

No mystery here, Miss Bennet.

Yours sincerely,

Mr. Fitzwilliam Darcy

P.S. Stop breaking and entering.

"I was let in," Lizzie muttered, and then swiftly folded the letter and tucked it into her pocket.

"Who was that from, dear?" Mrs. Bennet asked in an appalling attempt at sounding casual.

Lizzie could hardly respond, *No one of consequence,* even if that was how she currently felt about Darcy. Lydia looked all too eager to spill what she'd seen of Lizzie's comings and goings, so Lizzie decided to tell a little truth for once. "Mr. Darcy," she said. "We briefly consulted on a case."

"Darcy! Not the Darcys of Pemberley?" Mrs. Bennet asked.

"The one and the same."

"Why, I had no idea that you were acquainted with a Darcy!" Mrs. Bennet appeared rather ruffled. "Well, they're a fine family, but their manners leave rather a lot to be desired. I don't wish you to continue this acquaintance, my dear."

"You don't need to worry, Mama," Lizzie said sincerely. "I don't wish to be acquainted with him either."

But unfortunately for Lizzie, she still had to deal with the young gentleman, and she was not about to let his condescending letter hold back her investigation—after all, he had given her the information she'd asked for and more besides. She found it curious that the pocket watch had vanished two days before the murder—the explanation that Hurst needed money was valid enough. Perhaps the watch had been the easiest thing to sell off quickly. But a pocket watch was an outward sign of success. Lizzie thought of the fine unread and uncut books on his shelf. Of the gap in the drawing room where a piece of furniture had once been. What had induced him to sell one of his close personal belongings over any of the other fine, less noticeably missed items in his house?

Lizzie stewed in her questions until after luncheon, when Mrs. Bennet retired to her rooms and demanded that Kitty and Lydia wait upon her. Then she shared Darcy's letter with Jane while she went for her bonnet. "I'm going out."

"For how long?" Jane was never one to tell Lizzie what to do, but Lizzie knew that she was putting her sister in an awkward position by forcing Jane to continually lie for her.

"I need to find out what happened to Mr. Hurst's pocket watch. Its disappearance might have something to do with his death."

"You're going to go back to the Hursts', after you were marched away by a Runner? Lizzie, be sensible!"

Lizzie sighed as she pulled on her gloves. "I suppose I'll have Fred help."

"Fred? Or Mr. Wickham?"

Lizzie stopped straightening her bonnet. "Whatever are you talking about?"

"You don't really know him," Jane reminded her. "How do you know he won't take advantage?"

"If he were going to take advantage, he would have had ample opportunity!"

"I don't mean that way . . . well, yes, I do. But that way is not the only way men could take advantage."

Lizzie was all too aware, still stinging from Collins's blatant theft of her own work. "Are we to be mistrustful of every young man we meet?"

"No," Jane replied. "But we ought to be cautious until a man's character is known."

"I may not have been acquainted with Mr. Wickham for very long, but in that time, he has walked me home rather than turn me over to the magistrate. He came to my aid when I called, escorted me to a public assembly, and home once more. He's shaping up to be *quite* the gentleman."

"If you say so."

"I do," Lizzie snapped back.

To Jane's credit, she did not grow irritated with her sister. All she said was, "Try not to be out too late. Mama will be paying more attention to your comings and goings now that she knows you've been talking with a Darcy."

Lizzie didn't respond as she departed. Everything offended her today: the cheerful spring sun that warmed the streets with the promise of summer, her mother's desperate wish for her to marry Collins, her younger sisters' interferences, Jane's worry. Her instincts were usually spot-on, and she was unaccustomed to running into a dead end.

No more supposing or guessing, she told herself. She had information, yes. Hurst was in debt, and his problems had made a target of his wealthy brother-in-law, who was the perfect scapegoat for Hurst's death. But the only piece of evidence she had was a button that could belong to anyone. The missing pocket watch could illuminate the case, if she could find it.

Lizzie made her way down to the streets of her Cheapside

neighborhood, looking to places that Fred liked to haunt during the day, picking up work as an errand boy for shopkeepers, merchants, and shoppers. She trusted his instincts and work. She knew where she stood with Fred. She didn't want to entertain Jane's concerns, but ever since she'd spoken them, Lizzie couldn't help but recall how Wickham had evaded her questions last night—she had ignored it at the time, because she was focused on Caroline. Wickham was charming, and he got results . . . but how?

Lizzie wasn't certain, but she consoled herself with the simple fact that when it came to talking to people in service and tracking down (possibly stolen) goods, a young orphan who slipped in and out of sight might be a better choice than a Runner.

Lizzie found Fred arguing a fee with the butcher's assistant and pretended to inspect the tray of delicacies in the bakery shop next door until he noticed her and gave her a barely perceptible nod. Fred and the butcher came to an agreement, and Fred approached her. "An errand, miss?"

"A job," Lizzie said in a hushed tone. "I need to find a pocket watch. It was stolen, probably under a week ago."

Fred raised an eyebrow. "Did someone steal from you, miss?"

"Oh, no. The watch in question belonged to Mr. Hurst. It's a curious thing—the Hursts' maid led me to believe that it was stolen during the murder, but I have it from the Bingleys that

Hurst had been complaining about it being stolen right before he was killed."

The butcher came out and spotted Fred speaking with Lizzie. "Oy! Get on, or you won't get paid!"

"Walk with me, miss?" Fred asked, and Lizzie nodded, following him down the street. They didn't quite look like they were together, Fred keeping a proper distance between them and barely looking at Lizzie as he said, "And you think that whoever stole it might have had reason to kill him?"

"Or, he sold it himself," she said, "and if that's the case, I want to know whom he sold it to. But I can't go into a pawnbroker's shop myself—I'll draw too much attention."

Fred's features scrunched up in suspicion. "What's a fine gentleman like him doing pawning his own watch?"

"He needed money, badly." After a brief hesitation she added, "I have it on good authority his brother-in-law was struggling to keep up with expenses."

"Won't be easy," Fred said, "finding one watch in all of London. Especially if it was stolen."

"But you can make inquiries?"

Fred nodded. "Just tell me what it looks like, and I've got a few lads I can ask. But what do you want me to do if I find it? I can't just say, 'Oy, that's stolen property, give it back.'"

"I don't want to return it, I just want to know where it's gone. Come get me if you find it," Lizzie said. She was already imagining scenarios in which she would impersonate Louisa, carry on that it was an heirloom, the only object she wanted to remember her poor dead husband by. Yes, that might work. . . .

"Anything else, miss?"

"Can you get a message to the Hursts' maid, Abigail? I don't dare go by the house again now that the butler knows who I am. See if she'll meet me, away from the house. I have some follow-up questions."

"Aye," Fred agreed, almost reluctantly. He was moving, Lizzie observed, almost erratically. He would not look at her, but he kept sweeping his gaze around, as if he were looking out for someone else. "And was that Runner any help, miss?"

"He proved very useful last night. But this is still my investigation, and you're still my best asset, Fred."

That earned a grin, even if he didn't direct it at her. "Keep walking nice and casual-like, miss."

Lizzie thought that was what she was already doing. "Why?"

But he didn't say anything, instead turning down a side street that had fewer shops and pedestrians. Lizzie followed, confused. "Meet me at Gwennie's flower stall!" he whispered, and picked up pace so he was a few strides ahead of Lizzie before bolting down an alleyway. She was perplexed but did as she was told, trying to walk at an even pace. What on earth could he be doing? Nonetheless, she circled the block, ending up back at the market. Gwennie was a waifish brunette who had a flower stall near the milliner Lizzie and her sisters patronized. So she made her way to the stall and pretended to admire the daisies. Fred caught up a few minutes later, appearing at her elbow.

"You've caught a tail, miss," he said.

Lizzie stiffened. "Are you sure?"

"Aye. I don't recognize him, but he followed you around the block."

She gaped. "Where?"

"Don't look," he said. "But he's stepped into the doorway of the tobacco shop."

"I can't fathom why . . ."

"Something you've done lately? Perhaps with that watchman?"

"It's not him, is it?" Lizzie asked, although the idea of Wickham stalking her through the streets of London seemed preposterous.

"Nay, miss. This bloke is a bit rough. Former boxer, I'd guess."

Lizzie shivered, but only partly in fear. Excitement was swirling underneath. She had thought her investigation fruitless until this moment. "You know what this means, Fred?"

"You've caught someone's attention?"

"Not just someone," Lizzie said excitedly. "But *the* one. Someone to do with the case!"

Fred blanched. "I should go get the Runner."

"No!" Lizzie protested. "Go run your errand for the butcher, and then see what you can do about tracking down that pocket watch."

"But what about you, miss? I can't leave you."

"No one will hurt me in broad daylight," Lizzie reassured him. "My father's firm is only a few blocks away. I'll go straight there, and wait for him to escort me home, or hail a carriage."

"Will you tell him you're being followed?"

"Of course," Lizzie said, although she intended no such thing. Fred's concern for her was touching, but it was overwhelmed by a surge of new energy for the case. "You'll have to get the message to me at home. Pass it off to Agnes," she instructed, naming the maid. "Not Cook. She'd hand it straight to Mama." Mrs. Bennet may respect the sanctity of correspondence properly sent and received, but she had no such restraint when it came to illicit notes.

"Right," Fred said uneasily. "You go off first, miss. I don't think he knows I've spotted him, so if you act natural, he might not realize you know."

"Thank you, Fred!" she said, and purchased a daisy from Gwennie.

Lizzie strode off, filled with renewed purpose and just a bit of unease. To be followed was such an exciting thing! She'd never been followed before, at least not in the course of her work for the firm. Lydia following her around assemblies her first season certainly didn't count. Multiple times Lizzie had to stop herself from turning her head, but she couldn't resist glancing into shop windows on the pretense of taking in their wares, when in reality she was straining for a glimpse of her tail in the reflection of the glass. She never caught sight of her mysterious follower, but she felt his presence all the same.

As she walked to Longbourn & Sons, a new theory began to take hold. Hurst was likely in over his head in debt. Bingley had been bailing him out but had grown weary of pouring money into his reckless brother-in-law's coffers, hence the discussions with Darcy about how to cut him off. But Bingley couldn't ever truly be free of Hurst, not while his sister was still married to him. It wasn't until Caroline had convinced Louisa to leave Hurst that the dissolution of their union became a possibility. Why, even Mrs. Bennet had spoken of it! Perhaps Hurst's less savory creditors had learned that he would soon be dead broke, and they'd decided to cut their losses and exact the ultimate payment. Bingley had merely been in the wrong place at the wrong time.

Or, Bingley had snapped and killed Hurst in a fit of rage and tried to cover it up. Darcy was in on it and wanted her away from the case, lest she reveal the truth.

Lizzie did not like that theory.

Would her father still consider her a fit, logical candidate for solicitor at the firm if she uncovered that Bingley was involved in the murder? Or would she just be made to look the fool for wasting time on an unwinnable case?

Longbourn & Sons was just ahead now, and Lizzie strode to the entrance. The front door swung open just as she was reaching for it, nearly knocking her aside. She took a step back, and a vaguely familiar voice said, "I beg your pardon— Miss Bennet!"

She looked straight up into Darcy's eyes and found herself quite breathless.

"Mr. Darcy," she finally managed. His name felt heavy on her tongue, but she pushed on brazenly forth. "What on earth brings you here? Finally come to accept my assistance?"

He laughed as if she'd just told a very witty joke. "On the contrary, I've just spoken to your father. I'm sure he'll explain the purpose of my visit."

All of Lizzie's excitement at the day's developments pooled into dread. Darcy smiled, an expression that Lizzie realized she had yet to see him wear. It changed his face entirely, from brooding and haughty to . . . well, not exactly warm. But interesting. It was a smile that concealed secrets Lizzie wished to know. "Good day, Miss Bennet."

He stepped neatly around her and into his waiting carriage, drawn by a fine pair of matching black geldings. She did not give him the satisfaction of watching him pull away but stepped inside and immediately looked about for Charlotte, trying not to panic. What had he told her father?

Charlotte looked up from her desk and spotted Lizzie. However, she did not give her the warm smile Lizzie was accustomed to. "Lizzie. Mr. Darcy was just here."

"I saw," Lizzie said. "What did he want?"

But before Charlotte could come up with an answer, her father's voice rang out. "Elizabeth!"

She looked up. Only Mrs. Bennet called her Elizabeth. Only Mrs. Bennet, and very, very occasionally Mr. Bennet, when he was angry with her. Now her father stood framed in his office door, displeasure heavy on his face and Collins simpering at his side.

Her father stepped aside. "In here. *Now*."

TEN

In Which Lizzie Calls upon Darcy

LIZZIE HAD ONLY A precious few moments to wrap her mind around this current development and get a handle on the situation. But she was nothing if not a quick thinker, and the moment the sturdy office door had closed behind her and Mr. Bennet, she asked, "What did Mr. Darcy want?"

"How did you become acquainted with Mr. Darcy?" her father countered.

"Through Mr. Bingley. Was Mr. Darcy consulting on a business matter?"

"How did you become acquainted with Mr. Bingley?"

Lizzie hesitated, unable to come up with a bland response. Her hesitation was her downfall.

"God almighty, Lizzie," her father said, sinking into his chair. "I knew you were curious about this case, but I told you we wouldn't be pursuing it. Mr. Bingley has already engaged counsel."

"Well, I didn't know that when I went to Newgate," she replied.

"You went to Newgate?"

"That's how I made Mr. Bingley's acquaintance. He was so impressed, he invited me to call on him. I met his sisters and presented my case, and he agreed that I could make inquiries, although he's retaining Mr. Darcy."

Mr. Bennet gaped at his daughter. When he had recovered enough to speak, he simply said, "Your mother must never learn of this."

"Obviously," Lizzie said. "But Papa, this case has turned rather interesting—"

"And the other day, when you were asking me about witnesses—did you have a suspect in mind?"

"Well . . . yes."

"And it didn't happen to be Miss Caroline Bingley, did it?"

"Why do you ask?" Lizzie stalled.

"Because Mr. Darcy has asked me that I 'rein in' my daughter and explain to her if she does not cease casting aspersions on the character of Miss Bingley, or any other member of the Bingley family, he will bring a libel suit against Longbourn and Sons."

"Libel? That's a stretch!" Lizzie's fury made her skin feel hot and tight. "I've not accused anyone. Yet."

"Your actions speak," her father responded. "What else will people assume when you're poking about those closest to the accused? To the murder victim? We are not investigators, Lizzie!"

"I know, and I don't suspect Miss Bingley anymore, although she was holding back, just as I suspected. I was able to—"

"No," her father said flatly. "I don't want to hear any more."

"But Mr. Bingley said—"

"I'm your father, and I say you will drop this *at once!*"

Lizzie stiffened in shock. It was rare that she heard her father raise his voice in anger, or even frustration, and the few times she had witnessed it, it had never been directed at her. His anger at her made her feel like a small child, and her dreams of being on the same side of the desk as he seemed further away than ever. "I simply thought that if I could show you I'm capable of handling a case—"

But Mr. Bennet cut her off. "Lizzie, I appreciate that you want to work for the firm officially, but my reaction would be the same if you were my son. Longbourn and Sons cannot afford the litigation that would come with a libel case. Pemberley would outlast us in court without a dent to their coffers. If you continue down this path, you will surely bankrupt this firm and your family. Do you want that?"

"No, Papa."

"Right," he said, and it was as if a curtain had been suddenly drawn and he sagged just a little. Forcefulness did not come naturally to Mr. Bennet. He fought his battles in biting words, delivered mildly.

"Go home," he said. "Don't come back here until I have given you express permission to do so."

"But what about—"

"Please, Lizzie," he said. "I cannot argue about this anymore today. I need to hire a solicitor I know I can trust to follow instructions, and right now you have broken that trust."

These words stopped all protest. She had never before caused him to distrust her, or send her away, and the hurt of it was shocking. All she could do was whisper, "Yes, Papa."

She left him in his office, wishing she could forget the shape of defeat in his posture.

Lizzie tried to keep her feelings in check as she approached the imposing offices of Pemberley & Associates. The gold-plated sign announcing the firm was so shiny she could see her angry reflection in it. She didn't even need to push open the oak door herself—a clerk was stationed to do the task for her.

The air inside smelled of paper and ink and a manly scent of cologne, tinged with cigar smoke. It was a smell, she realized, she was familiar with. She associated it with Darcy. How embarrassing that she already recognized his scent! She hoped he didn't smoke cigars. It was a dreadful habit.

"How may I help you, Miss . . . ?" a clerk behind a desk asked.

"I've an appointment with Mr. Darcy," she said, passing him her calling card.

"Mr. Darcy doesn't take on clients without a referral from a solicitor with whom he is acquainted," the clerk replied.

Lizzie bristled at his rudeness. Well, if you had a gold-plated sign announcing yourself outside, she supposed you could afford to be impolite. "The younger Mr. Darcy," she clarified.

"Is he expecting you?"

He would be a fool if he wasn't. "Of course."

"I see, Miss Bennet." The clerk looked up. "If you'll be so kind as to wait . . ."

"Here?" Lizzie asked, letting her tone tell the clerk just what she thought of that idea. "I'll thank you to see me to Mr. Darcy's office at once."

The clerk hesitated for a moment, and Lizzie could just imagine he was trying to discern what would be less trouble-some—bringing a stranger to Darcy's office or having to deal with Lizzie's demands. Either she was doing a better job than she thought at channeling her inner Caroline or Darcy was the forgiving type, because the clerk relented. "Follow me."

He led Lizzie down a short hall and through a large open office space full of orderly desks. Lizzie did her best not to stare. Pemberley & Associates employed three times the number of solicitors and clerks that her father did, and there were at least eight office doors along the perimeter.

Lizzie expected to be led to one of these offices—perhaps a smaller one, tucked away into a corner. But instead, she was presented to a desk in the far corner of the room, next to what appeared to be a records room. Lizzie was about to protest when she spotted a small nameplate on the desk: Mr. F. Darcy.

"Mr. Darcy should be with you shortly," the clerk said with a sniff, and left her standing.

Lizzie was surprised—the son of the founding barrister of Pemberley & Associates, and he didn't even have an office? That meant that either Darcy had done something very foolish to deserve this humiliation or he was rather dense. Well, his plan to "defend" Bingley by bleating about his exceptional character *was* dense. But reporting her to her father wasn't exactly the action of someone who didn't know what he was doing. And she was going to tell him just what she thought of his actions . . . as soon as he returned.

After a minute of standing at the head of Darcy's desk, Lizzie realized that none of the clerks or solicitors who sat nearby were going to offer her a seat. The only available chair was Darcy's, and it wasn't even pushed in neatly. In fact, Darcy's desk was a mess—not quite as bad as Mr. Bennet's, but no one would call it tidy by any stretch.

If Lizzie was going to be kept waiting, she wouldn't hover

like a timid creature. Looking around at all of the industrious young (and some not-so-young) men who refused to glance in her direction, she shook her head and sat down, right in Darcy's chair. She justified this action with the knowledge that no visitor, client or not, would stand waiting for anyone at Longbourn & Sons. When no one protested her action—in fact, she rather suspected that no one noticed—Lizzie began to occupy herself by taking in the contents of Darcy's desk. His blotter was messy with heavy strokes of black ink and partially obscured by correspondence and various notes.

She recognized the documents in Darcy's hand thanks to the note he'd sent. His handwriting was careful, decidedly masculine but with an elegant slant to the letters that made Lizzie lean in a little closer. As she expected, the majority of the documents were regarding Bingley. She found a list of character references and another of debt collectors that she assumed were after Hurst for money—they were all respectable, not the type to send a goon to kill a man. A figure sheet amounting to nearly two thousand pounds made her eyes widen. She read the sheet twice to confirm her suspicions—it was what Hurst owed his creditors. It was a fortune twice what her father brought home annually. A number like that might not have destroyed Bingley, but if word got out, it would have been a black mark against the entire family's reputation.

Lizzie shuffled through the mess of Darcy's papers, hoping to discover more. Half of the sheets pertained to another handful of cases that he seemed to be dealing with, boring contracts for small businesses. No wonder Darcy hadn't much of an imagination for defending Bingley if this was what he dealt with day in and day out. The charges against Bingley must be as big a case for Darcy as it was for her.

Lizzie straightened the books and pens and began sorting the papers in separate piles according to case. Near the bottom of the mess, she found a bill of lading for Netherfield Shipping for fine broadcloth, linen, wool, flannels, and silk on the SS *Leander* headed to Spain, except . . . Lizzie racked her brain. The SS *Leander* had been lost, she was certain of it. Recently. She remembered reading of it in the papers. Had it been the French or the Barbary pirates? That particular detail didn't come to her, but the loss must have been dreadful, especially on top of Bingley's stress in bailing out his brother-in-law.

It could also explain why a good-natured Bingley might have been desperate to get Hurst off his payroll.

"I don't recall putting out an advertisement for a secretary," a cold voice cut through Lizzie's concentration. Her pulse leapt, but she did her best to not appear startled.

"You need more than a secretary to help you sort through this mess," she said, and looked into Darcy's icy stare. He stood squarely in front of his desk, and Lizzie felt a small thrill. "Have you given thought to developing a filing system?"

"What are you doing?"

"Poking about," Lizzie said. "Where have you been?

Intimidating someone else? Or should I say, attempting to?"

"I did not intimidate anyone," he shot back. "I simply communicated how ill-advised it is for a firm such as Longbourn and Sons to meddle in a Pemberley case."

"When a firm such as this"—Lizzie twirled her finger to indicate the large office area—"tells a firm like my father's to step back, it *is* intimidation. Besides, you seem to forget that Mr. Bingley asked for my help."

"Get. Up." Darcy reached out for the papers in her hand, and Lizzie ignored him and sorted them into their remaining piles. "Bingley is altogether too trusting. If he wants to let a strange young woman meddle and lie her way through a case, that's his prerogative, but it is my duty to protect him from possible damages."

"I think that the Bingley family is hiding something from me," Lizzie stated as she stood, keeping her gaze locked on Darcy. His eyebrows rose ever so slightly. Confirmation. "Why?"

Darcy laughed, a derisive sound that annoyed Lizzie. "If you think I'm going to tell you, you've misjudged my character."

"And if you think that I am going to be intimidated, you've misjudged mine."

To Lizzie's surprise, Darcy's face lost its haughty edge and he sighed. "Miss Bennet, you seem determined to make this into a personal case against my character. I assure you it is nothing of the sort. Bingley is my oldest friend, and I stand to lose more than you if he is imprisoned, or worse, hanged. Furthermore, I have formal education and a fundamental understanding of the courts that I fear you lack."

"Oh? Would you care to enlighten a poor, untrained woman?"

Lizzie saw his confident expression falter ever so slightly. But then he set his leather case on the desk, as if he were settling in for a long-winded lecture. "Laws are not inherently just because they are laws. The courts are biased to trust a man like Bingley—upstanding, of a decent family, impeccable manners, a good businessman. In order to clear his name, I intend to use that bias to my advantage in order to assert his innocence. The facts of the case are scarce, Miss Bennet. What do we really have? A body. Flimsy motive. There are no witnesses to the crime, and they cannot tie the murder weapon to Bingley. This case will be tried in the court of public opinion, and good public opinion is one thing that my client has in spades."

He finished his speech with a small slap against the desk. It gave Lizzie chills—God help them all if Darcy was ever in possession of a gavel.

"I'm the daughter of a barrister," Lizzie began, shocked at how measured her voice sounded when her body was trembling with anger. "So I'm aware of the nature of laws and the miscarriage of justice. You're the son of a barrister, so I find it curious that you don't challenge these conventions. Don't you care about the truth?"

"Bingley didn't do it," Darcy replied. "That's truth enough for me."

"So justice doesn't bear much consequence for you."

"You are inserting your own words into my mouth, Miss Bennet!"

At mention of Darcy's mouth, she couldn't help but look at his lips. They were generously shaped, and the lower lip protruded just slightly. *Concentrate*, she reprimanded herself. "No, I am merely repeating what you have said."

"You know what would be an injustice, Miss Bennet? Subjecting Bingley to a protracted case in which his integrity is questioned and his character doubted by everyone he has ever met or done business with. It would ruin his social standing, and that of his sisters. His business, which he has worked hard to establish and grow, would never recover. His entire life, destroyed because you want to play detective."

"Because there is a *murderer* on the loose," Lizzie shot back. "Or does that not concern you either?"

"Of course it concerns me." Darcy glanced around, as if afraid anyone would witness him writing off the presence of a murderer. "But what do you expect me to do about it? I'm a solicitor, not a vigilante."

"Then whose concern is it? If those in positions of power don't say to each other, 'Something is wrong and we must right it,' then who will do so?"

"You, apparently."

"And just how successful have I been?" Lizzie asked, hating the bitter taste of her admission of defeat. "You'll likely win your case, but allow me to share a lesson I've learned in the drawing room: Once your reputation is in doubt, it is near impossible to restore. You believe that a judge's decree of innocence will save Bingley's reputation?"

"A High Court judge is one of the most respected voices—"

Her laugh interrupted him. "People will gossip. They may still invite your friend to dinner parties and raise a glass to you for clearing his name, but they'll secretly wonder, *What if he got away with it?* They won't want their daughters to meet him, just in case. They won't do business with him, for fear that maybe, just maybe, they'll be next. A good opinion, once lost, is lost forever."

"You take a rather dark view of society, Miss Bennet."

"It comes from being the sort of young lady that society does not find agreeable."

Darcy began to look just as frustrated as Lizzie felt. "I'm not responsible for what society may think. If anyone is foolish enough to let rumors or unproven suspicions color their opinion of someone, they are not worthy of my respect."

"That's an easy opinion to hold when you already have a position and a fortune."

"Don't pretend that you aren't pursuing this matter for money or recognition, Miss Bennet," Darcy said, his voice suddenly dark.

Lizzie was surprised at how much it displeased her to have Darcy looking at her with such disdain that she shocked herself by admitting the truth. "Of course I hope that I will be compensated—both in payment and recognition—for my hard work. But the recognition is more important to me. How else do you suppose someone of my position has any hope of getting a job? I don't have the good fortune of simply being handed everything from my father."

"You dare insult my work ethic while standing in my father's firm?"

"You dared to condescend to me in my father's firm, so why not?"

There was barely a foot of space between the two of them now. Lizzie wasn't quite sure how it happened, except that arguing with Darcy seemed to slowly draw him closer and closer until she was standing just before him, the top of her head level with his eyes so that she was forced to hold her chin up to meet his gaze. He glared down at her.

"You're infuriating."

Despite herself, Lizzie's gaze was drawn to his lips again as he spat out the words. She had an entire list of questions she would have liked to ask him next: What defense strategy would he recommend that a barrister employ before the judge? If those in power didn't pursue the truth and uncover criminals, then who ought to? In light of Bingley's case, did he believe that they needed more rigorous marriage and family laws? Was he also wondering what it would be like if they were to close the distance between them and . . .

In the end, she settled with, "And you're excessively prideful."

As far as comebacks went, it was not Lizzie's strongest. Humiliation flushed through her, causing Lizzie to tear her gaze away from Darcy's mouth before he could produce another disparaging word. She turned on her heel and stalked out of Pemberley & Associates' offices, refusing to look a single person in the eye on her way out or to entertain visions of Darcy running after her to apologize with those alluring lips.

ELEVEN

In Which Lizzie Makes an
Intriguing Connection

LIZZIE STEPPED INTO THE busy street outside of Pemberley & Associates, fuming. Darcy was dismissive. And lofty. And entitled and many other things besides, things that Lizzie fully planned to ruminate on when she got home and could speak with Jane. . . .

She rounded the corner, headed east toward Gracechurch Street, just as a hard hand clamped down upon her elbow. For a heart-fluttering moment she thought that Darcy had come after her (to argue another point? to apologize for his rudeness?), but that possibility was dismissed when she was yanked toward the street.

She drew in a breath to scream for help, but a gloved hand was already over her mouth. Her assailant steered her toward an open carriage door, and panic flooded Lizzie's limbs in a fiery rush. She remembered, belatedly, Fred's warning about her tail. She'd forgotten about the man following her because she'd let her emotions about Darcy overwhelm her senses, and now it didn't matter that she fought against her attacker—he simply lifted her like a child and roughly shoved her into the waiting carriage. The door slammed shut behind her and the carriage began to move, making Lizzie's head spin.

"Please take a moment to collect yourself," a polite voice said. "I wish you no harm."

Lizzie gripped the seat as she searched for the source of the voice. Her bonnet was askew and there was a tear in her right glove—Mama would be cross if she saw it. Then a sobering thought rose: Would Mama even have a chance to see her glove and become cross with her?

When she finally focused on the face of her abductor, she grew puzzled. "It's you!" she sputtered.

The enigmatic and elegant woman from the night before sat arrayed in silk and brocade on the seat across from her. She wore a spectacular feathered hat with a fine veil over her face, but it was unmistakably the lady who lectured her on the impossibility of second chances, marriage markets, and choice.

"You're following me," Lizzie stated.

The woman raised an eyebrow. "*I'm* not following you."

Lizzie took in her fine clothing and the sumptuous velvet of the carriage's seating and amended her statement. "Fine, you're having me followed."

"You're a most intriguing young lady, Miss Bennet."

Lizzie noted the use of her name right away and felt fear clench her body, but she tried not to show it. "I'm sorry, I don't believe I caught your name."

"Oh, if you insist." The older woman extended her hand to Lizzie, who shook it. It was covered in the finest black lace gloves that Lizzie had ever seen. "I'm Lady Catherine de Bourgh."

"Miss Elizabeth Bennet," Lizzie replied out of habit. "But you already knew that."

Lady Catherine gave no response to Lizzie's dig. "Now that we have that out of the way, I thought we might continue our conversation from last evening."

"Now?" Lizzie couldn't understand how idle talk about the opportunities for women was so important that it required stalking and kidnapping. "You could have called, Lady Catherine."

"You've caught my attention, Miss Bennet."

"And why is that?"

"You are an active sort of young lady. You're not highborn, but you have good manners. You're . . . useful."

The words were spoken in a complimentary tone, but Lizzie wasn't planning on letting her guard down. "I like to keep busy."

"You've kept yourself busy in your father's firm. He's not a very good barrister, is he."

Family pride flared in Lizzie, and she simply said, "Papa doesn't care much for society."

"And your mother?"

"My mother has five daughters," Lizzie said with a laugh. "She has to care very much."

"Five! And all of you are unmarried?" Lizzie confirmed with a nod, and Lady Catherine shook her head. "How unusual. Pray tell, how old are you?"

Lizzie had been followed and abducted and was now being questioned about her personal life? Oh, no. "With three younger sisters out, Your Ladyship can hardly expect me to own it," Lizzie replied, unable to hide her irritation.

"Do you wish to marry, Miss Bennet?" Lady Catherine asked, ignoring Lizzie's waspish tone.

Oh, she loathed this question! The person who asked it always expected one unequivocal answer: yes. But it was not quite so simple for Lizzie. She knew she was supposed to *want* to marry, and the concept itself didn't seem terrible if she could marry a man who encouraged her to pursue cases, who did not try to limit her . . . well, it was no use dreaming up such impossible dreams. Such a young man did not exist—or rather, none such a young man that her parents would consent to her marrying.

Lizzie was tempted to snap out a quick response, but

something made her hesitate. Lady Catherine's gaze was appraising beneath her expensive veil, and Lizzie had the strangest feeling that *this* was what Lady Catherine really wanted to know. But why?

Instead of answering, Lizzie mustered up her sweetest society smile. "I wish to be useful."

"Hmm," Lady Catherine said. "You remind me of myself when I was young. I would recommend putting off marriage for as long as possible. It's a tool to keep women from wielding any true power or autonomy."

"I thought the opposite was true," Lizzie said. Never had she heard any woman advise to *not* seek a husband. "I thought marriage was the opportunity to be one's own mistress."

"That's the biggest lie we tell ourselves," Lady Catherine responded with a harsh laugh. "You wouldn't be your own mistress, you'd be mistress of your husband's household, and you'd spend your days tending to his house and children and social status. If that's freedom, it's not the sort that women ought to pursue. I learned that too late." She paused, and Lizzie wondered if she was expected to offer condolences. Considering she'd been kidnapped, she chose to pass over this particular social nicety. "Now I make it my business to advise other useful young ladies in pursuits that, while not marriage, may prove to be fulfilling."

"And how do you go about that?"

"I know a good many people, my dear. Marriage was not

completely without its advantages. I'm wealthy and connected. I'm in the position to help young women with particular talents achieve the freedom to look after their own interests."

"How very kind of you," Lizzie said, but she remained cautious. If a person's behavior was a manifestation of their moral character, then Lizzie ought to not forget that Lady Catherine had her followed and then shoved into a carriage against her will—all when she could have simply invited Lizzie to tea or orchestrated a more appropriate introduction.

"It is," Lady Catherine confirmed, and the edge in her voice put Lizzie on notice.

She ventured forth cautiously. "Although, I'm not sure how you might help me."

Lady Catherine's smile was a brief flash, and Lizzie knew that she had played right into the older woman's hand. "You are pursuing a certain case—the death of Mr. Hurst?"

Lizzie leaned forward. How on earth was this woman connected to Hurst and the Bingleys? "I've been commissioned by Mr. Bingley to provide an alternative theory of the murder," she confirmed, unwilling to reveal too much.

"And do you have one?"

"A few," Lizzie hedged.

"I may be able to let you narrow your options. Beware of Darcy."

Now *this* surprised Lizzie. "Why?"

"He's not as honorable as appearances would suggest."

Lady Catherine was the second person to say as much to Lizzie, and now she was definitely paying attention. Nonetheless, she needed more details. "Forgive me, Lady Catherine, if I'm unable to take your advice to heart without corroboration."

"Why, you are a suspicious mind."

"My father taught me to trust, but verify." Lizzie smiled and waited to see if Lady Catherine would reveal more.

"There was a duel," she said finally. "Two years ago."

Now, this surprised Lizzie. Dueling was illegal, but that didn't stop foolish men from engaging in the practice away from the eyes of the law. But even if one wasn't caught, news often traveled through social circles. If these rumors had a grain of truth, the scandal could ruin a man and his family. "A duel? Over what?"

"There was an incident involving Pemberley and Associates, and the younger Mr. Darcy challenged a man to a duel over it—someone far below him in social class."

Of course he had. Darcy seemed like just the type to satisfy his own vanity, even though gentlemen did not, as a rule, challenge those from lower classes.

"He won, and the firm made the problem . . . vanish." Lady Catherine waved her gloved hand. "He's not someone to tangle with, Miss Bennet. You don't have the means to take him on, nor does your father."

"Why are you telling me this?" Lizzie asked, reaching the end of her patience.

"As I said . . . I've an interest in helping young ladies where I can. You said it yourself last night—ladies must forge new paths. I'd like to help with that."

"Thank you. That is very prescient advice, and your information is gladly received."

Lady Catherine waited, and Lizzie wondered if she expected Lizzie to unburden herself of her theories and questions. Well, they could drive to Scotland and back and Lady Catherine would still be waiting. Lizzie did not trust the other woman—no one simply handed you information on a platter without expecting something in return. Lizzie would not share anything with this woman until she knew what she wanted.

"Very well," Lady Catherine said when Lizzie remained silent for a stretch. She rapped against the back of carriage, signaling the driver to stop. "I hope you'll heed my advice, Miss Bennet. Keep your guard up. And I hope we'll meet again."

It was clearly a dismissal, even though Lizzie hadn't the faintest clue as to where they were. *Please not the middle of nowhere,* she thought as she said, "It was a pleasure."

But when she stepped down to the street, she was shocked to find she was blocks away from her own home. Did the driver know where she lived? Lady Catherine's carriage pulled away, and Lizzie allowed herself to watch it for only a moment before heading down the street to home.

What Lady Catherine's interest in the Hurst case was, she couldn't possibly imagine. Was she simply keen on helping

Lizzie? Or was she motivated by something else? Money? She looked rich enough. Had Hurst owed her money? But if that was the case, why would she want *Lizzie* to solve his murder?

Against her own suspicions, Lizzie thought of the woman's claims against Darcy. The image of Darcy glowering earlier that afternoon came to her, speaking of the difference between law and justice. He was persistent and underhanded—just that morning he'd gone to her father to rein her in. But was he a criminal?

Dueling is a crime, she reminded herself. It didn't matter the circumstances or what was at stake. If he'd engaged in a duel, then he was a criminal. Darcy was Bingley's friend and solicitor. He had admitted that he stood to lose quite a bit if Bingley went down for this crime. What would he do to ensure that he would win his case?

She recalled Darcy's confidence and his desk in the corner. Could he have killed Hurst, implicated his best friend, and then planned to clear Bingley's name in order to claim the glory? Pulling off such a victory would certainly catch the attention of more senior members of Pemberley, but Darcy seemed so averse to risk, Lizzie had trouble fully imagining it. She had to get hold of herself. Jane would be disappointed to hear Lizzie was contemplating reckless theories without evidence.

Stick with what you know for certain, Lizzie reminded herself.

The only problem was that she wasn't certain of anything in this case. Not anymore.

TWELVE

In Which Lizzie Makes a Bargain with
Her Mother, with Unexpected Results

WHEN LIZZIE GOT HOME from her rather trying day
of being followed, confronting Darcy, and experiencing a tem-
porary abduction, she checked for messages from Fred—but
there were none.

She knew it was unreasonable to think he'd found information about the pocket watch in just a matter of hours, but
the strangeness of her encounter with Lady Catherine left Lizzie restless for something tangible to hold on to in this case.
She paced the length of the small bedchamber she shared with
Jane as she caught her older sister up on the events of the day
(glossing over the bit about being followed and downplaying
her abduction).

173

Jane was aghast. "I don't know how she can be considered polite society if she had you dragged into her carriage!"

"How is it any different from Mama dragging us from dinner party to social call?" Lizzie joked, but it fell flat.

"Be sensible," her sister said. "You don't know who she is, or what her connection to this case might be."

"I know," Lizzie said, throwing herself down on the bed next to Jane. "I wish I knew more about *her*. Maybe then I could figure out what she wants from me."

Jane was silent for a moment, and then she said, "There *is* someone you could ask. Someone adept at society gossip, who knows even the most inconsequential things that more recent members of society may have forgotten. . . ."

Lizzie sat up. "Jane, no."

Jane's sensible brown eyes were wide and innocent, despite what she was implying. "If you want information you can act upon . . ."

Lizzie groaned. Jane was right. The problem was that Lizzie made it a habit to *never* actively seek her mother's help on anything.

"Maybe," Lizzie grumbled, and Jane didn't press her. Perhaps because she knew that Lizzie had no other choice.

Lizzie held out for a little while longer, wasting the rest of the evening paging through notes in her sketchbook and adding thoughts, hoping something would stick out. But when morning arrived with no word from Fred, Lizzie knew she couldn't afford to wait—not with only three days until Bingley's hearing.

Jane agreed to distract Lydia and Kitty with hair ribbons, to guarantee Lizzie a little privacy, which proved she really was the best of sisters. Lizzie gathered her hopeless needlework as a pretense and went and found their mother in the drawing room.

"Good morning, Mama," Lizzie announced as she took a seat across from Mrs. Bennet.

"Oh, Lizzie!" Mrs. Bennet blinked and studied her second daughter. "I never see you anymore. What on earth have you done to that cloth?"

"I'm repairing it," she said. "How are you? We haven't had a proper chat in days."

"That's because you're always off to goodness knows where—the firm, tea with Charlotte, talking books with your father. You ought to pay more attention to things at home. If you had, you'd know my knees ache."

Lizzie opened her mouth to respond with sympathy, but Mrs. Bennet had launched into a litany of complaints that included her headaches, nerves, and indigestion and ended with Mr. Bennet's obstinate refusal to see his daughters married.

Lizzie hmm'd and oohed when appropriate while stabbing her cloth and tangling her thread. She soon realized that if she waited for the perfect opening, she'd be there until evening. So she merely waited until Mrs. Bennet took a breath and said,

"You know, I've met the most fascinating people while helping Papa at the office. I wonder if you know them?"

"I wish you wouldn't go into the firm," Mrs. Bennet said without missing a beat. "It is not at all a proper place for introductions to occur."

"But better to meet young men there than not at all," Lizzie pointed out. "For example, that's how I became acquainted with Mr. Darcy."

Mrs. Bennet waved her hand as if shooing away a fly. "He's fallen out of favor, you know."

Lizzie figured as much from the location of his desk, but her mother continued. "Mrs. Gardiner told me ages ago that inheriting the firm from his father isn't even a guaranteed thing! Apparently he must apply himself, like anyone off the street."

"What a novel concept. That ought to be applied at Longbourn."

"Don't be silly, dear," Mrs. Bennet said, giving Lizzie a peeved look. "We might not like the fact that Mr. Collins is your father's heir, but that doesn't change how things ought to be done!"

Lizzie didn't wish to argue in circles about Collins—her thoughts were preoccupied with Darcy. But her mother confirmed what she had begun to suspect, and against her better judgment she began to review their interactions thus far, seeing his condescension as bravado and recognizing the flashes of insecurity.

But why was he in this position to begin with? The duel? Lizzie had to stay focused.

"Never mind Mr. Darcy," Lizzie said, shaking her head. "Just the other day, I encountered Lady Catherine de Bourgh on the street."

Even this softening of the truth scandalized her mother. She dropped her needlework to exclaim, "Lizzie! Tell me you did not speak to her. Without an introduction?"

"She introduced herself," Lizzie said, which was the truth. "I was quite surprised. I was wondering if you knew much about her."

"Lady Catherine de Bourgh," Mrs. Bennet began, and then her eyes narrowed.

"What's the matter, Mama?"

Mrs. Bennet continued to stare at her, quizzical. Then she slowly shook her head. "I know what you are up to, Elizabeth!"

"Mama?"

"You think I'm silly, but I see—you're sneaking about on a case again, aren't you?"

Of all the times for Mrs. Bennet to finally catch on! Lizzie attempted to refute the charge by saying, "Of course not!" When Mrs. Bennet didn't buy it, she added, "Papa banished me from the office."

"So you thought you'd use me to gather the information you need?"

That was exactly what she'd been doing. But she had to

placate Mrs. Bennet—life would not be worth living if her mother did not at least think she had some control over her daughters' lives. "Not at all, Mama. You're well connected and informed, and I've always respected your extensive knowledge of society."

"I don't believe you," Mrs. Bennet said, and, to Lizzie's horror, began to dab at her eyes with a lace-edged handkerchief. Lizzie set her needlework aside and repositioned herself at her mother's side, rubbing her back. Lizzie's desire to please her parents was not restricted to her father, so she was not happy to make her mother cry. But Lizzie also knew Mrs. Bennet was not content with her lot in life, and it was unfair of her to blame her disappointments on her husband and daughters. Lizzie feared they would be forever disappointed in each other, and she didn't know how to rectify the situation. But she also sensed that if she gave in to her mother's expectations, she would turn out just like Mrs. Bennet—unhappy, but in her own way.

"Mama, Lady Catherine may be connected to a case, but I *am* curious." When that got her nothing, Lizzie tried again. "You know, her dress was very fine, with the loveliest lace gloves I have ever seen." Mrs. Bennet stopped dabbing at her eyes. "I can't believe I'd never heard of her before. Has she recently come to town?"

Mrs. Bennet set her handkerchief down. "I would *like* to believe you," she said.

"You can."

"I shall tell you my gossip . . . if you do something for me."

"Anything, Mama."

She should have predicted Mrs. Bennet's request and yet was still horrified when her mother smiled through her tears and said, "Invite Mr. Collins to dinner. Mr. Bennet keeps forgetting, and since you see him so often at the office, it should be proper for you to convey my invitation."

"But I can't—Papa has banished me." Never had Lizzie thought she'd be glad to use this as an excuse.

"He won't be cross if you're delivering a message," Mrs. Bennet said. "I'll tell him."

"I don't know, Mama. Mr. Collins has been preoccupied of late."

"All the more reason to invite him *immediately*. Don't give me that look! I don't wish to see this family homeless, so sacrifices must be made."

Mrs. Bennet was not about to back down, and since Lizzie wasn't going to share that Collins had been flirting with Charlotte earlier that week, Lizzie knew they had reached an impasse. Either she relented or her mother held on to her information.

You only have three days, she reminded herself.

"Fine," Lizzie said. "I'll invite him."

"Excellent," Mrs. Bennet said, delighted. "Now, as to Lady Catherine, I've never heard of her. I recall a Sir Lewis de Bourgh from Kent, but he died years ago, and I don't believe he left a wife or any children. Perhaps she is a distant relation that has been abroad. . . ."

Lizzie gaped. "That's all? That's *nothing*."

"I told you exactly what I know. It is not my fault that you're dissatisfied with my insight."

Lizzie worked to tamp down her anger because she knew that Mrs. Bennet had merely played her the same way that Lizzie sought to use her. Perhaps they were more alike than she cared to admit.

Lizzie stood. A deal was a deal. "Well, I better get along to Longbourn, then."

"We shall have a pleasant evening with Mr. Collins and wring a marriage proposal out of him yet!" her mother said cheerfully. "Oh, and Lizzie—I don't know what Lady Catherine's connections are, but do keep a civil tongue if you see her again. One never knows when it might be convenient to employ her good name."

"Yes, Mama," Lizzie said, already heading for the door.

"And for heaven's sake, stay away from Mr. Darcy."

Lizzie stopped and turned. "Why?"

"Because I just remembered—Mrs. Forster told me a most dreadful rumor that Mr. Darcy once challenged a man to a duel. That sort of reckless behavior is to be avoided."

Mrs. Bennet kept talking, heedless of Lizzie's shock. Lady Catherine hadn't lied about that, then.

"Go on now," Mrs. Bennet finished, not noticing Lizzie's

stunned expression. "Tell Mr. Collins Monday should be quite convenient."

Lizzie was not entirely surprised to arrive at Longbourn and find Collins hovering over Charlotte's desk. She sucked in a deep breath just as they noticed her presence.

"Miss Elizabeth," Collins said, just a notch louder than necessary. "What are you doing here?"

"Hello, Lizzie," Charlotte said. Her easygoing expression of a moment ago tightened into a nervous smile, and Lizzie found herself caught between wanting to wipe the smug look off of Collins's face and wanting her friend to be happy. Charlotte won out. Lizzie exhaled slowly, brought out her best society smile, and said, "Hello, Mr. Collins, Charlotte. How are you both today?"

Charlotte relaxed, and Lizzie knew that she had done the right thing—which made asking Collins to dinner so her mother could maneuver a marriage proposal out of him all the more awkward.

"Well," Collins said, "but very, very busy. I suppose you've come to visit Miss Lucas, as I believe your father expressly forbade you from interfering with casework."

Lizzie clamped her mouth shut but was gratified to see Charlotte wince slightly. "Actually, I've come to speak to you."

Collins stared for a moment, his mouth agape in surprise.

Lizzie looked to Charlotte, and her best friend raised her eyebrow in curiosity. When she glanced back at Collins, Lizzie mistrusted the satisfied expression that had replaced his shock. "Of course, Miss Elizabeth. Step into my office."

"Oh, no need—"

"I insist!" Collins reached out to take Lizzie's arm, and Lizzie took a small step back to avoid his touch. Collins's hand caught the strap of her reticule, yanking it off Lizzie's arm. It fell to the floor, spilling Lizzie's sketchbook and her pencil, a handkerchief, and the small amount of coin she possessed. "Oh, my apologies!"

He knelt down to help her pick up her things, and Lizzie dove for the sketchbook. Unfortunately, Collins got to it first. Lizzie snatched up her reticule and said, "No harm done, Mr. Collins," and held out her hand for her sketchbook.

But Mr. Collins was oblivious. "I did not take you for an artist, Miss Elizabeth!"

"Oh no, I'm not! Please don't—"

But to her horror, he was already opening the sketchbook to inspect the pages. Lizzie cast a frantic look in Charlotte's direction, and Charlotte jumped. "Mr. Collins, you're embarrassing her! A lady's sketchbook should not be viewed without express permission."

Collins looked up from Lizzie's sketchbook and toward Charlotte. "Oh! I didn't mean . . ." And to Lizzie's shock, he closed the sketchbook and handed it back. Lizzie did her best not to snatch it from his hands.

"My apologies, Miss Elizabeth. Shall we?" He gestured toward his office door and Lizzie looked to Charlotte. She didn't want to be alone with him. But Charlotte smiled encouragingly. It was a smile that said, *Thank you for being polite.* And, *It'll be fine.*

I'm being kind for Charlotte, Lizzie thought. She followed Collins, and he shut the door behind her. Lizzie resolved to get this over as quickly as possible. "I have simply come to extend an invitation to dinner. From my mother."

Collins's face registered mild surprise, quickly overtaken by joy. "Miss Elizabeth, your mother is too kind. For her to think of me, when I'm just a lowly solicitor . . ."

Lizzie rolled her eyes. "Nonsense."

Collins ignored Lizzie's less than civil attitude and pulled out a chair for Lizzie to sit down. "I've worked for your father for many months now, and during this time I thought that surely your family must resent me. Not your father—he's been very gracious. But of course, there's no one else to take up the mantle."

"No one indeed," Lizzie replied, but her sarcasm was lost on Collins. She ignored his gesture to sit, not wanting to find herself trapped.

Collins didn't seem to take notice. "I worried about the

opinion of your mother and sisters, naturally. Ladies rarely see things the same way men do. Why, in your eyes, I'm taking the business that is your only source of income, and when your father passes—hopefully not for a good many years—you shall have nothing but a modest settlement to live on."

Lizzie had simply come to ask him to dinner, not for her family's dismal prospects to be thrown in her face. "I assure you my mother means you no ill will, and says that Monday would—"

"That's a reassurance." Collins's face took on a peculiar look, as if he were weighing a hefty thought. It was that expression that caused Lizzie to pause a moment, and her hesitation allowed Collins an opening. "May I speak frankly, Miss Elizabeth?"

Lizzie would prefer he not but said, "I hardly have the authority to ask you not to."

"Your modesty is commendable," he said. "You may guess what I have to say. From the moment your father took me on and the future of his estate was made known to me, I knew that my duties extended beyond simply inheriting your father's legacy."

Lizzie had not the slightest clue what he was talking about, but her instincts told her nothing good. She cast a look at the closed door and wished she could run for it.

"Almost as soon as I set foot in this building, I singled you out as my future life companion. Before I run away with my feelings, perhaps it would be useful for me to state my reasoning?"

Of all the things that Collins had just said, it was the idea of him running away with his feelings that caused a swell of feeling in Lizzie's chest. She was so close to laughter that it was all she could do not to let it out, and thus she missed her chance to interrupt him.

"I believe it's important for me, as a gentleman, to marry. Your father has set a fine example, and I would like to follow suit. The second reason has to do with my benefactress. Before I came to London, she told me to make every effort to establish myself in society, and I believe that marriage shall accomplish that."

Lizzie felt light-headed. Was this really happening? "Mr. Collins—"

"And third, Miss Elizabeth, is the reason I alluded to earlier. With the bulk of your father's estate to come to me after his passing, I couldn't live with myself if I didn't choose a wife from among his daughters, so that his loss might not sting quite as much. I'm completely indifferent to your lack of fortune, and I promise to never speak of it once we are married. Nothing remains except to assure you of the violence of my affection!"

Nothing sounded more horrifying to Lizzie, and she took a giant step back. "What about Charlotte?" she asked.

"Miss Lucas is a . . . fine young lady," Collins said, "but you must know that I'm hardly interested in her in *that* regard. She's not appropriate as a life partner."

Lizzie felt the heaviness of the words he did not say. Lizzie did not wish her friend to be shackled to Collins, but his excuse was enraging. "Because her mother was from the West Indies and not the West End?"

Collins nodded. "I'm glad you understand."

"You mistake me," she choked out. Talking had become difficult, and the right words were hard to grasp. "I understand nothing."

"When it comes to marriage, you and I are far better suited. I'm certain both of your parents will approve of our engagement."

Well, this was a nightmare. "I haven't even given you an answer!" Lizzie reminded him.

Collins kept trying to edge closer, and Lizzie was running out of space in which to retreat. "I'm not worried," he told her. "I know that when young ladies refuse a man, they secretly mean to accept. I'm prepared to ask again and again, before leading you to the altar."

The image of Collins leading Lizzie anywhere was so distasteful, she nearly gagged. She would have loved nothing more than to turn on her heel or, better yet, smack some sense into him, but if he intended to keep pursuing the matter, it was better to lay it to rest now. "I assure you, I'm not one of those young ladies—if indeed they exist. I'm certain that you could not make me happy, and even more, I could not make you happy."

Lizzie thought she might be getting through to him. His countenance was no longer quite as smug; he looked confused, even frustrated. "Perhaps you wish me to flatter myself, Miss Elizabeth. What I'm offering you is significant. A position in society as a married lady, a household of your own, a modest fortune, the opportunity to keep your family in comfort. You're unlikely to receive a proposal such as this again."

Lizzie laughed once more. "If your words are an attempt at flattery, please know I would rather be paid the compliment of being taken at my word. I would not, could not, marry you, and nothing you say will convince me otherwise."

Lizzie planned to make for Charlotte's desk and escape the conversation, but she had taken no more than a single step backward when Collins's expression changed. He grabbed her by the wrist, surprising Lizzie with the strength of his grip.

"Stop this nonsense, Elizabeth," he said. "I'll be patient, but if you don't accept, I have the means to see that you never set foot into Longbourn and Sons again."

Lizzie yanked her hand from his grasp, furious that he would threaten her—but frightened, too. Mr. Bennet was already disappointed in her. Was refusing Collins the final straw that would see her banished from Longbourn forever, her career aspirations crushed?

Lizzie realized in an instant that even if it was her undoing, she could not, would not, relent. "I don't know how else to say it. I. Will. Not. Marry. You."

And with that, she wrenched open the office door and stalked past an alarmed Charlotte and right out of Longbourn, Collins's furious stare burning at her back.

THIRTEEN

In Which Lizzie Receives a Shock

JANE WAS EMBROIDERING IN their shared bed-chamber when Lizzie returned. She looked up from her stitching as Lizzie came in and said, "Oh, there you are—"

Lizzie checked to make sure the hall was clear, then shut the door with a solid click. "Jane," she said gravely, "I have good news and horrid news. Which would you like to hear first?"

"Heavens." Jane set her needlework aside. "You better start with the bad."

"No, I think I shall start with the good news." Lizzie removed her spencer and flung herself down on her bed, next to Jane. "The good news is that you don't have to worry about Collins ever proposing marriage to you."

"Oh?" Jane asked, not sounding the least bit relieved. Then

again, she'd never had to seriously concern herself with the prospect. "And why is that?"

"That's the horrid news. Because he just proposed. To me. But don't worry, I refused."

Jane's shock was rather satisfying, but not nearly enough to make Lizzie feel better. She kept waiting for the moment when she could laugh the whole strange encounter off, but the humor never came. The mattress ticking dipped as Jane shifted closer. "Lizzie! Does Mama know?"

"No. And she can *never* know."

"I don't know how likely that is," Jane said. "She can sniff out a proposal in a crowded room from a mile away, and besides, she's been making preparations for dinner with Collins all morning."

Lizzie rolled over and buried her head in her pillow.

"Come, sit up. Tell me everything."

She did so and gave Jane the full story, including Collins's flirtation with Charlotte, which had gone from horrifying to indecent considering the recent turn of events. Jane, however, did not seem quite as indignant as Lizzie felt.

"Collins has shown us his nature," she said, as if relaying the afternoon's weather. "He's led by the promise of fortune and standing, and an alliance with Charlotte could not give him either of those things. Clearly, she deserves someone who will appreciate her. But I'm worried, Lizzie—what if your rejection has soured Collins's relationship with the family?"

"Why is that my fault?" Lizzie protested. "Why not blame Collins for proposing when I've never given him any indication I was interested? Quite the opposite, in fact!"

"Because that's not how the world works," Jane murmured.

"I know." *Men can choose; women may only refuse.*

"Mama is going to be so upset," Jane added.

"You won't tell her?"

"Of course not. But Lizzie, she'll find out. Collins shall go to her and Papa to ask them to convince you, or . . . I don't know. But when have you ever known Collins to keep quiet about anything?"

Lizzie flopped back down on the bed and sighed.

Jane stroked her hair. "Papa won't make you marry him. Mama will be quite angry for a while, but you can trust Papa."

Lizzie nodded, but doubt crept in. She knew that he'd always *said* that he would not force her to marry. However, that was all before she had disobeyed him and he had banished her from Longbourn & Sons. What if he was so frustrated with her that he decided to marry her off so she would become another man's problem?

"I was going to tell you when you came into the room," Jane said, reaching for something in her pocket. "This came for you. From your informant."

Jane handed her a tiny bit of butcher paper, and Lizzie eagerly unfolded it to reveal a pencil drawing, quite good, of what was unmistakably the corner of Gracechurch Street and

Lombard. In the corner was a drawing of a watch, its hands set at ten o'clock.

Half past nine the next morning saw Lizzie at the appointed intersection, straining her eyes through the morning fog to find Fred's short figure. She was almost able to forget about Collins and his horrid proposal in anticipation of Fred's news.

She didn't have to wait long. He came sauntering down the street with the grace of a cat. "Morning, miss."

"Did you find it?" she asked.

He shook his head. "Just as I thought, miss. None of the reputable places will talk to me, and no place else will cop to buying a stolen watch. If your bloke sold it himself, he did it quiet-like."

Lizzie wilted with disappointment. She'd hoped Fred's drawing of the clock meant he had found it. With only two days left, all she had were theories and conjectures. Perhaps she could find another case to prove her worth to her father, but could she do it before he hired that Eton-educated, pompous man he had interviewed the other day? Not to mention she hated the thought of looking like a failure to Darcy. . . .

"I tried to pass along a message to that maid," Fred continued. "Only, turns out she's no longer at the Hursts'."

That gave Lizzie pause. "Abigail left for another position?"

"No," Fred said slowly. "She was sacked."

"*Oh.*" Lizzie's first feeling was horror—had she caused Abigail to lose her job?

Fred continued. "The kitchen maid told me it happened the day before last, and get this, miss—she said that when Abigail left, the butler demanded to search her belongings."

"That's not unusual, Fred. Oftentimes the butler will ensure the staff is not making off with something valuable if they feel like they've been unfairly dismissed."

"Aye, but she said that the butler was looking for Mr. Hurst's watch—apparently Mr. Bingley's solicitor is after it."

"*Oh.*" Darcy! Had Lizzie tipped him off? "I have to speak to Abigail at once. Do you have an address for her?"

"The kitchen maid said she took a bed at a rooming house on Thames Street." Fred gave her directions.

"Thank you, Fred," Lizzie said, and she tipped him a coin. He grinned and started to slip away, but Lizzie called him back. "I couldn't help but notice that you're an exceptional artist."

The boy smiled but then quickly shrugged it off. "It'll do, since I don't know my letters."

Lizzie knew none of the street children were educated, but Fred had potential. He was clever and savvy, and who knew where he could apply his artistic abilities if he could read and write? "I could teach you, if you like."

Fred's features furrowed in suspicion. "You don't have to, miss."

"I know," Lizzie said. His rejection hurt, just a little. "But I could, if you ever wanted."

She opened her mouth to tell him that literacy was freedom, nothing short of everyday magic. But something held her back—the memory of Charlotte telling her she was naive. She hesitated, and in the uncomfortable moment that followed, Lizzie realized she couldn't force Fred to accept, any more than she could force her own views on suitors and marriage on Charlotte. So she opted not to say anything more, hoping he'd agree. When Fred realized she wasn't going to insist, he nodded and said, "I'll think on it, miss." And then he was gone.

Lizzie watched him vanish from view. She felt both sad and helpless. London was full of injustices, both large and small. How did one even begin to address them all?

For now, Lizzie had a job to do, and she took comfort in having her first solid lead in more than a day. She set out toward the docks. Thames Street was not very far away from her own home, but the difference made by moving a couple of blocks closer to the river was remarkable. The damp felt heavier, especially this cloudy morning, and the streets were crowded with carts and wagons ferrying cargo and day laborers looking for a job. There were fewer shops, and therefore fewer ladies about, so she garnered curious looks. Lizzie kept her head high and tried to look as though she knew exactly where she was headed. She was just stepping around a particularly pungent fish cart when she heard her name.

She turned and was surprised to find the lanky figure of Wickham heading in her direction. She felt the corners of her mouth turn up in a smile. "Mr. Wickham! Are you on duty this morning?"

"Off duty, as luck would have it." He caught up with her, panting slightly. "I just was finishing up my shift, and I thought to myself, *Whatever could Miss Bennet be investigating today?* I decided to take a walk in your neighborhood, and I spotted you about a block and a half back."

"Oh." Lizzie was not accustomed to being pursued so often in one week, but Wickham's presence reminded her she ought to be a tad more careful. She really didn't have the time for another unscheduled carriage confab with Lady Catherine today. "I'm off to speak with a witness who used to work in the Hurst household."

"Care for a bit of company?"

Lizzie felt her cheeks warm despite the cool morning air. She couldn't say no to that dimple, but . . . "The only thing, Mr. Wickham, is that my conversation is regarding a delicate matter. I'm afraid if she knew you were a Runner, she might not want to speak with me."

"Then introduce me as your acquaintance. Colleague, if you like." Wickham stepped up to her and offered her his arm.

Lizzie took it after a moment's hesitation. "All right then. But let me do the talking."

"Of course, Miss Bennet. I defer to you—it's your case,

after all. But would you do me the honor of telling me what you've learned since our last outing together?"

"Not much, I'm afraid," Lizzie said, but how wonderful to have a man not only acknowledge that she was capable but *defer* to her! She told him how her progress had been stymied by Darcy showing up at her father's office to threaten legal action.

"That sounds like him," Wickham remarked.

His comment made Lizzie wonder if Wickham's experience with Darcy was more than an encounter. "You're acquainted?"

"In a way," he hedged. "But I don't trust him."

"Because he killed a man in a duel?" Lizzie wasn't sure why she repeated this bit of gossip, but it did the trick of shocking Wickham. Lizzie pressed her advantage. "I've heard the rumors. Do you know whom he challenged?"

Wickham regarded her uneasily. "Scandalous rumors follow him wherever he goes. Fortunately for him, his father has enough money to distract from his less honorable qualities."

"You seem to know a fair bit about the Darcys," Lizzie said, fishing.

Wickham's response was not what Lizzie was expecting. "I used to work at Pemberley."

Lizzie halted in surprise. "*What?* Why didn't you say?"

"I don't like dwelling on it. It was my first job and I worked for his father, doing the odd side job here and there. He told me he'd send me to school if I kept up the good work."

"What happened?" Lizzie asked gently, dreading the answer.

Wickham looked to the gray skies, then back at her. "It's painful to talk about, considering how it all ended. I worked my way up to clerk when his son started at the firm. He was only a year younger than me but had already been to university. Had his sights set on going to the Inns of Court and one day being called to the bar. You could tell the moment he walked in, he was surveying everything as if it was his for the taking."

Lizzie knew that look of Darcy's well.

"I was doing all right, keeping my head down, until I did a little work for Darcy. A libel suit, but the information I dug up on the client didn't align with Darcy's idea of the case. He refused to pay me. I said that I'd go to his father, but I wasn't even given the chance before Darcy had me escorted from the building and threatened to charge me with trespassing if I ever came back."

"The *nerve*," Lizzie said, her voice quiet, but she was simmering inside.

Wickham wouldn't quite meet her gaze, but she could see the emotion in his face as he continued. "I wrote letters, but they were never answered; I made inquiries and was threatened for it. I was in a bad shape and out of funds, so I joined the navy. It didn't suit me, and now I'm back here, making a living the best way I can."

"That's very unfair," Lizzie murmured. "I'm sorry that happened to you."

"Thank you," Wickham said, and patted her hand. "You see now why I'm suspicious?"

"I do," Lizzie said. "And I'll not lie—every person I meet seems to have a similar story regarding Darcy." She thought of a saying her father often uttered in the course of a case—*Where there's smoke, there's fire.*

Their conversation was put on hold as they arrived at a sad, squat gray house. The stone was slick with condensation, and the windows were grimy and dark. Lizzie could smell the stench of mold and damp from where they stood on the street, but it was the correct address. "Here we go," she said to Wickham. "Remember—let me talk."

He nodded, and she knocked on the flimsy door. From inside they heard rustling about and the cry of a small child before the door was wrenched open by a red-faced matron with a dirty apron and a little one clinging to her skirts. "Yes?" she asked, suspicion weighing down the word.

"Good day, madam. We are looking for Abigail . . ." Lizzie realized with a start that she didn't know Abigail's surname.

"Abigail Jenkins?" the woman asked, her gaze evaluating them. "And what business do you have with her?"

Lizzie was about to say they were friends, but Wickham cut in. "We're her cousins, recently arrived to town from Hertfordshire."

So much for letting Lizzie do the talking! At least Wickham sounded truthful, and she had to admit it was a good cover.

The woman stared at them for a moment longer, then stepped back and yelled into the depths of the house, "*Abigail!* Visitors!"

The matron swept up the child in her arms and pointed into a darkened room. "You can wait for her in the sitting room. If it's tea you're wanting, it'll be extra."

"Please don't trouble yourself on our behalf," Lizzie rushed to say.

The sitting room was dark, with a worn settee and hard chairs, but it was clean. Lizzie perched on the settee, and Wickham stood behind her, next to the window. They heard shuffling and some whispering in the hall, and then Abigail appeared, looking skeptical at the sudden materialization of cousins from Hertfordshire. When she spotted Lizzie, her eyebrows jumped.

"Thank you, Mrs. Evans!" she called out to the hall, and took a seat across from Lizzie. "I never expected to see you here."

"Hello, Abigail. This is my colleague, Mr. Wickham," Lizzie said, but Abigail barely acknowledged him with a small glance. "What happened?"

Her brown eyes were bloodshot but dry, and she spoke in a flat tone. "Just as I predicted, miss. They're closing the house. Mrs. Hurst refuses to return, and I can't say as I blame her."

"So quickly?" Lizzie asked. She wasn't surprised that Abigail didn't want to reveal she'd been dismissed, but she needed Abigail to trust her. "Surely they would have kept you on long enough for you to find another position."

Abigail didn't say anything to that, so Lizzie tried another approach. "Well, never mind. You know my offer stands, to give you a letter of reference. You were so helpful that day when I called. It's just, I wonder . . ."

Lizzie let her voice trail off, and Abigail shifted in her seat. "What, miss?"

"Well, this is delicate. You told me the other day the watchmen believed that Mr. Hurst's pocket watch was stolen by the murderer. Only . . . I heard the watch was missing before his death."

Abigail's face went a shade paler. Lizzie continued, "I was wondering if perhaps you knew its whereabouts. If he sold it, maybe." She waited a beat, then added, "Whoever has it may lead us to the killer. At least, that's what Mr. Bingley's solicitor seems to think."

"Do you think so, miss?"

Lizzie could tell by the way Abigail's fists had buried themselves in her skirts that she was nervous. Lizzie looked her straight in the eye. "I do."

She let Abigail realize the danger on her own. Abigail's eyes darted to Wickham, standing behind Lizzie, and Lizzie prayed Wickham would have the sense not to startle the young woman either. Finally, she spoke.

"I may have some information. But I don't think it'll lead where you're hoping."

"It's my duty to follow up on any and every lead," Lizzie

said. "I have no interest in any other crime but the murder. As long as you didn't kill him, we should be quite all right."

Abigail shook her head. "I didn't kill Mr. Hurst, miss. I can promise you that."

"I believe you."

Lizzie's words seemed to give Abigail confidence. "The Runners *did* think the watch was missing with the murderer, at first. He'd gone to bed fully dressed, but without his watch or a single coin on his person. They thought it was suspicious, and I suppose it was, if you didn't know . . ."

"But the staff knew of the money troubles," Lizzie prompted.

"We aren't stupid. The furniture was disappearing, and the butcher wouldn't serve Cook until the account was settled, so we hadn't had meat for a month."

"And the watch?"

"Mr. Hurst was home two days before he was killed, wailing that it was stolen. It was valuable and he threatened to march the thief to Newgate himself. We thought he'd sold it himself and was carrying on to save face."

"But?"

"You'll think me awful," Abigail whispered with one flicker of a glance to Wickham.

It was this admission that caused Lizzie to sit back with a small huff of surprise. "Oh, Abigail. Why?"

"Four years I worked in that house," Abigail said quietly, "and do you know how many maids came and went? How often the bell would ring for tea, and we'd walk in to find him drunk? And if the girls breathed so much as a word to Mr. Banks or the housekeeper about what he'd say, what'd he *do* when he was in that state, they were dismissed without a reference. I endured it, but when Mrs. Hurst left, I knew I'd be dismissed, and I was afraid no one would write me a reference. I took the watch when Mr. Hurst came home for a change of clothes. I thought that he'd be distracted by Mrs. Hurst's absence and wouldn't notice, but . . ."

Lizzie let out a deep sigh. She wanted to pull Abigail into a hug, but she didn't move. She'd heard of households where the men took advantage, of course. There were always whispers. She thought that kind of behavior was deplorable, but she'd never considered the effect it had on the young women.

"I see," she said quietly after a long stretch. "I'm very sorry, Abigail."

"It's not your fault," the young woman said, looking at her lap. Lizzie still felt culpable somehow. It made her problems with Collins pale in comparison . . . except that none of it was right. Not one single bit was acceptable, and Lizzie didn't know how to change it.

She reached out and took the young woman's hand. "Abigail, I'm not angry. And we're not going to report you. But . . . did you take anything else?"

"Just the watch, miss. I wanted a little to get by on, but

202

nothing too expensive to raise suspicions. If anyone asked, I'd say it belonged to my dead father."

"And have you already sold it?"

Abigail nodded quickly, and Lizzie wasn't sure if she believed her. But did it matter? Tracking down the watch would just get Abigail even further into trouble. The poor girl didn't need any other trials. But . . . "Abigail, do you know who might have killed Mr. Hurst?"

Abigail shook her head. "I never knew anything about that, miss."

"But you knew he owed money, correct?"

"He had the creditors, and gambling debts," Abigail said. "Mr. Bingley took care of those. Until he stopped, last year."

That made Lizzie arch an eyebrow. The sums she'd seen on Darcy's desk had been for merchants and dealers who did business with gentlemen on credit. And although people had alluded to Hurst's mismanagement of funds, no one had spoken of gambling debts—or mentioned that Bingley had paid them. Besides, she thought that Bingley's decision to stop giving his brother-in-law money was recent. "Do you know why?"

"I shouldn't, miss . . ."

"Abigail, please. I'll write you that reference letter, if that's what you're concerned about."

"You would, knowing I stole?" Abigail's expression was incredulous and, Lizzie detected, a hint distrustful. Her gaze darted to Wickham, as if Lizzie needed his permission.

"I would," Lizzie said, and she meant it. "You were in an impossible situation, but you were honest with me when I asked. I trust that if you were ever in that sort of situation again, you would find other employment, with my help, rather than resort to stealing."

To Lizzie's shock, Abigail began to tear up. "That's very kind, miss. More than I deserve."

"Everyone deserves a second chance," Lizzie said, although she wasn't sure if she believed everyone did. But if anyone was worthy, it was certainly Abigail.

"I don't think Mr. Bingley stopped paying because he was angry," Abigail said when she had gotten ahold of herself. "I think he stopped because he couldn't afford to anymore. Mr. Bingley was over for tea a few weeks before Hurst was killed. He told Mrs. Hurst he was being squeezed on all sides and the last thing he needed was his brother-in-law racking up more debt, too."

This lined up with Caroline's claim that she was able to get only one new ball gown that season. But where was the money going, if not to the Hursts?

Or . . . maybe Lizzie was asking the wrong questions. Maybe instead of wondering where the money had gone, she should be asking whether there was any money to begin with. The bill of lading on Darcy's desk for the SS *Leander* . . . what if that wasn't the only ship that Netherfield had lost?

"Mr. Hurst must have been very upset," Lizzie said, still lost in her own mental calculations.

"He was like a cat, that one," Abigail said with a small shrug. "A little crooked, always landing on his feet. He didn't seem overly concerned."

But why not? Lizzie reconsidered Bingley's account of Hurst's final evening—Mr. Bingley had found his brother-in-law at his club, drunk. Lizzie had assumed that Hurst was drowning his sorrows . . . but she didn't know anymore. "Thank you, Abigail. This has been . . . enlightening."

"Will it help you solve your case?"

"I don't know." Lizzie needed to think through her next steps. "May I return tomorrow, with a letter of reference for you?"

Abigail seemed embarrassed, but she nodded. "Yes, miss. Thank you."

"Thank *you*."

Lizzie and Wickham made to take their leave, and Wickham kept his promise to not speak. As Abigail showed them out, he smiled at her, showing his dimple. Abigail made a small squeaking sound that caught Lizzie's attention, but then Abigail shut the door on them quickly.

"You ought to be careful where you wield that smile," she told him as they stepped into the street.

"Are you jealous, Miss Bennet?"

"No, I'm merely thinking of poor Abigail. You were quite

serious the entire time, only to trot out the charm at the very end. I hope she recovers."

Wickham laughed as he took her arm, which was a shade more forward than he had been before they entered the boardinghouse. "I assure you, Miss Bennet, I was only being polite. I find that my attention has been captured by another."

His look left her with no confusion as to whom he meant. *Wickham is a flirt,* she realized . . . but she had to admit, it was rather nice to be on the receiving end of flattery that did not make her shudder. She didn't quite know how to respond, so she kept silent as they picked their way through the streets. When Wickham realized that she wasn't going to address his earlier comment, he asked, "You don't really believe that she's already sold the pocket watch?"

"I don't think it matters either way. I don't intend to pursue it."

Wickham brought her up short. "You can't be serious! And you're going to write her a letter of reference?"

Lizzie didn't like his accusatory tone, but she supposed that disapproval of illegal activities was an occupational hazard. "Yes. I meant what I said, and she was in an impossible situation. Taking her before a magistrate would be cruel."

"But you heard her—Mr. Hurst did not treat the servants well. What if . . ."

Now it was Lizzie's turn for shock. "Mr. Wickham, you

cannot be serious! No. She couldn't have. That would have guaranteed her a death sentence."

"So?"

Lizzie's instincts told her he was wrong, and she wanted to tell him so, but she halted and took an even breath. *Logic*, she reminded herself.

"So," Lizzie said with patience she didn't feel, "when a servant kills their master, it's not considered murder—it's petty treason. And petty treason carries the death sentence. If she had actually murdered him, she might hang about the house after the crime so as to not arouse suspicions, but if she had been dismissed, she would have been long gone by now. Only a fool would hang about if a noose were looming."

"She had more motive than anyone!"

Abigail had motive, but so did Bingley, and Lizzie still needed proof before she could accuse anyone. "Come now, Mr. Wickham. I asked you along as a friend, not as a Runner. I warned you that we might discuss delicate matters."

Wickham looked as though he were going to protest, but he relented. "Of course, my apologies."

"It's all right," Lizzie said, even though she didn't really mean it. Yes, what Abigail had done was wrong, but did it really affect anyone else but herself? Considering that the punishment for such a theft would be extreme, and she had already gone through so much, Lizzie saw no reason to punish Abigail further. The speed at which Lizzie had arrived at this conclusion probably should have alarmed her, but she was reminded of something that Darcy had said, of all people: *Laws are not inherently just.* Lizzie wanted to help people, but she also wanted to practice law—why was it that the two seemed so frequently at odds?

"What are you going to do, if not report her?" Wickham asked.

Lizzie slid a glance toward him, and it was on the tip of her tongue to tell him she intended to follow the money. Abigail's remark about the flow of money from Bingley to Hurst had her thinking, and . . . well, she didn't have much left to go on. This case had turned into a convoluted mess that left her spinning in circles while a man was dead and a murderer was on the loose—but Lizzie still had two days. She would spin a little while longer, up until the last minute, if that's what it took.

"I don't know," Lizzie lied. "This case has an excessive number of dead ends."

"You'll keep me informed of your actions, won't you?" Wickham asked. "I'd hate to see anything happen to you."

"I promise," Lizzie said, although she meant no such thing.

FOURTEEN

In Which Darcy Surprises Lizzie

WHEN LIZZIE RETURNED HOME, she spent a great deal of time on the letter of reference for Abigail. Her first drafts were glowing, perhaps a bit over the top. So she crossed out sentences and revised until she had a respectable, appreciative, and believable letter to give to the poor young woman.

After she sealed her letter of reference, Lizzie drew out the only other bit of physical evidence in her possession: the button. She turned it over in her hand as she thought about her next move. Darcy believed that he could win the case by emphasizing Bingley's upstanding character and contrasting it with Hurst's lack of morality. And yet everything she had uncovered seemed to confirm that Bingley had more motives than anyone for killing Hurst. Maybe it was time to truly consider that he was guilty.

But then, what would her father think if she turned on her own client, simply to solve a crime? Would he be impressed, or would doing so demonstrate that she was even more of a liability to Longbourn? After all, who would hire a solicitor that got you into trouble, not out of it?

Lizzie flipped the button and caught it. Abigail didn't kill Hurst, she was sure. But if Darcy was pursuing the pocket watch lead, what if he discovered she was the one who'd stolen it? It wouldn't matter then if she were represented by the finest barrister in all of England; a jury wouldn't hesitate to find her guilty. How was that justice?

Lizzie flipped the button again, but by the time she caught it, her mind was made up. The Bingleys were hiding something, something to do with money. Likely something to do with Netherfield Shipping. Either Bingley was deliberately keeping her in the dark or he believed that discussing business with a lady was impolite.

Well, the time for polite behavior had passed.

The following day, Lizzie awoke determined. She donned her finest day dress, a cream-and-rose Indian block print, and topped it with the green spencer that made her eyes dance. Today, they were lit with the fire of determination. What she was about to do might not be very proper, but she could at least look the part. When Jane saw that she was dressed to go out, she asked no questions. Instead, she fetched a gold-and-topaz brooch, the only piece of jewelry Mrs. Bennet had not sold in the early days of her marriage, when money was scarce.

"I can't wear that," Lizzie told Jane, but her older sister insisted.

"Mama says it should be saved for special occasions, and this is one. You're going to solve this case."

"Or fail miserably," Lizzie said as she let Jane attach it to her spencer.

"Don't be defeatist, or I'll jab you," Jane threatened, which brought a reluctant smile to Lizzie's face.

Her first errand was to drop off the letter of reference for Abigail. Lizzie kept an eye out for Wickham as she retraced yesterday's steps to Thames Street, wondering if he'd approve of her decision to confront Bingley and Darcy. Likely not. That was fine. She didn't need him to agree with everything she did or said, but she wouldn't have said no to backup, just in case today resulted in an arrest. But Wickham was nowhere to be seen, and soon Lizzie arrived at the lodging house.

The same suspicious matron opened the door, and her eyes narrowed even more when she saw it was Lizzie again. "Abigail's not here," she announced by way of greeting.

Lizzie was surprised but collected herself. "Good day, madam. May I leave a note for her?"

The woman shrugged. "You can leave it, but in my experience when young women stay out all night, they don't come back for messages."

Lizzie shook her head. "I don't understand."

"Abigail," the woman said, exasperated. "She didn't want tea yesterday. She went out, but never returned by curfew. If you find her, tell her to find new lodgings. I run a respectable house."

And with that, the woman shut the door in Lizzie's face.

Lizzie surveyed the street in confusion. Had her visit yesterday spooked Abigail? If she still had the watch, would she have tried to sell it? Lizzie would not be able to help her if she had been picked up for theft. But surely Abigail wouldn't have been that foolish—she had seemed grateful. All she had to do was wait until morning, when Lizzie handed her the letter of recommendation. She could have gotten a new position and either disposed of the watch or held on to it until it no longer attracted suspicion. . . .

Lizzie stepped away from the boardinghouse with one final glance to the darkened windows and headed east along Thames Street, unsettled. She didn't have time today to track Abigail down, and the day had dawned with weak sunlight, but the clouds were growing more menacing in the distance. Lizzie hoped she could get to a high street and hire a carriage before it started raining.

At the corner two blocks down, a group of women clustered

together at the mouth of a cramped side street leading to the docks. Lizzie was about to step around them when she heard shouting from the direction of the river and noticed that men seemed to be hurrying toward the noise.

Acting on some instinct that Lizzie didn't question, she asked the women, "What's happening?"

Lizzie received a few sharp glances, and finally a woman wearing an apron splattered with fish guts said, "They pulled a lass out of the river this morning, miss."

Lizzie's body went numb, and the shouts in the distance sorted themselves out into words: "Call the watch!"

"Do you know who it is?" she asked. The women shook their heads, and it was all Lizzie needed to turn down the side street. With no concern for her finest dress, she walked briskly through puddles and manure, overcome by a sudden fear. She told herself she was being irrational even as she picked up pace. It couldn't be. It wouldn't . . .

Lizzie burst onto a street that directly overlooked the river and immediately spotted the source of the commotion—a large group of dockworkers gathered near the edge of the water. She went straight to them, hardly noticing the curious stares that followed her.

She got very close before a dockworker her father's age stood to block her view. "Nay, miss. You don't want to see her."

"Please," she said. "I have to know."

He tried to stop her, but Lizzie took advantage of his

hesitation to touch an unfamiliar young lady and ducked under his arm.

As soon as she saw her, Lizzie wished she hadn't. Abigail was set out on the dirty ground as if she were sleeping. Her blond hair had come undone and was spread out around her like wet tentacles. Her clothing was soaked and her lips blue. Lizzie caught a glimpse of her hands—bound with rope—before someone took Lizzie by the elbow and pulled her away.

Part of her thought, nonsensically, *Perhaps they can revive her*. But she immediately banished the thought from her mind. Her lips were blue. Her hands were tied. She had not come home last night.

Abigail was dead.

"Do you know her?" asked the man who'd tried to block her view.

Lizzie nodded, her gaze on her own feet and her mud-splattered skirt. It took her a long time to respond, but she finally whispered, "Her name is Abigail Jenkins."

"The Runners are coming, miss," he said. "You can tell them, and they'll escort you home."

Lizzie looked up then. And would they investigate? Or would they learn that she was recently sacked from the Hurst household and with Mr. Hurst recently murdered make assumptions about who she was and what she might have done?

Lizzie pulled her arm from the man's grasp. He looked surprised, but before he could say or do anything, Lizzie was already walking back up the street, fighting her roiling stomach and stoking the anger inside of her. She ignored the shouts from behind her, turning briefly only once to confirm that no one was following her. She headed northwest, now more determined than ever to follow through on her plan to confront the Bingleys.

It took Lizzie nearly an hour of walking before she found a carriage that could take her to the Bingleys' address, probably because she looked a fright with her dirty clothes and thunderous expression. She spent the drive trying to collect herself but found that the more she tried to distance herself from what she had just seen, the angrier she got. By the time the carriage dropped her in front of the Bingleys' town house, Lizzie was in no mood to be trifled with.

The butler did not even try to hide his disapproval as Lizzie swept into the house without waiting to be invited in. "I'm here to see *Mr.* Bingley," she enunciated, ignoring his scowl at her mud-splattered hem.

"Right this way, miss," he responded, although she could tell it pained him to do so. But he led her straight to the drawing room, where Caroline looked up from her seat next to the fireplace and Louisa stared out the window at the scattering of rain.

"I said—" Lizzie began, but the butler cut her off.

"Miss Bingley, this young lady insisted on being seen."

"Miss Bennet," Caroline proclaimed, as if Lizzie's name

were poison on her tongue. "You look a fright. Have you walked all the way from Cheapside?"

Lizzie opened her mouth to unleash all of her pent-up anger upon Caroline and her snobbery but was interrupted by a soft cry of surprise.

She turned and noticed a girl about her age. She had the complexion of someone who didn't spend a lot of time out of doors, but her cheeks were rosy and her dark hair was a lovely mahogany shade that actually quite reminded her of . . .

"This is Miss Bennet?" the girl said, rising to her feet to greet Lizzie.

Lizzie looked to Caroline to make the introduction, which she did grudgingly. "Miss Elizabeth Bennet, allow me to introduce you to Miss Georgiana Darcy. Georgie, this is Miss Bennet."

Georgiana grasped Lizzie's hand, much to Lizzie's surprise. "It's a pleasure to meet you at last, Miss Bennet."

"Lovely to meet you," Lizzie said, but her voice sounded faint to her own ears. "Are you any relation to Mr. Darcy?"

"My brother," she confirmed, and Lizzie realized the resemblance. Aside from sharing the exact shade of hair color, they had the same long nose—although Georgiana's was perfectly straight. Despite her eagerness to be made known to Lizzie, she seemed shy. She fidgeted as she said, "Fitz has told me so much about you! I can hardly believe that we are finally meeting."

"Neither can I," Caroline muttered.

Lizzie was stuck on Fitz. Darcy's sister called him *Fitz*? *Don't laugh*, she warned herself. Heaven only knew what *Fitz* had told his sister about her.

"It is lovely to make your acquaintance," Lizzie told her, and under normal circumstances she would have enjoyed getting to know Miss Darcy, although she hadn't even been aware of her existence. If Lizzie had been asked beforehand, she would have expected someone haughty like Caroline, but Georgiana hadn't even looked at Lizzie's dirty dress once. *Curious.*

"Have you come to harass Charles?" Caroline cut in. "Or me? Perhaps you'd like to take a turn at Louisa, grieving as she is?"

As if on cue, Louisa let out a strange hiccup that Lizzie supposed was a show of grief.

"I've come with developments on the case," Lizzie said, not taking the bait.

"Oh!" Georgiana said with surprise and great interest. "We should call for Bingley and Fitz, shouldn't we, Caroline?"

Caroline sniffed, not trying to hide her skepticism. "Have you followed me about some more? Discovered who was calling upon Louisa last Thursday?"

"There's been another murder," she snapped, letting the words douse any humor that had been left in the room.

Georgiana gasped, and Louisa looked up. Caroline grimaced. "Is it someone we know?"

"Abigail Jenkins," Lizzie said, her throat closing in around the young woman's name. Unbidden, the memory of Abigail, water-soaked and still, flashed in Lizzie's mind. She closed her eyes to try to banish it, and when she opened them again, Caroline and Louisa were exchanging blank looks.

"What does this have to do with my brother?" Caroline asked.

Lizzie ignored Caroline and asked Louisa, "Why was Abigail dismissed?"

Louisa gaped at the question, and Caroline stepped in as if on cue. "It isn't polite to discuss domestic troubles in front of company."

"Oh, I believe what's considered polite and impolite is fluid when speaking of murder."

Caroline stood to face Lizzie. "Perhaps that's your problem, Miss Bennet. You believe that there are exceptions when there should be none."

"I hardly see how caring about the life—or death—of another human being should be considered an exception!" Lizzie's voice shook, and she was truly in danger of bursting into tears.

But Caroline was interrupted by Louisa ringing the bell to summon the butler. Caroline shot her sister a dark look, but Louisa said, "Oh, don't, Caroline. I am sick of this whole mess, and I don't want Charles to hang."

Georgiana took in the scene with wide eyes, and Lizzie took satisfaction in being heard as she composed herself. But she was suddenly struck with nerves—Darcy was here. The butler was fetching him and Bingley, and soon Darcy would be looking at her with that brooding stare, ready to refute her every word. . . .

Lizzie took a steadying breath.

Bingley and Darcy entered, and Bingley was all smiles. "Miss Bennet, I am very happy to see you again. Do you come with news?"

Lizzie hesitated, waiting for Darcy to make a snide remark about her abilities, but he took a seat next to Georgiana and placed a protective hand on her shoulder.

Lizzie squared her own shoulders. "There's been another murder. This time, the Hursts' maid, Abigail. She was drowned. I've just come from the docks, where I saw her body myself."

"Dear God," Bingley said, collapsing into a chair.

"How do you know she was murdered?" Darcy asked. His tone wasn't cold or mocking, just curious. Still, Lizzie bristled.

"One doesn't simply trip and fall into the Thames, Mr. Darcy," she said, her voice sounding strained even to her own ears. *Don't cry*, she reminded herself. "Her hands were bound."

For a moment, Darcy looked stricken. Lizzie might have felt satisfaction at surprising him once, but all she felt was horrid guilt. She had been running from it the moment she learned of Abigail's fate, and now the weight of responsibility fell heavily on her. What if Lizzie's meddling had led a killer straight to Abigail?

"This turn of events cannot be a coincidence," Lizzie continued when she found her voice once more. "Abigail was dismissed before she had the chance to secure another position, but I spoke with her yesterday and she told me something I find curious."

Lizzie paused; no one spoke.

"Abigail had knowledge of the Hurst household. Mr. Bingley, she hinted that the decision to cut off Mr. Hurst was due to your own need for money. Caroline confirmed that you've been experiencing money troubles—it was why she convinced Mrs. Hurst to leave her husband."

"Are you accusing Bingley of murder, Miss Bennet?" Darcy's voice was hard as stone. Bingley had gone white. He sank back into his chair and rubbed his face.

"Not at all," Lizzie responded. "After all, I've no proof. But what I know is that Mr. Bingley engaged my services without giving me all of the pertinent information. Isn't that right, Mr. Bingley?"

Mr. Bingley was rubbing his temples and looking down at the floor. Even Darcy remained silent, but he cast a questioning look at Bingley.

Lizzie sighed, weary all of a sudden. "I don't see how you expect to solve this mess without being forthcoming."

"I know, I know," Bingley mumbled. "I hadn't meant to deceive you, Miss Bennet. But it was a closely guarded secret, and I hoped it was completely separate from this whole mess. Not even my sisters know."

Caroline huffed at that last bit. "I'm not an idiot, Charles. I know we don't have any money."

Bingley looked to Darcy for direction, and Lizzie prepared herself for an argument. But to her surprise, Darcy nodded. Bingley sighed and looked to Lizzie. "I didn't tell you because I truly didn't think it was connected to George's death. I thought perhaps a disreputable creditor had gotten to him before we could sort things out. I never thought that they would be out for *blood*."

"Who?" Lizzie asked.

But Bingley was no longer looking at her. Instead, he addressed his sisters and said, "Netherfield Shipping is about to go bankrupt." Caroline gaped while Louisa's hand flew to her mouth. Lizzie took a seat in the nearest settee.

"Trouble began a year and a half ago," Bingley continued. "Piracy. We lost two ships. Insurance helped, but I had to move money about to keep us going. I thought it was just rotten luck, only . . . it got worse. We lost five more ships, and three this year. Only two have made their destinations, and the profits aren't enough."

"But the insurance," Caroline protested.

"Insurance won't pay if you're being targeted," Darcy spoke up.

"You knew?" Lizzie asked him.

"Darcy has been appealing to the Admiralty on my behalf. Fat lot of good it's done us. They're too busy with the French to pursue some faceless, nameless pirate who seems to have it out for Netherfield Shipping. Then the pirates began demanding protection fees."

"How much have you been paying them?" Caroline demanded.

"I haven't."

Silence fell over the room, as everyone took in Bingley's meaning.

"Why not?" Caroline shrieked.

"Because it's immoral and illegal," Bingley replied, his calm a striking contrast to Caroline's desolation. "Besides, I won't be bullied."

Caroline turned to Darcy. "Talk some sense into him! We're going bankrupt!"

"I can't," Darcy said, "and even if I could, I wouldn't. It's illegal to pay off pirates, and I wouldn't persuade my client or my friend to do something that I myself wouldn't be willing to do."

Men and their honor were a mystery to Lizzie. It was not honorable to pay off pirates, but it was honorable to challenge others to a duel?

"Forgive me, Louisa," Bingley continued, entreating his older sister. "I gave George a position in the company thinking he would assume responsibility. When it became clear that he wasn't contributing, I limited his role, terrified he'd lose us money when we had none to spare. I'd paid off gambling debts in the past, but then I told him he'd get a salary and nothing more, hoping he'd realize the gravity of the situation. When it became evident that he was still spending and not even bothering to come home, I grew angry. I was pouring all my own money into keeping Netherfield going, and he kept racking up debt. Had I known someone would take such drastic measures . . ."

He turned to Lizzie. "Miss Bennet, I wasn't forthcoming because I didn't want my sisters to know of our business troubles, and I didn't want word to get out."

The anguish on Bingley's face and the pain in his voice were convincing—but Lizzie wasn't feeling generous. "A young woman is dead," she whispered. "She had no part in this, but she died for it nonetheless. I need to know everything, no more secrets."

Bingley nodded, and it took Lizzie a moment to collect her thoughts. What if she had simply approached Bingley days ago to press him for more information? Why had she been so determined to solve this without questioning Bingley more closely? She slid a glance toward Darcy. *That's why*, said a voice in her head that sounded annoyingly like Jane's. Because she wanted to find the truth and she wanted no man's interference. *Foolish.*

"You said you limited Hurst's work in the business?" she asked Bingley finally. "When?"

"Ages ago," he said. "I didn't want to tell the ladies, because I didn't want them to know how bad things were. George agreed to keep quiet and was all too happy to leave work as long as I agreed to cover his household expenses, which I managed to do until earlier this year."

Lizzie could feel Darcy's gaze upon her. She glanced at him briefly, and yes, he was staring right back, curiosity written across his face. She turned back to Bingley. She had to get her mind around the timeline of events.

"You say your insurers dropped you last year?"

"Yes, last September."

"And was Hurst involved in securing insurance?"

Confusion crossed Bingley's face. "God, no. I wouldn't have trusted him to receive my mail, much less insure my business."

"But on his desk in his study," Lizzie said, slowly reviewing the memory, "I saw a letter pertaining to an insurance policy on Netherfield Shipping. I can't quite remember . . . it was dated this year, I'm sure of it."

"Would this have been when you broke in?" Darcy asked.

"I was let in," Lizzie insisted. "And I did not break anything. I'm telling you, there was something regarding an insurance policy on Netherfield. What if Hurst's murder has something to do with the business?"

"So pirates killed Hurst?" Darcy asked, sounding doubtful.

"I don't know!" Lizzie snapped. She still couldn't figure out how Abigail fit in.

"It makes sense," Georgiana said, cutting the tension between Lizzie and Darcy. "If Hurst took out a fraudulent insurance policy that directed premiums to the pirates, and they got rid of him, and implicated Bingley, and Caroline and Louisa knew nothing of it—"

"Then they would have kept on paying the fraudulent policy, allowing the pirates to profit," Darcy finished. He jumped up and began running his hands through his hair in an agitated manner. It was the first time Lizzie witnessed him less than perfectly put together.

"From there it would not have been a stretch for them to insinuate someone into the business who knew of their plan, and to take control of the company," Lizzie added.

"And they would have had regular payments, and full access to a trading route for smuggling purposes," Darcy finished.

"Quite a coup," Lizzie agreed.

Their eyes met, and for a heart-pounding moment she felt the thrum of shared victory. Then she reminded herself not to get too carried away. "We need to find that insurance policy."

"We need both the fraudulent and the canceled genuine policies," Darcy corrected her. "We can present them before the judge and build the case that this was a business matter turned sour."

"Let's go to Grosvenor Square to retrieve the one Hurst had, and then to Pemberley," Bingley said, standing and calling for the butler.

Darcy shook his head. "It'll be faster if you go to your brother-in-law's, and meet me at Pemberley."

Lizzie turned suspicious. Perhaps because Darcy would be

left with a key piece of evidence, or because he'd been agreeing with her. She would not be left out. "I'll come with you."

"No need," Darcy said. "Your help and perspective are appreciated, however—"

"Not a chance!" Lizzie cried out. "I'm the reason why you even know to look to the insurance policies in the first place."

"Because you committed a crime—"

"For the last time, I was let in! I'm coming with you, and you shan't get rid of me."

She stared him down, and he returned her forceful gaze. Lizzie thought of Lady Catherine's warning, Wickham's story of betrayal, the rumors that had reached even her mother's ears. As much as she would like to believe that Darcy agreeing with her was a mark of common sense, she could not completely overrule her suspicion. If there was the slightest chance that he was crooked, Lizzie would not allow him to abscond with her evidence.

"Very well," he relented.

"Excellent," Georgiana proclaimed. "I shall come too!"

FIFTEEN

In Which Lizzie and Darcy
Face Complications

THE FOG HAD CREPT up, turning the late afternoon gloomy. Lizzie sat next to Georgiana in the Darcys' carriage and studied Darcy, daring him to say something. He kept his silence, but luckily Georgiana was talking enough for the both of them. "This is really quite the twist," she said. "Like something out of a novel, but even more exciting. It's very clever, isn't it?"

"Extortion masquerading as legitimate business actions?" Lizzie said. "Well, a bit cleverer than I would expect out of Hurst. But it would hardly have worked long-term."

"Are you so unwilling to give credit to a man that you can't acknowledge when criminal activity has outsmarted you?" Darcy inquired, keeping his gaze out the window.

"I've never declined to give credit where credit is due, Mr. Darcy. That seems to be your expertise."

"You expect me to account for a great many things I've never done," he bit back.

"You don't like to accept help, do you?" she asked, managing to keep her tone pleasant only because Georgiana was beside her, and Georgiana seemed perfectly lovely.

"I don't decline help when I need it. If it's my attitude you take issue with, perhaps my greatest weakness is that I can't forget when other people have acted foolishly or offended me."

"So your only choice is to hate everyone?"

"And yours is to willfully misunderstand everyone," he said finally, meeting the full force of her gaze.

His look—how to classify that look? In it, Lizzie felt as though she saw herself the way he must see her. A headstrong, foolish girl who inserted herself into situations where she wasn't welcome, where she offered no valid opinions or assistance. For some reason, this perception cut her. She'd rather that Darcy look at her with disdain, annoyance, even anger, than look through her as though she had no value.

She sighed. "I simply meant that extortion masquerading as an insurance policy was only moderately clever because it wouldn't hold up under close scrutiny. My father's expertise is in business law. I imagine that the documents provided the criminals paychecks, but this isn't a wise long-term plan."

"Thus the murder to preserve the farce," Darcy concluded.

"Thus the murder," she echoed. Finally something they could agree upon.

Lizzie saw Georgiana regarding her and Darcy as if they were performing in a play for Georgiana's own entertainment. "How fascinating," the younger girl replied. "Someone awfully clever must be behind it all, then?"

"Yes," Lizzie and Darcy said at the same time, and the thought made Lizzie uncomfortable. Who could it be? A small part of her still suspected Darcy. He was clever enough. And if his behavior toward Wickham was any indication, he was ruthless enough. But now that she knew that Hurst's death did not protect the Bingley family from ruin but might instead expose their precarious position, she had serious doubts—unless Darcy had yet to play his final hand.

"If Bingley asked you for money, would you give him any?" she asked.

It was a tactic she'd learned while trying to elicit information from her father, to ask him abrupt, straightforward questions when he was lost in thought. He was usually so startled that he'd answer honestly.

"Yes," Darcy said, proving her method. "I would have given him as much as I had, if he'd asked. But he didn't."

Lizzie nodded but was unsettled by the feeling that she had missed something.

Darcy's carriage came up a side street, revealing the darkened side of the Pemberley & Associates offices. It wasn't a workday, so few people lingered in the streets. The fog had morphed into a cold, spitting rain and stern breeze, and the lamplighters had not yet been around. Before the driver could make the turn to deliver them to the entrance, the carriage came to an abrupt halt. Lizzie heard the driver's voice raised in anger and a response from an unfamiliar man. For a moment, Darcy's eyes met hers before they moved to opposite windows.

Outside, Lizzie couldn't see much aside from empty streets and what appeared to be a staggering figure making the horses balk. Darcy called out, "What's the delay?"

"A drunk, sir!" the driver called back.

Lizzie turned to find Darcy looking back at her. "I could be unreasonable," she said, "but does this seem like a distraction to you?"

"Better to be unreasonable than sorry," Darcy declared. "Stay here, both of you."

Then he threw open the door and leapt out.

Lizzie gaped. If Darcy really thought that she was going to stay put while he investigated danger . . .

"Go," Georgiana whispered. "I'll pretend I tried to stop you."

"I rather like you," Lizzie said, and she went after Darcy.

By the time she scrambled down, there was no sign of a drunk, and the driver looked rather alarmed to find himself two passengers lighter. Lizzie took off, rounding the street corner just in time to see Darcy sprint inside Pemberley & Associates. She picked up her skirts to follow at a faster clip.

The office was draped in dark shadows thanks to the lack of lamps and the turn in the weather. But Lizzie followed the sound of Darcy's steps deeper into the building, haphazardly bumping into furniture as she made her way to the open office area. "Bollocks!"

"Miss Bennet?" Mr. Darcy called out. She could just make out his figure across the room.

"I'm fine," she said, winding her way in his direction. "Where are the lamps?"

"The front door was unlocked," he said, and she detected a rattle in his voice.

"We need some light, Darcy." Lizzie continued picking her way toward him, but her foot slid. She caught herself and blinked a few times to allow her heart to settle and eyes to adjust. Paper. She'd skidded on a loose sheet of paper on the floor. She picked it up, and as she looked around, she noticed more scattered sheets. Not just on desks but on the floor, too.

"Ransacked," she muttered. She felt exposed, as if malicious eyes waited in the dark, unfamiliar corners of the firm. "Darcy?"

She would meditate later on the pathetic wobble to her voice, but in that moment she was relieved when Darcy responded with a whisper, "Over here!"

She could make out his figure over on the far side of the office and continued picking a path toward him. Light. They needed light. *You are being a fool, Elizabeth Bennet,* she told herself sternly, but she did not like this. Had Abigail felt like this, at the end? The idea of Abigail alone and afraid and in the dark as a killer closed in made Lizzie's throat clench.

"Darcy?" Lizzie whispered, and reached out her arm. She was never so glad to feel his hand grasp hers, even if her own fear annoyed her. "Do you have a light?"

"Are you afraid of the dark?" he asked, not mocking. It was a genuine question.

"Does it matter? We're supposed to be looking for something, and we can't see."

"Give me a moment. I have a tinderbox in my desk." He placed her hands on the desk and added, "Don't move."

For once, Lizzie was glad to comply. She heard rustling and willed him to hurry. A scrape of the flint was followed by a tiny spark of light, and Lizzie focused on the glow. It took Darcy two more tries to get a candle to light, and she felt her breathing come easier when she saw his worried face illuminated. "Are you all right?" he asked.

She nodded, then looked about in the meager light that his candle cast. "Oh my." There were papers scattered everywhere. Darcy's desk had been emptied, and his drawers stood open and bare. "Where *was* the insurance policy?" she asked.

"In my desk," he replied. "I have no idea where it's gone in this mess."

"If it's even still here."

"Indeed." He found a candelabra and lit four candles before setting it on another desk. Lizzie began picking up papers, shuffling through them, as Darcy muttered, "Why tonight, of all nights, to break in and steal an insurance policy?"

"Isn't it obvious?" Lizzie asked.

Darcy looked up, and even in the meager light Lizzie could read his irritation. "Please, do enlighten me."

"We're on to him," she said. "Abigail was murdered last night, and she had information about Hurst's business. The killer stole all of your paperwork on Netherfield so that whoever was left to pick up this mess would confuse the fraudulent policy at Hurst's house for the legitimate one."

"But *I* would know," Darcy said.

"Would you be believed?"

That made Darcy stop. Lizzie could see it on his face, horror at the possibility of not being believed when he knew he was speaking the truth. Lizzie was glad that he was experiencing just an ounce of what she endured trying to break into legal work, but the triumph didn't last. Instead, she felt the urge to reassure Darcy. "Bingley will secure the fraudulent policy. After all, I doubt the killer knows we've figured out the scheme—"

Lizzie caught sight of movement in the corner of her eye and turned to trace its source. It came from the direction of the records room, the door to which, she realized with unease, stood slightly ajar. Darcy had stopped speaking when he saw her react, and now he was looking at the corner. "Miss Bennet?"

It was just the dancing candlelight, she told herself. She started to turn back toward Darcy . . . and the movement came again.

"Someone's there," she breathed. Abigail's killer? Improbably, she took a step forward and Darcy followed, leaving the candles behind. "I swear, I saw movement."

Gathering her courage, she pushed the door open. "Is this door normally locked?"

"Yes," Darcy confirmed, sounding nervous.

"Who has a key—" Lizzie was interrupted by a sense of movement in the corner of her eye. She turned and saw a dark figure right behind them, shockingly close. He was backlit by the candlelight they'd left on the desk, and surprise was on his side. He shoved both Darcy and Lizzie, sending them tumbling into the records room. Lizzie lost her balance and fell to the floor, and Darcy came down on top of her. By the time Darcy righted himself, the door had slammed shut and Lizzie heard the unmistakable sound of a key turning in the latch.

"Are you hurt?" Darcy asked.

Lizzie was still trying to catch her breath, but she shook her head and then realized that Darcy couldn't see her. They were in total blackness.

"I'm all right," she managed, and shakily got to her feet. "How are you?"

"Fine. Who in the devil was that?" Lizzie could feel Darcy moving in front of her, and she couldn't help herself—she stretched out her arms until she felt his shoulder. His hand found her elbow. "Did you see his face?"

"No," she said, hating the panic in her voice. "Do you have a key?"

"Of course," he said. "But it won't unlock from the inside."

"What kind of door doesn't unlock from the inside?"

"We play a prank on all the new clerks," Darcy said. He sounded distracted. "We send them to fetch a file, and someone closes the door behind them to lock them in. We usually let them out after an hour."

Men, Lizzie thought hopelessly. "And no one ever thought about how that trick might play out if there was no one in the office?"

"Well, I think the idea was that it would be an added security measure. If a thief ever entered the records room, someone with a key would have to let him out, thus catching him. . . ."

"And yet *this* thief had to have a key to get in, correct?"

"Clearly the system needs to be revisited," Darcy muttered.

"Never mind," she said. "We need to find a way out."

She took a step forward, feeling for the door. She found the handle and twisted, but no luck. She attempted to rattle the door, but it didn't even budge. She began throwing her weight against the door, then felt Darcy's hand at her shoulder. "The door opens inward."

"Oh," Lizzie said, feeling foolish. "Well, is there another way out? A window, perhaps? I could wiggle through something small, I'm sure."

"Nothing," Darcy replied. "We'll just have to wait. Georgiana or the driver will get curious enough to investigate. We'll pound on the door when we hear them."

"That's the best you can come up? Waiting?"

"Do you have a better idea?" he snapped.

Lizzie did not, but it was against her nature to admit it.

Waiting was also against Lizzie's nature. She couldn't help but run her hands over the door, hoping for something that would help their situation. She could hear Darcy breathing but not see how close he stood or what he was doing. The idea was rather unnerving.

"You can't be still, can you?"

Lizzie made a face she knew he couldn't see. "I can be still."

"I can feel you fidgeting," Darcy said.

"And I can feel you brooding."

Lizzie took a tiny step backward and realized that Darcy wasn't breathing naturally—she could hear the ragged intake of his breath and the shaky exhale. Concern overcame her. "Are you hurt?"

"No."

If he wasn't hurt, then why was he panting like an overworked horse? "Are you frightened?"

"Aren't you?"

"A little, but I'm not about to panic yet."

"How wonderful for you." His attempt at sarcasm fell flat, and that's when Lizzie really became concerned.

"What's bothering you?"

He drew in an audible breath. "I don't like small spaces, all right? They make me . . ."

"Panicky?" Lizzie suggested. "But wait, just how small is this room?"

"It doesn't matter. I can't see a bloody thing, there are no windows, and we're locked in. I feel as though the walls are closing in on me."

"Oh," she said quietly. She was used to arrogant, bored, mocking Darcy. More and more, these cracks in his confident facade puzzled her. "Well, I'm a bit afraid of the dark."

"I gathered," he said, but for once his tone didn't offend her.

"When I was a child, my sister would have to hold my hand until I fell asleep. I thought every little noise was a thief sneaking about the house."

"So you've always had an overactive imagination."

"Yes," Lizzie acknowledged, "but perhaps it's not so overactive after all, is it?"

He sighed. "I will admit that you're right about this case. It has turned out to be far more complicated than I first suspected."

Lizzie caught her breath on the compliment, even if it was grudgingly given. It made her feel as though there were an imbalance between them, and she struggled with what to say in response. Finally, she came up with, "I'm sorry I went after Caroline the way I did."

"You should apologize to her, not to me."

Lizzie would rather eat dirt. "It's just that this case is very important me."

"Why? You'd never met Bingley before last week."

Something about the darkness made it easier to admit the truth to Darcy. "My father refuses to formally train me. He said if I could prove to him that I could solve a case, using logic, he'd consider it. Bingley's arrest was the first case I came across, and I don't have a lot of time before my father hires someone else."

"Ah," Darcy said. She waited for him to say more, but silence stretched between them.

"Does talking make it better or worse? It helps me."

"I think it helps. I feel . . . disconnected. This dark makes me feel like I don't know which way is up or down or right or left. . . ."

Lizzie reached out until she felt Darcy's arm. He tensed, but from there, she was able to figure out where his hand was, and she took it in hers. "There. Now you know where I am."

"Thank you," Darcy murmured.

She told herself the only reason she was holding Darcy's hand was that the last thing she needed was for him to lose his wits before they could be rescued, but in reality, it felt nice to know where he was, too.

"I'm sorry your father won't train you," he said finally. "He must be a very stubborn man."

Lizzie laughed because this was by far the strangest

evaluation of her mild-mannered father she'd ever heard. "What makes you say that?"

"If he's holding out against you . . . ," Darcy said, and she detected a teasing hint in his voice.

"I'd never thought of it like that."

"They don't make it easy for us," Darcy said. She assumed he was referring to his father as well but didn't ask. He continued, "I suppose when the stakes are so high, they need to know that we're completely dedicated. But . . . it shouldn't be so much harder for you. You're far more passionate about the law and justice than most of the young men I was at school with."

Lizzie could scarcely believe her ears. Darcy was complimenting her. Had their assailant knocked him on the head? It felt like a victory to have him acknowledge her abilities, and yet it also made her feel exposed. Instead of responding, she asked, "What's it like, working for Pemberley?"

"Busy," Darcy said. "We have a great number of cases. Keeping track of everything can be overwhelming, but I've spent my entire life preparing."

If Darcy had said this in any other context, she might have rolled her eyes at his self-importance. "And do all employees start off as solicitors with a desk in the middle of the office?"

"No," he said with a small laugh. "I actually started out as an errand boy, running papers and messages. Then I went to school, and when I came back I was a clerk and spent a year filing case notes before solicitor training. Not all clerks make it to that point. There are no shortcuts at Pemberley. But if you put in the work and prove yourself loyal, you'll be rewarded."

Their truce of a moment ago vanished with these words as Lizzie recalled Wickham's account of his time at Pemberley. What of *his* hard work? What of his loyalty? Her old suspicions of Darcy bubbled back, replacing her sympathy. "Does it work that way for everyone?"

"Of course. Why do you ask?"

"I've just heard otherwise, that's all."

"What do you mean?"

"You can't tell me that there isn't any nepotism at Pemberley."

Darcy's response was sharp. "Where is this coming from?"

"I've met one of your father's former employees, that's all. He told me a different story. He was set on the same trajectory as you, but when he surpassed you, you saw that he was dismissed."

"That's absurd! Who on earth told you that?"

Darcy withdrew his hand from hers, and Lizzie continued. "Mr. Wickham."

"Wickham?" Darcy repeated, and Lizzie had the strangest feeling that if she'd said she heard it from the prince regent, Darcy would not have been more shocked. "Wherever did you meet *Wickham*?"

Lizzie was about to say that it was none of Darcy's business when she heard the scrape of a key turning in the lock, and the door was thrown open. She and Darcy leapt apart as lamplight poured into the records room. Lizzie blinked a few times at the sudden brightness and heard Georgiana say, "Oh, thank goodness! Alan, they were locked in!"

"The thief shut us in," Darcy explained, reverting to the brusque, haughty-sounding young man that Lizzie was familiar with. "Are you all right?"

"I saw him run out of the office," Georgiana said, excitement evident. "He ran past the carriage, and I opened the door as he went by and hit him quite hard! He kept on, and Alan was about to run after him, but when you two didn't return, I became worried. I was calling your names—you didn't hear?"

"No, sorry," Lizzie said. "Good work, Miss Darcy."

"Thank you," she said as Lizzie and Darcy followed her out into the office. "But what happened in here?"

"The murderer stole my paperwork on Netherfield, and left quite a mess besides," Darcy said. Alan, the driver, was lighting candles and lamps, allowing them to better survey the mess of documents. "I doubt I'll be able to find any of it before Bingley's hearing tomorrow."

"Oh," Georgiana said, her excitement dimming. The three of them were silent in their defeat, taking in the mess. Then Georgiana added in an earnest tone, "I'm sorry I didn't hit him harder."

SIXTEEN

*In Which the Bennets Receive
a Surprise Caller*

THE WATCH WAS CALLED immediately, and the other clerks and solicitors of Pemberley were sent for. Darcy led the men through the office, assessing the damage and attempting to preserve their paperwork and files.

It became obvious once the office was properly lit that the thief had targeted Darcy's desk but made a half-hearted attempt at distraction by also prying open a few other desks and scattering documents about. The barristers' offices were locked, and the only ones who held keys for them were their individual owners and Darcy's father. Nevertheless, Darcy insisted upon a full assessment of the break-in, not willing to jeopardize the reputation of the firm. Lizzie watched him from the side of the room, where she had made herself useful by sorting the papers she'd recovered from the floor. She tried to stay focused on the matter at hand, but her mind was still in the dark of the records room, wondering what excuse Darcy would have given about Wickham if only they'd had five minutes more.

It wasn't long before Bingley arrived, soaked from the pounding rain that had started not long after Lizzie and Darcy had been liberated. He found Darcy in the corner of the office, muttering about hiring a night guard. "What's happened?" he asked with alarm.

"Someone broke in," Darcy said matter-of-factly as Lizzie sidled over. "We're trying to determine what, if anything, has been stolen. But we haven't found Netherfield's insurance policy."

Bingley's posture sagged. "What now?"

"We aren't giving up," Lizzie and Darcy said in unison, and then exchanged uneasy looks.

Bingley retrieved an oilskin document pouch from inside his jacket. "I found the policy, Miss Bennet. It was on Hurst's desk, just as you said. I've never seen it before in my life."

He handed it over to Darcy, but Lizzie had no qualms about leaning in to read over his shoulder. "It looks authentic," Darcy murmured, sounding surprised. Lizzie would agree, upon first glance. But as they examined the document, Lizzie said, "The fourth clause—and the sixth. They're loosely worded."

Darcy flipped to the last page. "And it's missing a clause on cancellation."

"It's far shorter than what I'd expect for a document of such importance," Lizzie added.

"Indeed," he said, looking impressed. "How do you know so much about contracts?"

"It's the only thing I'm allowed to study," she replied, and looked up from the document. Darcy's face was very close to hers, and she was overwhelmed by his proximity. She took a step back. "As I said, my father's expertise is in business law."

"Hm." He gathered up the papers before Lizzie had a chance to read them more closely, tucking them in his inner coat pocket. Lizzie once again felt a sense of unease that the evidence of something she'd uncovered was now in the possession of a man.

"We'll keep searching," Darcy promised Bingley, although Lizzie would have bet her own hand in marriage to Collins that it would not turn up at Pemberley. "The fraudulent policy should be enough for the judge to conclude that something is amiss and that Hurst had other enemies."

Or it would backfire spectacularly and the judge would assume that Bingley had set up his brother-in-law in order to save his business. But Bingley looked so downtrodden that Lizzie didn't have the heart to say this aloud. After all, part of being good legal counsel was to not discourage your client. Then again, one ought not give them false hope, either. . . .

"What shall I do?" Bingley asked, looking about the office, which was being set back to rights.

"Go home," Darcy urged him. "Rest."

"Don't give me that," he said miserably. "I need a task to keep my mind off tomorrow."

"Take the ladies home, then."

Lizzie crossed her arms. "Oh, I'm not going home yet."

Darcy simply rolled his eyes heavenward.

"Don't do that. Would you tell a man to simply go home?"

"I just did!" Darcy protested, gesturing toward Bingley.

"Would you tell another male *solicitor* to simply go home?"

"If there was nothing left to do, then yes."

Lizzie knew that she was coming across as headstrong and obstinate, but she wasn't prepared to see their evidence disappear with Darcy. "Clearly there isn't nothing left to do! Otherwise you yourself would be headed home."

Darcy looked to Bingley. "Please, take Georgiana home. Go in with her and consult with the staff; make sure everything is secured. And then go home and do the same with your household. Whoever broke in here is likely Hurst's killer, and they're still at large."

Bingley nodded and gave a small bow to Lizzie. "Miss Bennet, my thanks. Be safe, and good night."

As he went to collect Georgiana, Lizzie murmured to Darcy, "See, that's how you show appreciation for a job well done."

Darcy gave her a dark look and stormed off to say goodbye to his sister.

It turned out that Darcy was correct—there was little left to do. The firm did not maintain a master list of all documents that went in and out in a day, and it would be impossible to determine what exactly had been stolen. Once things were cleaned up, Darcy arranged for two clerks to stay the night in the office to deter further break-ins. Finally, he turned to Lizzie and said, "If you don't object to my company or the rumors that are sure to follow, I'd be happy to see you home."

"It's rather late to worry about propriety," she said. "We were locked in that records room together for at least twenty minutes. Imagine if all the society gossips caught wind of *that*."

Lizzie's words were all bravado, though—it was now dark, and a killer was on the loose. Even if she didn't trust Darcy, she was glad for the company of an opponent she knew rather than an unfamiliar one. The moment they climbed into the carriage, she said, "When shall we meet tomorrow to build our case?"

"My case," he corrected with a heavy sigh.

"You wouldn't have a case to build without me."

"You've contributed a great deal, but as unfair as it is, women aren't allowed in court."

"That's untrue. Women are not *encouraged* in court."

He gave her a baffled look. "You think that if you show up often enough, one day they'll just call you to the bar?"

"Why not?" she fired back. "There's no law banning me

from practicing. In fact, the only obstacle I face is men who don't think I'm capable."

"I'm not belittling you, Miss Bennet," Darcy said. He pressed his fingertips against his temple. "You distrust me, and that's the real reason you can't leave it to me."

"I have reason to. What of the way you treated Mr. Wickham?"

Darcy simply shook his head and said quietly, "You have greatly misjudged me."

"Have I?" Lizzie asked with a small laugh. "Will you challenge me to a duel over it?"

His expression darkened, but he met her gaze head-on. "If you wish to know anything about my past, all you need to do is ask. Despite the grievances you bring against my character, I promise to do you the courtesy of speaking the truth."

"Did you challenge another man in an illegal duel?"

"Yes," he said.

She was shocked at his honesty. *"Why?"*

"I cannot give you the reason. It concerns the reputation of someone I care about deeply, and whose trust I will not break."

Before today, Lizzie might have thought this was just a convenient excuse. But something in his expression made her falter. "Did you—did you win?"

He gave a short, scornful laugh. "You could say I did, but does anyone really win a duel?"

Lizzie supposed he was alluding to the hit to his reputation, although did he not still retain a respectable position in society? Money? Influence? A future?

"Whom did you duel?"

At this, Darcy gave her a rather puzzled look. But before he could respond, the carriage lurched to a halt. She looked out the window and saw her own front door. When she looked back, Darcy was reaching for the carriage door. "Is your father in?"

"Why?" Lizzie asked, panic flaring in her. Darcy wasn't going to haul her straight to her father and tell him his daughter was out of control, was he?

Darcy stepped down from the carriage and held out a hand to help Lizzie down. "You said he's a business law expert. We need a barrister. He seems like the obvious choice for court, don't you agree?"

Lizzie nodded and followed him, but she was dumbfounded.

"Will he take on this case?" Darcy asked.

Lizzie had no idea how Mr. Bennet would react to this development, but she'd take the gamble if it meant another chance at getting her hands on the evidence Darcy was carrying. "Come in and let's see what he has to say."

They hurried through the rain, which was slowing to a light drizzle, to the front door. Lizzie wondered if there was any way that she could whisk Darcy upstairs to her father's study without her mother spotting them and going into a tizzy over the impropriety of Lizzie arriving home unchaperoned with a young man. On the bright side, this might be the blow to her reputation that got her out of pointless social engagements!

"You have a lovely home," Darcy murmured to her as they entered, dripping rain on the carpet.

"Shhh, I don't want—"

Kitty's voice rang out. "Who is this?!"

Lizzie looked up to see her sister on the stairs, staring down at them, and cursed inwardly. "Kitty. This is Mr. Darcy. Is Papa in his study?"

Rather than answering, Kitty said, "Mama is in a state over you, Lizzie!"

"Why? Doesn't she have four other daughters to torment?"

"You'll be lucky if I don't tell her you said that! No, you have a caller! A *gentleman* caller! Which is awfully exciting, and perhaps a bit scandalous, seeing as you just now brought a different gentleman home—are you finally taking an interest in marriage after all? It's about time."

Lizzie froze, conscious of Darcy's gaze heavy on her back. She thought of Collins—was it Monday already? If he had come here hoping to sway Lizzie's opinion on marrying him, and Mrs. Bennet discovered that Lizzie had received a proposal and not told anyone . . . God help her.

"Where's Mama?" she asked.

But as soon as the words left her mouth, the drawing room door opened down the hall and she heard Mrs. Bennet's voice drift out. "I'm sure she'll be home very soon. She's a very headstrong girl, but if you'll just be patient a little while longer, I am sure that— Lizzie!"

Her mother charged down the hall with the force and determination of an ox, and Lizzie prepared herself for full and utter humiliation in front of Darcy. *His sister calls him Fitz*, she reminded herself in an attempt to lessen the impact of her impending embarrassment.

"Where have you been?! You have a caller! And he's been waiting almost an hour for you! Your father has given you far too much freedom and— Who is this?"

"Mama, this is Mr. Darcy. He's come to consult with Papa."

Mrs. Bennet gave the bare minimum of courtesy to Mr. Darcy, although Darcy bowed and greeted her with the utmost civility. "Mrs. Bennet, a pleasure. Thank you for receiving me, and so late in the evening."

"Mr. Bennet is in his study. Kitty can show you." Mrs. Bennet began picking at Lizzie's person in an attempt to straighten her hair and clothing. "Now look at you, drenched and disheveled—and is that mud? Lizzie, this is your best dress! But, oh, he already knows you're here, so you better go in and speak to him, before Lydia convinces him to propose to her instead."

That gave Lizzie pause. Lydia *despised* Mr. Collins. "Mama, who—"

A hearty laugh from the drawing room made Lizzie look up, and in an instant she realized exactly who was waiting. She looked to Darcy to see if he had recognized the voice as well, and judging by the glower he was working himself up to, he had indeed.

Lizzie brushed past her mother and rushed down the hallway. She entered the drawing room to find Wickham by the fire and Lydia sitting rather closer to him than was proper. He looked up when she entered and wielded that dimple in her direction. "Lizzie!"

Wickham's smile disappeared when he spotted Darcy right on her heels. He got to his feet, taking Lydia by surprise. "Hello, Darcy."

"Wickham," Darcy said through clenched teeth.

"Lydia!" Lydia said, pointing to herself. "This is Mr. Darcy? Heavens, Lizzie—you didn't tell us how handsome he is."

Lizzie shot her sister a look. Now was not the time for Lydia's dramatics. "Lydia, will you please go see to Mama?"

"No," she said. "I prefer the company in here."

Lizzie didn't wish to argue with her sister in front of guests, so she shifted her gaze to Wickham. At the same time that Darcy asked, "What're you doing here?" Lizzie exclaimed, "Oh! You're hurt!"

"I shall live," Wickham assured her, holding out his hands and arms to show that he was fine. But the knees of his trousers were muddied and the elbow of his jacket was torn. He had a rather large bruise on the left side of his jaw and a small gash above his left eye.

"What happened?" she asked, neatly pushing Lydia aside for a closer look.

"The hazard of performing one's duties," he informed her. "I was set upon by a gang of thieves."

"That cut looks fresh," Lizzie said. It hadn't yet scabbed over. "Has it been cleaned?"

"I've already offered," Lydia said, clearly annoyed.

"It's a small thing," Wickham assured her, but he flinched when Lizzie took his arm to draw him closer to the firelight so she could examine it.

"Are you hurt elsewhere?"

He didn't answer. He wasn't even looking at her. Rather, he was staring at Darcy.

"I didn't know you were back in town," Darcy said, and the words would have been pleasant if not for the coldness in his voice.

"I didn't know that you would be here," Wickham said in a measured tone, but Lizzie saw a flash of panic in Wickham's eyes before it was replaced by a familiar jovial expression. "It's quite the night. The change in weather always makes people restless. I know that I'm not presentable by your standards, but . . ."

Something felt off. Lizzie's grip on Wickham loosened, and she tried her best to keep her voice from wavering as she said, "And what is the reason for your call this evening?"

He looked at her, and Lizzie held her composure despite

the thousands of questions that were racing through her mind. "I've come to see how you were faring in your case."

But Darcy cut in. "Tell me, Wickham—did you ever return your key to Pemberley and Associates when you were dismissed?"

Lizzie's confusion crystallized into clarity. Wickham's stance and figure were identical to those of the intruder, his injuries too fresh. The mud on his knees hadn't even dried.

"Mr. Wickham?" Lizzie asked. She began to take a step back, but Wickham's hand closed around her arm, much stronger and tighter than she could have imagined.

"Don't, Lizzie," he said, and yanked her close, so her arm was pinned behind her. "No one move!"

"What are you doing?" Lydia protested.

At that moment, Mrs. Bennet came back into the drawing room. She took in the scene and cried out, "A quarrel! Over my Lizzie! Over Lydia or Jane, I would have believed it, but *Lizzie!*"

Darcy took a step forward, but Wickham shouted, "Not one step!"

Darcy stopped, and his eyes widened. Lizzie followed his gaze, and she went very still.

Wickham was brandishing a pistol, and the business end was pointed directly at Lizzie. She struggled to keep her breath even as he dug the muzzle into her ribs, but she didn't like the fear in Darcy's eyes. "How about we all calm down and speak logically?" she said, far more collected than she felt.

But it was too late. Lydia and Mrs. Bennet began scream-ing, and elsewhere in the house Lizzie heard a stampede of footsteps that indicated Jane, Kitty, and Mary—and if this kept up, it would surely rouse Mr. Bennet from his study.

The idea of her family coming to harm was more terrify-ing than having a firearm pointed at her. "Don't hurt anyone!" Lizzie pleaded just as Darcy held up both hands and said:

"Don't do anything stupid, Wickham!"

Wickham, for his part, seemed very calm indeed. "Stand back! I don't want to hurt her, but I will if you don't let us through!"

"I'll go with you—just don't hurt anyone," Lizzie said. She attempted to look up at Wickham, but he pulled her arm back even harder, and she saw stars at the edges of her vision.

Darcy pushed back a hysterical Mrs. Bennet and Lydia, placing himself between the ladies and Wickham and Lizzie. "You don't have to do this. Let's talk it out."

"Is your carriage outside?"

Darcy nodded and locked eyes with Lizzie. She knew that Wickham meant to take her with him, but the idea of leaving the house without Darcy made her tremble. "Wickham, leave my family out of this. This is between us and Darcy—"

"Quiet!" he barked, twisting her arm again. Lizzie gasped in pain as the stars returned.

"Don't hurt her!" Darcy shouted.

"Don't force me to!" was Wickham's equally loud response.

He propelled Lizzie down the hall and out the door into the damp night. The streetlamps offered a meager light, but enough that when Wickham pointed his firearm at Alan and barked, "Move!" the driver all but fell off his perch. Wickham hoisted Lizzie up and leapt up next to her in a breath. She caught a glimpse of Darcy rushing out of her house before Wickham jostled the reins, and they were off into the dark evening, bound for a destination unknown.

SEVENTEEN

*In Which Lizzie Realizes
Her Misconceptions*

IT WAS THE SECOND time in a week that Lizzie had been forced into a carriage against her will, but the first time at gunpoint, and she did not appreciate the escalation. She clutched at her seat as Wickham prodded the horses into a trot and then sought to increase their pace.

Fear was a vise around her throat, but she didn't want to be one of those ladies who swooned at danger. She had to say something, do something—so she spoke the first words that came to mind. "I know you don't like Darcy, but this is rather much."

"You're wrong about that. I hate him."

"Yes, but kidnapping, Wickham? I mean, really." This was mad—she was bantering with him as if this were a social visit.

"Where's your sense of adventure?"

"I'm afraid I left it back in the drawing room."

"Pity." He flicked the reins, spurring the horses along faster. They reached the end of Gracechurch Street, and he steered the horses west. The streets were still wet from the earlier rain, and Lizzie wasn't sure if it was her overactive imagination or if she really did feel the wheels skid on the turn.

She tried to keep a cool head, but their speed alone was cause for alarm. "This is grand larceny, you know."

Wickham laughed. "Criminal charges are the least of my worries."

Lizzie flinched as they narrowly missed a flower seller's cart, and Wickham allowed the horses to slow just a bit as they turned left and navigated down a tight, dim street. That was when she heard the sound of hooves and wheels rattling behind them. She twisted in her seat to peer around the back of the carriage and caught sight of a hired chaise—lighter, with only one horse, but faster than Darcy's grand carriage with four horses, gaining on them.

Wickham noticed her movement and turned as well. "That'll be Darcy, I wager. Mad that I stole his carriage. Then again, maybe it's *you* he's concerned about."

The anger in his voice disturbed her, as if Lizzie were just another prize to be won. *He's played me,* she realized with horror. Her head spun in an attempt to pay attention to where they were going and also piece together Wickham's connection with this case. If he was the one who broke into Pemberley, then he was likely responsible for Abigail's death as well.

And Lizzie had led him right to her.

"Please, stop. We can still work this out, without anyone else getting hurt."

Wickham laughed darkly and made an abrupt turn that nearly sent Lizzie flying from her seat. "No, we really can't. It's time for you to stop meddling and do what you're told."

The side street they'd turned onto was familiar to Lizzie and even narrower than the thoroughfare from which they'd come. During the day, it was packed with people and children playing. This time of night, it was empty, but it was dark and Lizzie could scarcely breathe through her fear that the horses would stumble or run over some poor soul.

"We don't have to involve the law," she tried again, although she didn't really mean it. Wickham deserved to go to prison, and Abigail deserved justice. "I'm sure there are other means of settling this!"

"I've tried that already. Darcy wanted to shoot at me instead."

"You're the one he dueled?" Lizzie couldn't believe she hadn't seen it earlier. "But you said you didn't know who—"

"No, I merely refused to answer you. For an aspiring barrister, you can be thick at times."

She wanted to shove him from his seat then, but his pistol was still pointed at her. Besides, she was not confident enough in her ability to grab the reins, and then she truly would be at the mercy of the panicked horses. Instead, she swallowed a new wave of fear. She had to attack this problem with logic, not fear. The first step—figure out where they were headed. Wickham seemed to be circling back around the way they came from, to throw off their pursuer.

As if to confirm this, Wickham elbowed her. "Is Darcy still following us?"

Lizzie took a moment to strengthen her grip on her seat and gather her courage. *Please let him be behind us,* she prayed. Despite the gravity of her situation, the irony of hoping that Darcy would appear did not escape her. But she had nothing on her person that would prove a match to Wickham's pistol.

She peeked around the edge of the carriage and for one heart-stopping moment felt herself sway too close to the edge. She looked down, and the ground was a dizzying rush. Wickham yanked her back.

"He's still there," she reported, unsure whether this would madden him and worsen her situation.

But Wickham sounded merely surprised as he said, "Is he now?"

Lizzie swallowed hard and tried once more to reason with Wickham. "It's not right that he should shoot you, or even duel you in the first place."

"Why? Because I'm lower-class?"

The disdain in Wickham's voice made Lizzie realize her misstep. "No. Because it's illegal."

"When I first met you, your idealism was charming," Wickham said. "Now, it's just intolerable."

He seemed determined to resist all of Lizzie's attempts at reason, so she switched tactics. "If anything happens to me, my family will be *very* displeased."

The threat felt weak even before it left her mouth, and Wickham laughed. "Your father would have to close a book long enough to figure out where you've gone, and your mother would be overjoyed—one less daughter to marry off."

The insult stung, but more than anything Lizzie was shocked by his callous tone. Wickham was unveiling his true self, and she couldn't believe that she had been fooled for so long. "This is not a crime you can walk away from."

"They'll have to catch me first."

Lizzie's spirits began to falter. They were drawing closer to the docks—the docks, of course! He didn't need to lose Darcy. He just needed to outrun him long enough to escape London. By water was the safest bet. A single man could slip away down the Thames.

But what did he intend to do with her?

She supposed it amounted to two options: she would leave London either over the Thames or under it. Just like Abigail.

For the first time in her life, Lizzie accepted that the time for talking had passed. She pushed away the image of poor Abigail pulled out of the water, hands bound together. She would come back to her, but for now she needed to figure out how she was going to get away. Perhaps what she needed wasn't brute strength but cunning. If she could throw him off, distract him, surprise him, just long enough to escape and run for cover . . .

They pulled out of the narrow side street to one that opened out to the docks. Ships bobbed gently in the water, and lanterns glowed from distant decks. Lizzie sucked in a breath to scream but felt the pistol nudge her ribs. She looked down at it.

"Don't," Wickham warned.

Lizzie kept silent. But looking down had reminded her—she was wearing Jane's brooch! Not much of a weapon at all, but if she could work it off her jacket, the sharp end could be jabbed at just the right moment. . . .

"Where are you taking me?" she asked Wickham, hoping to distract him.

"You'll see," he grunted, and her hand crept up to her breast and began working the brooch's clasp.

"How long will it take to get there?"

"I said, you'll see. God, you're aggravating!"

But Lizzie noticed him beginning to pull back on the reins and deploy the brake, easing into a trot. The poor horses' sides were heaving, slick with sweat. Lizzie looked to the water, trying to discern which ship they'd board. In the distance, she heard the clop of horse hooves and the creak of wheels. Darcy in the chaise! Lizzie craned her neck to see how far off he was, but she couldn't see him at all.

"Darcy is persistent," Wickham remarked. "I had no idea he was so fond of you."

"I'm sure it's just the horses he's invested in," Lizzie said, and the brooch clasp released. She used the moment that Wickham's gaze was fixed behind them to swiftly remove it from her spencer and hold it concealed in her left hand.

"Somehow I doubt that." Wickham glanced back at Lizzie, who was now the picture of terrified innocence, her hands clutched in her lap. "I've never seen him care this much about a woman's well-being, aside from his sis— *Ahhhhh!*"

Lizzie had taken advantage of Wickham's momentary distraction and plunged the sharp end of her brooch into his thigh. She yanked it back as she leapt from the carriage, which had slowed to a gentle roll. The force of her landing sent a sharp jolt of pain through her right ankle, but she didn't let that stop her. With Wickham's cry of pain and fury echoing after her, she began to run—well, more like hobble at a brisk pace—in the direction they had just come from.

It was dark, and she had only a vague idea of where she was. As she passed crates and dark ships, she prayed that she'd stumble upon help. Then, when she heard Wickham's shouting and the sound of him jumping from the carriage and running after her, she simply prayed that no one would stop her escape.

"Elizabeth Bennet!" Wickham screamed into the night.

Still, Lizzie ran.

And then . . .

Crack!

Lizzie would swear for years to come that she felt the bullet pass by so closely it could have caressed her cheek. Her hobbling came to an abrupt halt out of pure shock, but she did not try to run again. She knew little about pistols, but she knew enough to not want to gamble on the possibility that Wickham's was a double-barreled flintlock, guaranteeing him one more bullet before he'd have to reload.

"Don't make me shoot again," Wickham threatened.

Slowly, Lizzie turned. Wickham stood twenty paces behind her, wincing in pain but holding the pistol level. "Now, don't do anything stupid and you won't have to meet the same fate that Abigail did."

Lizzie flinched at this confirmation. She wanted to fly at him and slap that smug look off his face, but she forced herself to remain steady.

"Why did you kill her? You saw—she wasn't going to say anything about what she knew. She wanted a new life."

"She recognized me," Wickham said, as if it were an unfortunate accident. "I didn't think she would, but when we left, I saw it in her eyes—she knew that I was more than a Runner, and she was a loose end."

If Abigail had recognized him before, then that meant . . . "It wasn't coincidence that you were called to the Hurst residence when the butler sent for help," Lizzie said. "You were watching the house. Are you even a Runner?"

"Of course I am. They'll take anyone upright and sober."

"What were you waiting for?"

"I neither confirm nor deny anything," Wickham said.

Lizzie took one step closer to him, heart hammering, but she had to know. "Did you kill Hurst?"

Wickham closed the rest of the distance between them, and Lizzie flinched, waiting for the gunshot. But he just grabbed her arm. "Don't be absurd."

"I won't move until you answer me."

"Then I'll carry you."

"Don't you dare!" Lizzie exclaimed, although her ankle ached fiercely and she was afraid he would have to do just that if they had much farther to go. "Why won't you answer me?"

"You'll see soon enough," he said, which made Lizzie think that he didn't want to kill her. But he was prepared to use force. She made the split-second decision to not resist but not help Wickham either. If he had to drag her, that would slow him down and maybe give her more time to—

"Wickham!"

Both Lizzie and Wickham turned to see Darcy standing just thirty paces behind them. In his hand was a pistol, trained in their direction. Lizzie's first thought was, *Don't shoot*. She needed to know what Wickham knew.

Wickham swung his own pistol toward Darcy.

And without stopping to think, Lizzie stepped between them.

EIGHTEEN

*In Which Lizzie Endeavors
to Use Reason*

"ELIZABETH, MOVE."

Darcy's voice was steady, yet it contained a note of desperation.

"Yes, *Elizabeth*," Wickham said, a mocking emphasis on her name. "Get out of the way."

"No," Lizzie said, and a preternatural calm descended upon her despite the terror she felt just a moment earlier when she was sure that Wickham had been about to shoot Darcy. "You only have one bullet left, Wickham, and if you use it on me, Darcy will surely end you before you have a chance to reload. Darcy, you can't kill him, no matter how much you hate him. We still don't know why he killed Hurst."

"I didn't," Wickham said at the same time that Darcy said:

"I don't care."

"Well, I do!"

She turned to Wickham, who was glowering at her. No, not her—at Darcy, standing beyond her. The resentment in his eyes took her breath away. "Are you blackmailing the Bingleys?"

When Wickham didn't say anything, Darcy said, "It wouldn't be the first time he resorted to such measures."

"Darcy, wait your turn," Lizzie said, keeping her gaze on Wickham.

"He sacked me and then challenged me to a duel," Wickham told her, sounding more like the young man she had met.

"And you never bothered to show," Darcy snarled.

"Because dueling is illegal!" Wickham shot back.

"Oh, I'm glad to know where your moral line falls," Darcy said. "Not before embezzling from my family, not before seducing my sister, not before kidnapping her and now Elizabeth, not before extortion, but dueling? Duly noted!"

"And Darcy shot you?" Lizzie asked Wickham.

"I never shot him, although now I wish I had!" Darcy cut in, before Wickham could respond. "He broke my nose when I caught him with Georgiana, and rather than tear him apart right then and there, I challenged him to a duel. But scoundrels have no honor!"

Hearing Darcy speak, Lizzie couldn't believe that she had ever thought him cold or emotionless. Careful not to move her position to provide either man a clear shot, she looked over her shoulder. She saw a stranger. Outrage had twisted his features into a furious scowl. He would do anything for his sister, she realized. Even go against the law to challenge a man to a duel.

"I *was* shot," Wickham insisted. He sounded nervous now. "When I was with the navy. You must have misunderstood, Lizzie."

Lizzie had certainly misunderstood a great deal about this situation, but there was nothing wrong with her memory. She chose not to focus on that bit just now. "You wooed Georgiana?"

"We were in love!"

"He was in love with her fortune!" Darcy cut in. "And when our family didn't give permission for them to marry, Wickham sought to force the matter by kidnapping Georgiana."

"She went willingly."

"She was fifteen!"

Lizzie caught her breath at the thought of someone as sweet as Georgiana Darcy taken in by Wickham's deceitful words and promises—but she had very nearly been fooled by them herself, and she was older.

"I stopped them before they could reach Gretna Green," Darcy explained, naming the Scottish town just over the border where a couple could marry without their family's permission. "Wickham refused to leave quietly, unless I paid him ten thousand pounds."

"Ten thousand pounds?" Lizzie could barely find the breath to voice the figure. "Did you?"

"I did," Darcy said through gritted teeth, "and that was when we fought, and I challenged him."

"But you didn't arrive at the appointed time and hour?" Lizzie asked Wickham.

He refused to meet her gaze, keeping it firmly fixed on Darcy beyond her. "He didn't," Darcy confirmed. "God knows what he did with the money. I heard he joined the navy, and then deserted. I thought—hoped—that he'd simply drowned. Until you brought him up this evening."

Lizzie had found herself so often at odds with Darcy that it came as rather a shock that she believed his every word. She saw now with startling clarity how Wickham had fooled her merely by appealing to her ego—and she had disclosed important details about her investigation. Abigail's death was on her hands. She looked at the young man that she had once thought so charming. Caught between the dark waters of the Thames and a bullet, Wickham didn't look so handsome anymore.

"You wanted to exact your revenge," Lizzie said, addressing Wickham. "So you targeted Darcy's best friend's business, killed his brother-in-law, and framed Bingley. I suppose that once you had Netherfield and its owners out of the way, you had a plan to implicate Darcy in some sort of legal scandal? That's why you wanted to swipe the legitimate insurance policy. You could make it seem as if Darcy were offering dodgy legal counsel, even encouraging illegal activity. It would have ruined him."

"*Exactly,*" Wickham said.

"He's not nearly smart enough to have figured that all out himself," Darcy growled. "You forget that he worked for Pemberley for two years. Even if he had come up with a plan of that magnitude, he wouldn't have had the drive to execute it."

"Shut up, Darcy! You have no idea what I'm capable of."

The fog began to shift, and in the long stretch of silence that followed, Lizzie could see Wickham and the entire scene more clearly than ever. He looked like a cornered animal—furious and frightened—and the hand holding the pistol trembled. Lizzie felt her courage waver, and she struggled to piece it all together. *Logic,* she reminded herself, but it was shockingly difficult to think logically when you stood between two pistols. "I find myself in agreement with Mr. Darcy," Lizzie said, stalling. Could he have pulled this off by himself? But where was he escaping to? And . . . "Who's waiting for you aboard that ship?" she asked.

The dock's edge was a mere ten paces away, and so many ships were moored in the Thames that it was difficult to say for certain which one Wickham had been aiming for when he slowed the carriage. But if Lizzie's hunch was correct, his destination would not be far off. Perhaps even close enough that whoever was waiting aboard was listening to every word. . . .

Lizzie was rewarded with the sound of two hands: *clap . . . clap . . . clap.*

Lizzie, Darcy, and Wickham searched the dark until they

spotted the source of the sound—a figure standing on the deck of a schooner cozied up to the dock a mere stone's throw away. "Bravo!" a voice called out.

A *female* voice.

Lizzie gasped, for she recognized it. A figure clad in breeches stepped forward, but it was no man—it was Lady Catherine de Bourgh.

"You're much cleverer than I initially gave you credit for, Miss Bennet!" she called, leaning languidly against the deck's railing. "Are you certain that you don't want to reconsider my offer?"

Lizzie didn't want to appear flustered, so she shouted back, "No thank you, Lady Catherine."

Lady Catherine made a disappointed tsking sound and said, "Well, maybe not as clever as I thought, then." The sound of a metallic click carried across the water, and quick as a flash, Lady Catherine held out her own pistol.

"Honestly," Lizzie said in a shaky attempt at bravery, "don't you think there are already plenty of pistols being waved about?"

"Lady Catherine?" Wickham asked, waiting for directions.

"Not now, Wickham. You've only made a larger mess of this. Miss Bennet, either you board this ship right now, or I shoot."

"Who?" she asked. "Me or Darcy?"

"Does it matter?" she asked with a throaty laugh.

"Perhaps," Lizzie hedged.

"I'll shoot your young man. I need your skills."

Lizzie wavered. Darcy was hardly her young man, but she wasn't going to let him get shot. "What about Wickham?"

"What about him? He's more useless than a stray dog you'd pluck from the river. If I'd known that, I never would have rescued him from his sinking ship." She gestured with her pistol. "Now come along, or I start shooting."

"Don't move," Darcy instructed her.

"Don't be absurd—" Lizzie started to say, and she took a step toward the boat, but then Wickham made his move. He lunged to her right and Darcy yelled, "Lizzie, *down!*"

"No!"

Crack!

Lizzie hit the cobblestones, uncertain at first whether instinct or the impact of a bullet had driven her to the ground. Her heart slammed in her chest, and as she looked about, she saw another figure—Wickham—take off toward where the schooner was docked. Another *crack!* split the air, and he doubled over. Lizzie screamed, and Wickham crumpled to the ground. But he was so close to the water that he disappeared over the edge of the dock, and Lizzie heard a heavy splash.

She scrambled to her feet, praying that Lady Catherine didn't have another pistol and that she wasn't reloading. She would have run to where she saw Wickham disappear if strong arms hadn't closed around her and dragged her behind a stack of shipping crates, out of Lady Catherine's line of sight.

"No," she gasped. "No, no, no!"

"Elizabeth, wait. Where are you hurt?" She struggled in Darcy's arms until he loosened his grip, but he didn't let go of her entirely. "Are you injured?"

"No," she said. "I don't think so. But Wickham!"

Lizzie fully expected Darcy to say, "Let him drown!" It was on the tip of her tongue to plead with him, to insist he was their only witness, but Darcy said nothing. He simply released her and said, "Stay back!" and then ran to the edge of the dock where Wickham had gone over. He removed his jacket and kicked off his boots, peered over, and then jumped in.

Lizzie looked up to see if Lady Catherine was readying her next round. But the schooner was not in the same place it had been just a moment earlier. It was drifting away from the docks, slipping out of reach between a ship's tender and another boat. She stood at the edge of the dock and tried in vain to read the ship's name, but it was too dark and the schooner was already too far away. Then she looked down into the black waters and shouted, "Darcy!"

She could hear splashing but couldn't see anything at all. *Don't let him drown,* she prayed. *Please, please don't let him drown.* "Darcy! Where are you?"

She looked around frantically for something, anything, to throw down to him, but the coil of tarred rope twenty paces away was too heavy for her to yank to the dock's edge. She thought of screaming for help, but that might bring every nighttime criminal and vagrant to her, and all she had was her brooch, still clutched in her hand, for defense. *Foolish*, she thought. She had gotten everything horribly wrong, and now Abigail was dead and Wickham was shot and Darcy might drown trying to fish him out and it was all her fault.

"Darcy!" she screamed into the dark water. "If you drown, I will be very angry with you!"

More splashing and a cough that might have been a laugh drifted up to her ten paces down from where Darcy had disappeared into the water. Lizzie ran in the direction of the sound and discovered a ladder built into the dock and Darcy a meter below, Wickham slung over his shoulder. Slowly, he pulled himself up, and when Wickham was within reaching distance, Lizzie pulled him toward her. When he was safely on the dock, she extended an arm to Darcy, who gratefully took it, and pulled him to safety as well.

Wickham's eyes were closed and his face exceedingly pale. "Wickham!" Lizzie began slapping his face to revive him. She stopped when she saw the blood on his left shoulder. It had been difficult to see in the dark, but when she pulled away his jacket, it bloomed bright and vivid against the white of his shirt.

"No, no," Lizzie whispered, and shrugged out of her spencer, pressing the fabric against Wickham's wound. He groaned at the pressure, but that just made Lizzie push against it even harder.

"Wake up," she ordered him. "You need to live. You need to tell the judge the truth."

She looked at Darcy. "We need a surgeon."

Darcy, however, shook his head. "Elizabeth. It's too late."

"No!" she snapped. "You're just saying that because you don't like him."

"I'm not, Elizabeth. Look."

She looked down and knew he was right when she saw that her hands were completely soaked in Wickham's blood. The wound was bleeding far more rapidly than they could compress, although Lizzie tried. But falling into the water and bleeding out into the Thames had done Wickham no favors.

"Miss Bennet?" Wickham's voice was whisper-thin, barely audible over his wet, labored breaths.

"You're all right," she said.

"Liar," he rasped. "I didn't kill Hurst."

"Shh," she said. "Conserve your breath."

"No. I didn't. I promise . . . on my dying breath, I swear. I didn't kill . . . Lady Catherine . . ."

Lizzie's desperation for answers got the better of her. "Lady Catherine killed him?"

Wickham laughed a little. Then she realized it was not a laugh but a choking gurgle. He was drowning in his own blood, she realized. "Help me!" she snapped at Darcy, and they propped him up.

"Lady . . . Catherine has spies . . . mastermind. Did not kill . . . Hurst."

"Do you know who did?" Lizzie asked, but Wickham coughed wetly. Lizzie would have sworn in that moment that he smiled—a brief, rueful smile that reminded her of walking the streets of London, discussing criminal activity and trading theories. A smile that was full of charm and secrets and half-truths.

Then he shut his eyes and breathed his last.

NINETEEN

*In Which Lizzie Ruminates
on Her Regrets*

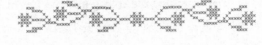

"ELIZABETH?"

Darcy's hand weighed on her shoulder. When their eyes met, concern was written across his face. "Elizabeth, we must go."

Still she did not respond. Wickham was dead.

"Elizabeth?"

"Don't worry," she said faintly. "This isn't my first dead body."

"Well, it's mine," Darcy said.

Lizzie looked up and was flooded with relief that he was here and unharmed. Although perhaps not perfectly well—he was drenched and shivering in the cool spring night, and Lizzie knew he needed to get warm before he caught a chill.

"What do we do?" she asked, and he shook his head. In the

distance, she heard the hue and cry and knew that others must not be far behind.

"He's dead, and I'll be blamed," Darcy said, voice hollow. It was as though they were in a courtroom. *This* was the Darcy she recognized. "They'll believe this was a lovers' quarrel, or another duel. They'll never believe that some other woman shot him from the deck of a ship before shoving off from the dock. Or that I attempted to save his life. I shall go to prison."

"Lady Catherine de Bourgh," Lizzie said faintly.

"I beg your pardon?"

"The woman who shot him," she clarified.

"Oh, very good," Darcy said, still sounding quite serious. "Lady Catherine de Bourgh shot him to death. The judge will certainly believe that."

His tone lifted upward, and Lizzie realized he was panicking. This was the cue she needed to take one last look at Wickham and set his body down. She was damp and his blood stained her dress and hands, but she stood and gripped Darcy's elbows so that he was forced to look her in the eye.

"You will not be blamed for this," she told him sternly. "We'll tell the truth, and my mother and sisters will corroborate that Wickham kidnapped me. My father's a barrister, so we'll be believed."

Darcy scarcely had a chance to reply before the clattering of another carriage drew their attention, and Lizzie was relieved to recognize the Bennets' horse and their small chaise. Her father leapt down, wild-eyed with worry.

"Lizzie!" he cried as he ran toward her, and made a strangled noise when he saw the blood upon her dress.

"It's not mine—" she began to say, but then Mr. Bennet engulfed her in a tight embrace, and she was overwhelmed with the temptation to let her father take care of all her troubles.

She gently patted him on the back until he released her, and she said, "I'm unhurt, Papa. Mr. Darcy aided my escape."

"Mr. Darcy!" Mr. Bennet grasped the younger man's arm. "My deepest thanks. Are you hurt?"

"No, sir," Darcy said, nodding courteously at Mr. Bennet.

Lizzie could tell by the way he watched the streets beyond for the Runners that he was on edge. It was such a strange feeling, knowing that his fate was in her hands, that she could dictate what happened next and it would have immense consequence on Darcy's life. Was this what men felt like all the time? Did they even stop to appreciate the power?

Then she remembered how Darcy had come to her aid, repeatedly, and wasted no time. "Papa, Mr. Darcy saved me, and then he tried to save Mr. Wickham as well. We must tell the Runners he isn't at fault for his death."

"You shot him?" Mr. Bennet asked, but there was no blame in his tone.

More people had come to the edges of the scene, looking on with curiosity, and just beyond them Lizzie could hear a man's authoritative voice braying, "Coming through! Stand aside!"

"Someone else did. I'll explain everything, but Mr. Darcy is innocent." Mr. Bennet stared at Lizzie, confusion clearly written across his face, and she added, "Please, Papa!"

Her father nodded, and with a quick glance to Darcy, he turned to meet the Runners bursting through the assorted onlookers.

"We heard report of pistol shots." A burly man with a thin beard addressed Lizzie, Darcy, and Mr. Bennet. Someone brought a lantern closer to the scene, and Lizzie saw the man flick his eyes suspiciously between Darcy, soaking wet, and Lizzie, drenched in blood, before finally settling on Wickham's lifeless body.

"Thank you for coming," Mr. Bennet said, disarming the man with civility, and before he could take in a breath, Mr. Bennet continued. "That man lying dead there tried to kidnap my daughter. He took her from our home, brandishing a pistol at anyone who threatened to get in the way. Thank God Mr. Darcy was present—he leapt to her defense, and pursued that criminal in his carriage. I followed them here, only to find that the abductor was killed by his own comrade, who has fled."

Lizzie rarely had the opportunity to observe her father employ the tactics of argument and persuasion he had taught her, so she was taken aback by this forceful, assured version of her father, and she admired how he framed the situation.

The thin-bearded Runner seemed skeptical, and he looked

between Wickham's body and Lizzie. "Why'd this man kidnap you?"

She stuck as closely to the truth as possible: "He wanted me to run away with him, and I didn't want to go."

"And you?" Thin Beard asked Darcy. "How do you figure into this?"

"I'm a business associate of the Bennets'," Darcy answered, which was another artful stretch of the truth that Lizzie couldn't help but admire. "I just happened to be at their residence when the abduction occurred."

"Please, I know that there must be an investigation," Mr. Bennet said. "But allow my daughter and Mr. Darcy to return home and rest. They've been through such an ordeal."

"Soon enough," Thin Beard pronounced, and then he and an associate examined Wickham's body, confiscated his pistol and Darcy's, which had been dropped and forgotten on the ground. At one point, one of the Runners pulled Thin Beard aside and whispered something to him while nodding at Darcy. They conferred some more while Mr. Bennet hovered, hawkeyed, with just a hint of menace in his usually mild eyes.

"What do you think will happen to Wickham?" Lizzie asked Darcy. Someone brought him a horse blanket and he wrapped it tightly around himself to ward off the evening air.

"I'll make sure he gets a proper burial," he replied.

"Really?"

"Yes. I have the means, and even though Wickham was

rotten, I respected his father. He was my father's valet, you know. Despite what he claimed, my family did try to do right by him."

"The things money can buy," Lizzie mused.

"Money doesn't buy loyalty," Darcy countered. "If it did, Wickham wouldn't be dead."

Lizzie looked up at him. "You're right. That was unfair of me."

Darcy seemed mollified and so Lizzie asked, "Do you believe he was telling the truth?"

"About what?"

"About not being the one to kill Hurst."

"He was a liar and a cheat. Why would he change his tune at the very end?"

"Agreed, but . . . he all but admitted to killing Abigail."

"Abigail worked as a maid and had little money," Darcy said, but not unkindly. "Hurst was a gentleman with connections. Surely you can understand how admitting to their murders is not the same thing."

Lizzie's eyes burned, and she rubbed at them with the one clean stretch of sleeve she had left. "It's wrong. A murder is a murder, and they were both human beings. One's death should not matter more than the other."

Darcy was silent for a long moment, and then a soft cloth was pressed gently against her cheek, mopping up her tears. Lizzie gasped in surprise and opened her eyes to find Darcy holding the handkerchief, looking at her with tender concern. That look alone made Lizzie forget to breathe, and as a result she hiccuped rather loudly. She took the handkerchief—it was soft and smelled of cedarwood and mint, and she realized that this was Darcy's true scent, under the books and ink and pipe tobacco she'd recognized at Pemberley. Her powers of observation were hopelessly scrambled when Darcy was around.

"I know it's unfair," Darcy said after Lizzie had wiped away her tears and gotten her emotions under control. "I didn't mean to dismiss his actions. I'm simply trying to explain the Wickham I knew. He was only ever concerned with appearances."

"And I was completely taken in," Lizzie said. "I never once stopped to question why he always showed up on the streets just when I seemed to need him. At the Hursts, when the butler caught me, and then just yesterday when I went to visit Abigail. She admitted, right in front of him, that Hurst hadn't been overly concerned with Bingley cutting him off, and she all but said she suspected him of some sort of scheme."

Darcy listened to Lizzie puzzle through the case, his expression grave. "And then Wickham said she recognized him at the end—she made a sound, and I thought he was charming her. She must have thought then that I was working for the killer. Maybe she had made plans to leave, but Wickham got to her first. He knew she could corroborate my suspicions, but that I wouldn't drag her into the case because she stole Hurst's pocket watch and was terrified of getting in trouble."

Darcy didn't say anything, for which she was grateful. She wasn't sure what would be worse: Darcy ridiculing her for putting her trust in the wrong man or attempting to reassure her that it wasn't her fault.

"And there's so much more!" Lizzie realized. She shook her head, as if she could dislodge all of the details. "I didn't question how we were able to get into that public assembly so easily, despite not holding a subscription. And yet, he disappeared and then returned, and we were able to just slide inside, and that was when I first met Lady Catherine. . . ."

"How well do you know that woman?" Darcy asked, now sounding somewhat alarmed.

"I met her for the first time at the public assembly Caroline attended—what if Caroline's suitor is in on this whole scheme? Someone must look into that, although you could not pay me enough to be the one to break the news to her. I thought at the time perhaps that Caroline had arranged to have Hurst killed and Bingley framed in order to take over the business."

Darcy laughed as if the theory amused him. "But this Lady Catherine?"

"Right. I never saw her speak with Wickham, but she spoke to me. I think she was trying to influence me, and then the following day she, ah, arranged a meeting. It was such a strange conversation, but she wanted to help my investigation. She told me about the duel. I didn't tell her anything of consequence because I'd never heard of her before."

"This is awfully organized," Darcy remarked.

"For a woman?"

"No, it's simply very organized. Period. If this woman has the reach you believe she does, then I grow more unsettled by the moment."

"It's brilliant, is it not? She's gone almost completely unde-tected, for as you've so astutely pointed out, women are not expected to appear in places of power."

Rather than become upset with Lizzie, Darcy sighed wearily. "You're putting statements in my mouth once more."

"Well, you all but implied it."

"Perhaps I did not mean to imply."

"Perhaps you ought to be more careful with your language."

"Fair," he said, and Lizzie was so surprised that she did not know what to say, so Darcy continued. "The problem, of course, is that no one will believe that a mysterious woman no one has heard of, styling herself as Lady Catherine, is the mastermind behind multiple crimes, including murder, without *proof*."

Darcy stated what Lizzie was too afraid to admit, and she nodded miserably and added, "The judge will laugh you out of court."

"He'll laugh us both out of court."

Lizzie smiled, only because she never thought that she and Darcy would agree on such things.

"I have one more question," she said after a long silence.

"Ask me anything," Darcy said.

"Wherever did you obtain a dry handkerchief?"

It was not dry anymore, of course—and it was rather wrinkled from Lizzie's twisting and scrunching. But Darcy laughed and held up his jacket. "I took it off before I jumped into the river."

Lizzie's eyes widened. "Does that mean the false policy . . . ?"

"Safe," he confirmed. He withdrew the oilskin document pouch and handed it to Lizzie.

"What are you doing?" she asked, even as her fingers closed around it.

"Just in case I'm hauled off to jail," he said. "I'm trusting you to keep that safe and prove Bingley's innocence."

Darcy's trust was not something that Lizzie ever expected to obtain, nor was it something she had sought out, but it felt like a gift and a serious responsibility. She wasn't sure she was up to the task, but the steady way he looked at her somehow gave her courage. "I promise I'll do my best."

They were interrupted by Thin Beard, who approached with Mr. Bennet. Lizzie's father conspicuously took a place by her side as they waited to hear what would happen next.

"There will be an inquest," Thin Beard announced. "But Mr. Bennet, you may take your daughter home."

"And Mr. Darcy?" Lizzie asked.

Thin Beard regarded him carefully. "You may return

home as well, but you will have to give an official statement tomorrow."

"Of course," Darcy said.

And just like that, they were dismissed. Lizzie waited for Darcy to demand that she hand back the evidence, but he didn't. She clutched the document to her. This was all she had to prove Bingley's innocence and to build an argument around. It didn't feel like enough.

Mr. Bennet took Lizzie's arm. "Come along, my dear."

"Wait," Lizzie said, stopping both her father and Darcy. *Evidence,* she thought. *The button.*

She hobbled over to where Wickham had fallen. His body was covered with a length of sailcloth, but dark blood seeped underneath the cover.

"We must wait for the coroner, miss," said one of the Runners, blocking her from reaching out and touching Wickham.

"Please," she said, not having to try very hard to make her voice quiver. "I just need one last look."

The Runner looked to Thin Beard, who nodded an impatient assent. The man stepped aside, and Lizzie gathered her courage and folded back the sailcloth. She couldn't look at his face, which was fine because she didn't need to. She studied his jacket in the poor light but couldn't make out what she was looking for. She reached out and touched the edge of the jacket, lingering over each button even as she felt congealed blood. She counted eight buttons, and none appeared to be missing.

"Lizzie, dear," her father said behind her, puzzled.

She gave up her search and rose, clenching her hand that had touched Wickham's cool blood into a tight fist as she followed her father toward the carriage. A part of her had hoped that she would find a missing button and that she could demand his jacket be removed as evidence. It would be altogether too easy to pin the entire crime on a dead man, and he was indeed guilty of at least one murder.

But Lizzie was not convinced that Wickham was the killer they'd been pursuing.

TWENTY

In Which Lizzie Confronts Her Fears

LIZZIE SLEPT A DEEP, dreamless sleep but awoke early the morning of Bingley's hearing, dread pooling in her stomach.

For all that Lizzie had discovered in the past week, she felt inept. She'd been taken in by a disreputable young man because he had a charming smile and asked her about herself, yet she'd been oblivious to his manipulation. She had allowed herself to be swept away by gossip about Darcy simply because he had not made a good first impression upon her and she found his manners distasteful. And what did Lizzie have to show for it all?

She still didn't know who killed Hurst.

Abigail was dead, because of her.

She'd insulted Collins by refusing his awful offer of marriage, jeopardizing her family's standing with her father's heir.

And worst of all, Mr. Bennet would surely not hire her now,

not when she'd disregarded his orders to not involve herself in the case *and* had gotten herself kidnapped because of it.

Lizzie was disturbed from her trail of miserable thoughts by a knock. Jane entered, a steaming cup of tea cradled between her palms. "Good, you're awake," she said. "How did you sleep?"

Lizzie sat up and drew the covers around her. "Fine. Has everyone settled down?"

"Hardly," Jane said, handing her the tea. "Lydia and Kitty are devastated that Wickham turned out to be a criminal and Mary is trying to read them Bible verses as consolation. I wouldn't be surprised if Mama wasn't trying to figure out how she might convince Darcy to marry you now, since he saved your life."

"I thought she didn't like him," Lizzie said, taking a sip. "Besides, I saved his life as well."

"You and I both know that will only encourage her," Jane said with a gentle smile. "Mama has been reconsidering Darcy ever since he came to our rescue."

Lizzie leaned against her sister and sighed. "I think I completely misjudged him."

"Isn't that a good thing? It's far better to find someone is actually a better person than you expected than to discover they lack character in a time of crisis."

"In theory, yes. In practice, I look the fool."

Jane hugged her sister. "Don't forget that he misjudged you

at first, too. Why, if his opinion of you was the same as it was a week ago, he wouldn't be in our drawing room right now."

"What?" Lizzie nearly spilled her tea. "Why didn't you say first thing?"

Jane raised a teasing brow. "Oh, I thought you didn't care for him."

"I'm merely concerned about the case," Lizzie lied as she launched herself out of bed and hobbled to the wardrobe. Her ankle was still sore from the previous night's leap from the carriage, but it didn't stop her from riffling through it for something suitable to wear.

"Put this on," Jane said, pulling out her own best green dress. "Your best dress may never recover from yesterday's excitement, and you can't be wearing second-best if you're going to appear in court today."

Lizzie hugged her sister. "You're the best of sisters."

When she was dressed, she evaluated her appearance in the mirror quickly and did something she thought she'd never do: she tried to imagine how she might look to Darcy. Not as an opponent, but as a young lady.

"You look lovely," Jane said, as if she knew exactly what Lizzie was thinking.

"I'm acting like Lydia."

"Nothing wrong with wanting to put your best foot forward. Now go down before Mama scares him off."

Jane's wisdom gave Lizzie the courage to retrieve her

sketchbook, the oilskin document pouch, and the stray button from her writing box, leave the room, and go downstairs to face Darcy. That, and abject terror at how her mother was representing her to Darcy.

But as she descended the stairs, there was a knock on the front door, and she limped over to answer it. She was shocked to find Charlotte standing on her front step, a rather large satchel clutched in her hands.

"Charlotte!" Lizzie forgot for a moment that she and Charlotte were still on awkward footing after their disagreement about Collins—and that she had not told Charlotte about Collins's proposal. It felt like weeks ago, not days. She drew her friend in, relieving her of the heavy load. "What are you doing here so early? And are you carrying bricks?"

"I got your father's message this morning," she said, huffing slightly. "I did as he asked and went to the office before everyone arrived, and gathered these books. Whatever's going on?"

"Oh, you have no idea." Lizzie sighed. "I was kidnapped! But I got away. And Mr. Darcy helped. But I saved his life, too—he would have been shot otherwise. And this entire case has gotten so complicated I don't even know where to begin."

"Kidnapped? Lizzie, are you all right?" Charlotte's alarm made Lizzie reach out and grasp her hands.

"A little sore, but perfectly fine now. And . . ." She looked meaningfully into Charlotte's eyes. "I'm terribly sorry."

"Oh, Lizzie. I know you are."

"Yes, but I should have said it earlier. From this moment on, I shall listen to you and respect your wishes. I was acting foolishly before."

Charlotte didn't rush to assure her otherwise, but she squeezed Lizzie's hands. "I appreciate that. Thank you."

Mr. Bennet's voice startled them. "Oh, Miss Lucas, you're here. Excellent." He stood in the drawing room doorway. "Lizzie, come along. We've got important matters to discuss."

Darcy stood as soon as she and Charlotte entered the drawing room after Mr. Bennet, and Lizzie had never before felt such a confusing rush of emotion. Misery at being wrong. Embarrassment at how she'd accused him of mistreating Wickham. A flush of excitement at seeing him once more, mixed with worry when she fully took him in. He was dressed impeccably in a fine dark jacket, but he didn't look as though he'd slept at all. His dark hair was a bit ruffled, as if he'd raked his fingers through it moments before.

Darcy turned to her and said, "Miss Bennet, are you well? Does your foot pain you?"

"I'm well, thank you," Lizzie said, flustered by the formality. "I'm getting around just fine." It seemed rather strange that they had experienced being held at gunpoint and facing organized criminals the night before, only to speak to each other so formally the following morning.

"She's recovered just fine," Mrs. Bennet said loudly, startling Lizzie. She hadn't noticed her mother sitting by the fire.

"Last night has hardly affected her one bit—why, she went to bed without even seeing me. I suffer from a condition of nerves, you see, and took to bed shortly after that villain Wickham kidnapped her."

"I apologize, Mama," Lizzie said, doing her best to sound polite and not irritated. "I had a very trying experience and my ankle hurt and I wished to go straight to bed."

"But not to see your own mother?" Mrs. Bennet protested, and Lizzie clenched her mouth shut. A bath and bed were all she had wanted last night.

"Now, now, my dear, I'm sure Mr. Darcy didn't come to hear about your nerves," Mr. Bennet interrupted.

"No one ever asks," his wife said, pouting.

Lizzie, now truly embarrassed, was gratified to see that Darcy was not disgusted with her mother's manners. "I'm very sorry to hear that. Mrs. Bennet, I assure you it was a most trying night for those directly involved. And I'm afraid we're far from resolving it."

"Sordid affair." Mrs. Bennet shuddered.

"Yes, Mama, but one that needs our attention." Lizzie looked to her father. It would not do for her to ask her mother to leave. That ought to be her father's job. But either Mr. Bennet was clueless or—and Lizzie rather suspected this was the case—or he did not wish to tangle with Mrs. Bennet.

"Right," Mr. Bennet said. "Mr. Darcy has engaged my services as barrister for this afternoon's hearing before the judge.

It's Weatherford presiding, so we need a tight case."

"I trust that you're fine with bringing in your father, Miss Bennet?" Darcy asked.

"Of course," Lizzie said. "But . . . why not a barrister from your own firm?"

"You said it yourself: your father is an expert in business law. And I think, from what you've uncovered, Netherfield is at the heart of this case. It might look untoward if Pemberley and Associates were to argue the case. I hope you'll forgive the early hour, too—I didn't want to draw criminal attention upon Longbourn and Sons, so I thought meeting here was best."

"Rather like a social call," Mrs. Bennet observed hopefully, but no one seemed to have heard her.

"Of course," her father said, reaching for the satchel Charlotte had brought. "And Miss Lucas was kind enough to fetch all that I needed from the office."

"Besides," Darcy continued with a slight clearing of his throat, and Lizzie realized he was addressing her, "this case is just as much yours as it is mine. This way, you stay involved."

Lizzie had to work not to let a grin break across her face. Instead, she nodded. "Thank you."

"Right, now start at the beginning," Mr. Bennet said.

Darcy and Lizzie began laying out the facts of the case, volleying the story back and forth as best they could, depending on which of them had the better perspective. Lizzie consulted her notes often, and when they got through the entire tale, Mr.

Bennet sighed and said, "There's scant evidence here. I don't like it."

"We have three pieces," Lizzie argued. "The false insurance policy. The penknife the Runners took into custody. And the button."

"The button cannot help us unless we know whom it belongs to," said Mr. Bennet, "and the murder weapon could belong to anyone—every gentleman in the city owns a penknife. They'll likely try to claim it was Hurst's."

"It wasn't Hurst's, and it's not Bingley's," Darcy was quick to point out. "I've already asked about Hurst's and it was in his writing box in the study. And the guards at Newgate were all too happy to divest Bingley of his. Besides, Bow Street told me the one they recovered has a mother-of-pearl inlay, and Bingley carries his father's, which is solid silver."

"But it doesn't definitely link anyone to the crime," her father pointed out. "And so we must rely on this insurance policy."

"It's a decent fraud," Lizzie told her father. "Perhaps not the most thorough, but then again, it likely was never written with the intent of standing up in a court of law—just to confuse and misdirect employees, or whoever inherited the business."

"A bit overwritten, in my opinion," Darcy added, looking to Lizzie. She nodded in agreement.

Mr. Bennet studied the document. "If I had been tasked to write a fraudulent insurance document, I might have done it exactly so."

"What a thing to say!" Mrs. Bennet exclaimed.

"I would have done it just like this, flowery language and all. Such words, as you both know," Mr. Bennet said, looking to Darcy and Lizzie, "are generally meaningless, but it flusters most men because they believe it's the language of importance. If I were this criminal, I'd want to fluster the reader into not looking too closely."

Which gave Lizzie a thought. "Then I wonder . . . who wrote it?"

Darcy and Mr. Bennet exchanged glances and then looked to Lizzie. "That's a very good question," Darcy murmured.

"Don't sound so surprised."

"Miss Bennet, if I'm surprised at anything you say, it's because I'm amazed at the quickness of your mind, not because I doubt your abilities. I was so caught up in the document's purpose that I hadn't even given a second's thought to who might have drafted it."

He seemed genuine, but Lizzie ignored his compliment in favor of thinking through this trail of thought. "Do you think it was Wickham?"

"This was never Wickham's style," Darcy said. "Nor is it his handwriting. Trust me, I would know."

"This Lady Catherine character could have paid any solicitor to do it," Mr. Bennet pointed out. "There's no shortage of men who would trade a little dishonesty for money, even in our profession."

"But it had to be someone she trusted," Lizzie argued. "She couldn't hire just anyone, because whoever wrote it would know what she was up to, or at least suspect. Piracy is a serious crime, with a capital punishment."

"He would be well paid," Mr. Bennet said.

"Or she has some sort of sway over him," Darcy added.

"Lizzie, are you talking of the Lady Catherine you were asking about the other day?" Mrs. Bennet interrupted.

"Yes, Mama," Lizzie said, her mind still on that very peculiar carriage ride. "I suspect . . ."

"What do you suspect, my dear?" Mr. Bennet asked.

She hesitated. This entire case had been built on Lizzie's suspicions, and look where it had led her. But with everyone in the room looking to her, including Charlotte and Mrs. Bennet, she knew she couldn't leave her thoughts unvoiced.

"I don't think she wrote it herself," Lizzie said. "If she had the ability to pen convincing contracts, then she wouldn't have tried to convince *me* to work for her. She said she had opportunities that no man would give me. And last night Wickham insisted with his dying breath that he didn't kill Hurst, and I don't think he was lying. He said Lady Catherine was the mastermind, that she had spies. And before he was shot, Lady Catherine said that he had done a poor job of cleaning up this mess."

"You suspect that whoever actually killed Hurst is the same person that penned this document?" her father asked. Lizzie hesitated, reviewing her memories, but her logic was sound.

"There's no way I can know that for sure," Lizzie conceded finally. "But it would draw us closer to the center of this whole affair. I wonder if Lady Catherine doesn't collect people, recruit them to her cause. She didn't just want to hire me—she wanted me to see things her way."

"Lizzie, is this Lady Catherine related to Sir Lewis de Bourgh, or not?" Mrs. Bennet cut in.

"I don't know, Mama!" Lizzie snapped, letting her frustration get the better of her. "If I did, I would have said."

"Sir Lewis was only a knight," Mrs. Bennet added. "So I suppose it's possible."

"You are probably correct," Mr. Bennet said to Lizzie, which brought a flood of relief and delight—until he added, "But we don't have time for a wild-goose chase—the hearing is today."

Lizzie knew he was right. Time had run out. If only she had known Lady Catherine was involved from the start! Lizzie could have pretended to take her up on her offer and tried to get more information out of her. But it was too late now. "What's our strategy?" she asked, forcing herself to abandon the hollow feeling that she had missed something.

Darcy explained his proposed defense to Mr. Bennet in three parts: First, he must establish the facts of the crime, paying special attention to the circumstantial nature of the evidence. Second, introduce Hurst's disreputable alliances and bring forward the witnesses that could corroborate his debt and failure to pay. Third, they must emphasize Bingley's outstanding reputation in business and his refusal to pay illegal protection fees.

"But if we introduce this," Darcy said, tapping the insurance policy, "you see the risks."

"The judge may take it as motive," Lizzie said.

"Exactly."

Mr. Bennet sighed heavily. "You must make a choice, then, as Mr. Bingley's solicitor and as his friend. If we include it, it's a gamble. But we will be bringing the case before the judge in full honesty. If we exclude it, we may have a better chance at winning, but we won't be completely transparent about your discovery process."

"The problem is that he's *innocent*," Darcy said. "I just know it."

"I'll happily lend you my legal expertise if you choose to introduce this into evidence," Mr. Bennet told him. "We won't have much time, but there may still be a chance that we can present it in such a light that Weatherford won't hold it against Mr. Bingley."

Darcy nodded his thanks and sat in quiet contemplation. Lizzie appreciated that he was giving it careful consideration, but she suspected his mind was made up. All Darcy wanted was to clear Bingley's name, and could she blame him? She looked to Charlotte and thought of Jane. She would go to any distance to protect them, especially if she knew they were innocent.

So Lizzie was stunned when Darcy finally said, "Let's introduce it."

"But Bingley might go to prison!" Lizzie protested. "Or worse."

"I know," Darcy said. "And he might be found guilty if I take the easy route. But Bingley would prefer the honest track—the man refused to pay off pirates even as they drained his coffers! And I can't make a habit of settling things the way I used to, in partial truths and dishonor." He gazed at her, and she knew that he was referring to the duel. "Why are you looking at me like that?"

"I'm simply surprised. Pleasantly so. I'd have thought after our last conversation concerning the law, you would have made a different choice."

"Yes, well . . . I'm finding that when certain people make excellent points, my opinion can be swayed."

Lizzie was struck speechless. But before she could even begin to piece together a reply, Mrs. Bennet said, "Well, I suppose you had better go up to your study, Mr. Bennet."

"Excellent idea," Lizzie proclaimed, and stood to hide that she was flustered.

"Oh, not you, dear!" Mrs. Bennet took hold of Lizzie's arm. "We are receiving callers. Have you forgotten?"

"Mama, this is far more important—"

"We're expecting Mr. Collins today," Mrs. Bennet reminded her.

Bollocks! Lizzie had forgotten. "Mama, I don't think that Mr. Collins will call today."

"Nonsense. You invited him." To Darcy, she explained, "Mr. Collins is my husband's junior partner. We expect that he'll propose to Lizzie very soon, which is very convenient as he is Mr. Bennet's successor. He shall truly be the family's savior on the event of Mr. Bennet's death."

At Charlotte's small gasp, Lizzie guiltily looked at her friend. "Mama, I only invited him at your request. I don't wish to marry him at all, nor do I think he will propose to me."

"What an unfortunate surprise," Darcy murmured, and Lizzie hoped that he was teasing her.

"Whatever do you mean?" Mrs. Bennet demanded.

Lizzie looked to her father. "He truly hasn't said anything to you?"

"I'm ignorant of the matter," her father replied mildly. "But please, for the sake of your mother's nerves and my own well-being, enlighten us."

Avoiding Darcy's gaze and thinking ruefully that Jane was correct about the hazards of keeping secrets, Lizzie reluctantly faced not her parents but Charlotte. "Mr. Collins proposed to me three days ago. I turned him down."

Mrs. Bennet's wail of despair raised the hair on Lizzie's arms. "You foolish girl! What have you done?"

Pain flitted across Charlotte's face, but she said, "You can't help who proposes to you."

That wasn't entirely reassuring, and Lizzie felt miserable at dashing her friend's hopes. Mrs. Bennet was not quite so understanding. "Mr. Bennet, your daughter must be brought to reason!" she insisted. "It's been three days! What if he's found someone else?"

Lizzie was relieved to find her father entirely unconcerned. "I don't understand what I'm to do about it—it sounds as though the matter is settled."

"I don't believe that Mr. Collins truly loves me, anyway," Lizzie said, hoping to spare her mother a bit of heartache.

Instead, her words brought about a new round of hysterics from Mrs. Bennet. "You'll marry him, Elizabeth! You must, or I shall never speak to you again!"

Darcy observed the scene with impatience mixed with amusement, and Lizzie thought that her humiliation could not be more complete.

Finally, Mr. Bennet intervened. "Enough!" He looked to Lizzie, and she couldn't read the look on his face as he said, "I'm afraid an unhappy alternative has been brought before you, my dear. From this day, you must be estranged from one of your parents. Your mother proclaims that she will never speak to you again if you don't marry Mr. Collins. And I will never speak to you again if you *do*."

Lizzie stood, frozen, as her father spoke. She took an extra moment to ensure that she had heard him correctly, and then a delighted smile blossomed across her face. Her father would not force her into an unhappy marriage! She flung her arms around him. "Thank you, Papa!"

Mr. Bennet returned her hug and then whispered so her mother could not overhear, "I'm proud of you, Lizzie."

Lizzie had to wipe at her eyes quickly when she finally released her father. Mrs. Bennet was deeply irritated. "How can you say such a thing? We agreed that Lizzie must marry him."

Mr. Bennet took his wife's arm. "My dear, we agreed on no such matter. I must ask that you grant me two requests: First, the freedom of my own reason in this particular situation. Second, that you allow me, Mr. Darcy, Lizzie, and Miss Lucas to retire to my study so that we can formulate a defense for Mr. Bingley."

But Mrs. Bennet would not be pushed aside so easily. "You're always cutting me out of important decisions and situations. *Always!* First, Collins shows interest in Lizzie after months of disinterest, and then he proposes marriage—a truly unexpected miracle—and you decide that she doesn't need to be married? A husband and wife ought to be in complete confidence in all things!"

"That defense only works in a court of law," her father replied wearily. "And I for one am very glad that Lizzie shall not spend the rest of her days having to keep Collins's banal confidences."

If Mrs. Bennet had a response to that, Lizzie didn't hear the particulars. A roaring filled her ears, and she felt very, very faint. Could it be? No, she was insane. She was desperate. Was it inspiration when you were struck by an idea at the eleventh hour or madness?

But underneath her light-headedness, her heart raced with certainty.

"Are you all right, Lizzie?" Charlotte asked.

"Elizabeth?" Mr. Darcy was at her side, intent with concern.

He called me Elizabeth again, she thought with delight. "I . . . don't know, I . . ."

Mr. Darcy guided her to the nearest seat, but she barely noticed the movement or the way his thumb caressed her knuckles briefly before releasing her hand.

"Her nerves! She's overcome! Lizzie, don't fret—it's not too late to salvage this situation. I shall ring for the maid, and we will get you into bed, and Jane can—"

"My nerves are fine," Lizzie told Mrs. Bennet. "I'm simply thinking."

At first, the thought seemed too preposterous to entertain, but the more credence Lizzie gave it, the more value it held.

Mr. Collins's proposal had been unexpected. Just days earlier he'd been pursuing Charlotte—what had induced him to then propose marriage to Lizzie after months of ill will between them? She had never flattered him; he was well aware that she despised him. His reasoning, which she had accepted at the time, now did not make any sense. Why would he propose to Lizzie when she had four other sisters he could have aligned himself with? Jane, Kitty, and Lydia would have all refused him, of course, but Mary might have accepted him.

Was she mad to think that he was motivated by some darker purpose?

She thought of how she'd seen him from a distance at the public assembly. Collins had disparaged such social events in the past. And yet, there he was—at the same public assembly that Lady Catherine and Wickham attended. He could have been receiving instructions or reporting to her. With unease, she thought of the day she'd been followed. Had Collins passed along information about her movements? Or had that been Wickham? Had they been working for the same woman?

Perhaps Lizzie would never know how great a hand Wickham had in misleading her, but the more she thought on Collins, the faster the evidence stacked up.

"Mama, where did you say Sir Lewis was from?"

"Kent, dear," Mrs. Bennet replied.

Kent, where Collins was from. Where his benefactress resided!

And, oh, heavens—the day Lizzie caught him flirting with Charlotte, hadn't she been sharpening his quill for him? Why would he ask such a thing of her, unless he was no longer in possession of his penknife, the penknife that Mr. Bennet had in fact given Collins upon his appointment as heir? Lizzie closed her eyes briefly. She had helped Mr. Bennet pick out that penknife, and it was silver, with mother-of-pearl inlay. She'd have to look at the one in custody to say whether it was the same one, but why hadn't she seen it before?

There had also been Collins's fury when she declined his proposal. His threats.

"May I see the insurance policy?" she asked Darcy, and he handed it to her without question. "Charlotte, would you look at this?"

Charlotte sat next to her. "What am I looking for?"

But Lizzie didn't want to plant thoughts in Charlotte's mind, not when they'd fallen out over Collins. She simply handed the document over and watched her read it. *Hereto, therefore, whither, henceforth,* and *insomuch as.* The document was riddled with ridiculous, gilded language. Distracting language. Lizzie had read many such documents before in her work behind the scenes of Longbourn & Sons and had crossed many such words out of said documents. All written by Collins.

Lizzie forced herself to sit with these suspicions, for the simple reason that quick judgments had gone horribly awry for her lately. She despised Collins. She was affronted by his spurious interest in Charlotte, and she wanted to believe him manipulative and untrue. She wished that her father had never hired him in the first place, never named him successor to the business, never put so much stock and faith in his ability to run the firm when it became obvious that he was judgmental, hypocritical, and unfaithful. But, that didn't make him a murderer.

Charlotte examined the document wordlessly, but Lizzie

knew the moment when Charlotte understood. She set down the document, and Lizzie was frightened that Charlotte disagreed with her and that Lizzie had angered her best friend. But instead, Charlotte reached for the satchel and riffled through it, extracting a stray sheet of paper and a magnifying glass. She took her time examining the documents with her magnifier, taking in the cramped swoop of the letters and the jagged angle of the clauses. When Mrs. Bennet whispered, "What on earth is going on?" Mr. Bennet hushed her.

Finally, Charlotte looked up. Lizzie was relieved to find that her friend didn't look heartbroken—she looked furious. Charlotte nodded once.

And yet . . . "I could be wrong."

"I don't think so," Charlotte said, her voice clear and forceful.

"You've figured it out, then?" Darcy asked.

"Yes," she said simply. Then she looked her father in the eye and said the words she'd nearly given up on: "And I know how to prove it."

Her father smiled and held his palms open. "I'm all ears."

Lizzie looked to Mrs. Bennet. "Mama, I think I shall reconsider Mr. Collins's proposal after all."

TWENTY-ONE

In Which Lizzie Sets a Trap

"MR. COLLINS," LIZZIE SAID, forcing herself to sound pleasant despite the queasiness she felt at the sight of him. Her mother showed him into the drawing room, and he bowed slightly in Mrs. Bennet's direction before turning to face Lizzie. Behind Collins, Mrs. Bennet gave Lizzie an exaggerated wink. Then she shut the door behind her, leaving Lizzie and Collins alone.

"Good afternoon, Miss Bennet. You're looking very well, if I may take the liberty of saying so."

"You may," Lizzie allowed. Although Collins wore an overly gracious, condescending expression, she couldn't forget the last time she'd seen him, when she had refused his proposal. The way his face twisted so quickly into fury.

"Shall we sit, Mr. Collins?" Lizzie asked, gesturing toward

the furniture near the fire. Her hand shook slightly, and Lizzie tried not to let her own nerves derail her mission. She had to be polite, collected, a touch contrite.

"Yes, thank you." He moved to sit next to her on the settee, which might have been appropriate for a man who expected to propose but was too close for Lizzie's comfort.

"Please, do sit in my father's chair. I assure you it's the most comfortable seat in the room, befitting your stature." She nearly choked on those last three words, but they did the trick of complimenting Collins. He smiled self-importantly.

"Thank you, Miss Elizabeth. I'm glad to find your spirits improved from the last time we met—hopefully that's not your only change in attitude?"

He was so odious, but Lizzie forced herself to say, "Of course, Mr. Collins. That's why we are here."

He laughed as if she had told the best joke. Even his laugh was intolerable! Her gaze strayed to his jacket, and the buttons there, but then Collins continued, "I didn't expect that I'd have to woo you again so soon."

Focus, Lizzie. "But surely you won't object to doing so?"

"I'm always happy to offer delicate compliments that are pleasing to ladies." He leaned so far forward that Lizzie was worried he would fall out of his seat.

"What a credit to your character," she lied.

"It's my responsibility, especially where the Bennet sisters are concerned." His smile bordered on a leer, and he added,

"Considering how things are settled, of course."

Lizzie ached to take this cue to segue into a discussion of estates, businesses, and marriage, but she knew she had only one chance to secure a confession. She wanted him relaxed, not suspicious. Instead she asked, "Do your words arise from the impulse of the moment, or do you practice them?"

He chuckled and leaned back. "I sometimes amuse myself by arranging little compliments that can be adapted to ordinary conversation. Although I always wish to give them an unstudied air."

"Of course," Lizzie said. She realized there was a glimmer of calculated manipulation behind his over-the-top demeanor that she'd always been happy to ignore in favor of poking fun at his sycophantic personality. "You strike me as a gentleman who seems prepared in all areas."

"Preparation is the path to success. I've offered to give your father a few suggestions, but he's turned me down. Although he does always seem prepared in court. Overprepared, even! Last week he spent the morning with a single text to find one line on the off chance that he might need to cite it before the magistrate!"

Lizzie resisted the urge to argue that this characteristic was what made her father a good barrister. Instead, she said, "It's always best to prepare for success, isn't it? That way one knows what to do with it when it arrives, and doesn't waste a single second."

"Precisely! I'm surprised to hear you agree."

"The more time I've had to think since our last conversation, the more I've realized that we might, in a strange way, be far more compatible than I initially realized."

His gaze did not waver. "How so?"

"Am I mistaken in believing that you are an ambitious man, Mr. Collins?"

"Not at all. Ambition—that's what my benefactress has always admired in me."

"I think perhaps you have more ambition than most people," Lizzie said, trying not to let herself grow too excited at the mention of his benefactress. Slow and steady now. "It took me a while to note it."

She had him leaning forward once more. "Solicitor now, barrister very soon. And who knows beyond that? Magistrate." He paused, then with quiet reverence added, *"King's Counsel."*

A small part of Lizzie marveled that such a ridiculous young man thought he could ever have a monarch's ear. She'd never detected it in him, which made her worry that he was much smarter than she previously thought. But the part of her that was focused completely on the task at hand ignored this doubt. "I had no idea you had such lofty goals. If I had known . . ." She deliberately looked down and feigned embarrassment.

"Known what, my dear?"

She set her face in regret and looked up. "You must understand, Mr. Collins. I turned down your proposal because I believed that you were like my father. He could have been magistrate. Perhaps not King's Counsel, like you . . . but I've always yearned for more. I see now I made a grave mistake in assuming because you started off as my father's apprentice that you'd never exceed him."

Lizzie hoped her father, who was listening with Darcy at the grate above the drawing room, didn't take offense at her indictments against his work ethic. She didn't mean it, but she had to make certain that Collins believed her to be earnest.

"Oh, my dear." Now Collins sprang out of his seat but did not sit down next to her. Instead, he knelt on the floor in front of her. Lizzie allowed him to take her hand. "I forgive your misconception. It's your father's fault, naturally. Instead of applying himself, he allowed you to embark on some trifling matters of business at the firm. But when I am made barrister, you will never have to work again."

"But I do like having tasks and a purpose," Lizzie said, unable to consent to a life of idleness, even when she was attempting to fool Collins.

"There will be many social duties for you to undertake, in addition to running the household," Collins assured her. "You'll have to pave our way into the social scene."

Lizzie could think of nothing more boring, but she pretended to accept it. "That's all very well, Mr. Collins. But I must remain practical. How do I know that you are willing to do whatever it takes to become King's Counsel?"

Lizzie was fearful for a moment that her doubts had offended him, for his face fell, but his grip on her hands strengthened. "I assure you, I am prepared to work very hard."

"Hard work!" Lizzie scoffed. "London is full of men who work hard! If I wanted a husband who was willing to work hard, I could marry a laborer. No, my dear Collins, I want to know that you will do *whatever* it takes to secure our future."

She stared into his washed-out gray eyes and mentally begged him to understand her meaning, hoping that he would be so caught up in the moment that he would reveal everything. Lizzie was afraid if she looked away, he would suspect her true motives and call off the proposal, and then he'd walk free, and Bingley would go down for Hurst's murder, and Lady Catherine would continue extorting and stealing and pirating and—

"Say you'll marry me, dear Elizabeth," Collins said, and it sounded more like a threat than a proposal. "I cannot begin to tell you all I will do to secure our future."

She wavered, partly because of Collins and partly because in a disjointed flash, she recalled Darcy looking at her with concerned eyes, and this memory alone took her breath away.

"Very well!" she gasped, surprised at finding the words sneak out of her while her mind was still on Darcy.

"Excellent!" Collins exclaimed, grinning, and his proclamation sent a spray of spittle in her direction. "This is very good. Now, you may have heard me mention my benefactress? I told your father she was a widow of means from my county, who wished for her kindness to remain anonymous."

"Oh?" He still had her hands clasped in his own, and aside from causing her great physical discomfort, she was beginning to feel trapped.

"Yes! She goes by the name of . . . Lady Catherine de Bourgh."

Lizzie could tell by his sly, knowing look that she was supposed to know whom he was talking about. "Why, I've met her," she said, sounding puzzled—it was not an act.

"I know; she told me!" He chuckled. "She is the one who wishes we marry. She has a great number of plans for us, and she'll even give us land in Kent! Her Ladyship was very displeased when you refused me at first, and expressed doubt that you might come around—she knows you're very strong willed. But she'll be happy to hear this news, and insist we marry as soon as the banns can be read."

"Plans?" Lizzie asked. "But what kinds of plans?"

"Nothing for you to worry about," Collins told her. "We'll call on her tomorrow morning—no, this afternoon—and tell her the good news."

Lizzie smiled grimly. Collins had revealed two essential bits of information—first, that he was in regular contact with Lady Catherine, and second, that he had no knowledge of her flight from London the night before. The lady likely saw the noose closing in around her lackeys and decided to flee while she still had the chance. That she had not extracted Collins, and had shot Wickham, spoke a great deal of *her* character.

"I'm afraid that won't be possible," Lizzie said softly. "I have a case in court this afternoon."

Collins shook his head. "Oh no, as your fiancé, I cannot allow you to attend that Bingley matter."

"Why not?" Lizzie asked, and it took all her might to keep the edge from her voice.

"Don't worry about it. Between you and me, it's one of Lady Catherine's little schemes." He looked all too delighted to reveal this to Lizzie. "I'm sure she'll explain when we see her."

"I don't think so," Lizzie said. "Lady Catherine has taken her leave of London."

Collins shook his head. "What?"

"I saw her leave myself, last night. By way of the docks." Lizzie enjoyed the sight of Collins's confusion. It kept her from losing her nerve, and she continued with shaky breath, "This was straight after she shot Mr. Wickham to death. She left without you, and she killed Wickham rather than allow him to join her. She knew that I was drawing closer to the truth, that I would discover she is no lady but a *pirate*, that she had *you* murder Hurst, and that when I discovered the truth, you would hang in Newgate, and that's why she left you—"

"*No!*" Collins roared, and released her hands. Lizzie's fingers were cramped from the strength of his grip—so much stronger than she'd anticipated, strong enough to stab a man eleven times—but she knew it was her only chance to act. She plunged her right hand in between the cushions of the settee and drew Darcy's spare pistol, pointing it at Collins just as he brandished a knife.

No, a penknife.

Lizzie could tell at a glance that it was not the silver knife with mother-of-pearl inlay that her father had gifted him. This one was tarnished and its tip was bent, no embellishment whatsoever.

"Why, Mr. Collins, wherever is that penknife that my father gave you?" she asked coldly. "Did you leave it in the body of your last victim?"

"Put your pistol down!"

"Not a chance," she said. From above, she heard a soft thud and the shuffling of feet. Her father and Darcy. *Not yet, not yet.*

"I see that your mother and Lady Catherine were right about you all along," Collins spat out. "You are a foolish, obstinate girl."

"And you're a murderer."

"You don't go against Lady Catherine! She knows magistrates, dukes, earls . . ."

"Oh? Did she promise to see you made magistrate if you murdered Hurst?" Lizzie asked, her anger making it a struggle to keep her pistol-wielding hand steady.

"She has that power, yes!" Collins snapped. "And she'll see it done! Not right away, but in five years' time. Hurst was a liability to her, always drinking . . ." And perhaps he wasn't entirely foolish, because his face whitened when he realized what he had admitted.

"Who's foolish now?" Lizzie asked.

Before Collins could respond, she let out an earsplitting whistle, learned from Fred. The drawing room door was flung open, and Darcy was the first one through.

TWENTY-TWO

In Which Lizzie Is Vindicated, At Last

IN SHORT ORDER, DARCY divested Collins of his penknife and bound his hands. Collins glowered and spat at them, proclaiming that they'd pay, that Lady Catherine would see them ruined. Lizzie almost pitied Collins and the inevitable desolation he'd feel when he accepted that Lady Catherine had abandoned him . . . but then she reminded herself he was responsible for a murder and had set in motion events that led to Abigail's death.

She picked up the penknife that Collins had dropped when Darcy grabbed him, holding it with a handkerchief. The blade was a buckled, tarnished silver. "Not the one you gave him," she said to her father, showing him the cheap knife. "I bet that one's in custody."

"You can throw them both in the Thames," was Mr. Bennet's vehement reply.

"Not a chance. It's evidence." She inspected it, looking for traces of blood. But if he had used it to take any other lives, there was no sign. She shuddered, then placed it in her pocket. When she looked up, Darcy was staring at her with the most peculiar expression. "What's the matter?"

"You were . . . that was brilliant. Are you all right?"

Lizzie didn't quite know how to respond. Her pulse was still galloping, even though Collins was contained. She had felt clear-eyed and determined when she was questioning him alone, but now she trembled. Instead of responding, she handed Darcy the pistol, butt end first. "Here, you better take this before I accidentally hurt someone."

"It isn't even loaded," he reminded her.

"Well . . . just in case." Lizzie had refused to take the pistol with bullets loaded, certain that the presence of the weapon was all she'd need to intimidate Collins. Now, hearing the foolishness of her words, she looked around uncomfortably. She glanced at the clock on the mantel and exclaimed, "We don't have much time!"

The attention on the hour prodded everyone to get moving and gave Lizzie an excuse to slide out from under Darcy's notice. As they poured out into the hallway, a distressed Mrs. Bennet watched from the stairs, proclaiming to no one in particular, "He was always a rotten one; I said it to Mr. Bennet the day he hired him, I did! 'I don't know about that Mr. Collins fellow—he seems rather shifty.' And look now. I hope he goes to prison for a very long time, I do!"

Lizzie ignored her mother, but then Mrs. Bennet said to her father, "You make certain that the judge and everyone at court know that you were the one to catch the serpent in your midst. Don't let Pemberley snatch all the glory!"

"Mama!" Lizzie protested. "If not for Mr. Darcy—"

"In incidences such as these, we can all share in the credit as well as the blame," Mr. Bennet assured everyone, but Mrs. Bennet continued to carry on.

At the door, Charlotte and Jane waited, Jane with Lizzie's bonnet and her own already donned. "I'm coming with you," she said. "Leave Mary, Kitty, and Lydia to deal with Mama's hysterics for once!"

"Really?" Lizzie asked, clasping her sister's hand.

Jane leaned in and whispered, "I wouldn't miss your first appearance at court for anything."

"Good work, Lizzie," Charlotte added, and then, "Let's make sure he can't hurt anyone ever again."

Charlotte's words were a reminder that although Collins was taken into custody, they still had a very important job to do and not much time to accomplish it. The Bennets, Charlotte, Darcy, and Collins took two carriages to the courthouse. It wasn't until they pulled up to their destination, Newgate looming close by, that Lizzie realized her dream of finally stepping through the entrance to the courthouse was about to come true. The moment was not as solemn as she might have imagined but rather rushed. She followed her father, and Darcy holding Collins, right through the gap in the brick wall and was surprised to find a large party already waiting for them in the courtyard: Bingley, his two sisters, Mr. Banks, and Hurst's valet.

"Thank God!" Bingley cried when he caught sight of them all. "Court will be called to session in five minutes—where have you all been? And who's this man?"

"No time to explain," Darcy said, doing his best to corral the large party into the building. "But he killed Hurst, and we can prove it."

In quick order, the entire group entered the building, too quickly for Lizzie to properly soak in all of the details that she had dreamed of observing. Her father borrowed robes and a wig, befitting his position as barrister, while Caroline, Louisa, Charlotte, and Jane headed to pay their admission to the spectator gallery. Lizzie didn't follow them, and Darcy didn't object, but he did ask Mr. Bennet, "Will the judge allow Miss Bennet to speak?"

"Women serve as witnesses all the time," Mr. Bennet said. "And my Lizzie could convince a man to invest in ice in December."

Normally, these words would have brought about a flush of pride in Lizzie, but at just that moment they were ushered into the courtroom. It was . . . smaller than Lizzie imagined but still very fine. The ceilings were tall, and a bank of windows on one end let in a weak spring light, and there were four brass chandeliers to illuminate proceedings. The rustling of paper and shuffling of many bodies made Lizzie feel faint as her father ushered her to the round mahogany table where counsel sat. To her right sat a jury of men. She peered past them to see if she could spot Jane and Charlotte in the gallery, but then Bingley was ushered to a bench on her left by a bailiff, and Darcy delivered Collins to another.

Before the judge could call the court into session, Collins began to yell, "This is lunacy! I strenuously object to my forced attendance—I have been framed, Your Honor!"

The gavel banged, and the sharp sound brought silence to the courtroom. "Mr. Darcy," said the judge, "see that your witness does not speak out of turn again."

"My apologies," Darcy said, "but Mr. Collins is not merely a witness. He is the culprit for the crime that my client has been accused of."

The judge didn't appear to be surprised. "In due time. Collins, is it? Don't speak out of turn or I shall find you in contempt of court."

So this was Lord Weatherford, Lizzie realized. The judge was a stern-faced man with a hooked nose and eyes that missed nothing. Lizzie was under no illusions that he'd simply overlooked her presence at the counsel table. She did her best to not fidget, but when she glanced at Darcy, sitting between her and her father, she saw him swallow hard. It brought her small comfort to know she wasn't the only one nervous.

Weatherford began reading the charges. "Mr. Charles Bingley, you've been charged with unlawfully entering the home of Mr. George Hurst at Number Forty-Five Grosvenor Square, and murdering him in his bed. How do you plead?"

"Not guilty, sir," Bingley, Darcy, and Mr. Bennet all answered.

"One answer will be sufficient, thank you," the judge said.

"My apologies, sir," Bingley said, sounding meek on his elevated bench. His face was illuminated and he kept blinking. Lizzie looked up to see a cleverly mounted mirror that was tilted to shine light from the window on the face of the accused. "I'd like to plead not guilty."

"Very well." Weatherford was unsurprised. "Who's representing you today?"

"Mr. Darcy, and Mr. Bennet, and, well—Miss Bennet, too." Bingley looked at them. "I'm not really sure how this works."

A tittering rose throughout the court, and the judge banged his gavel once, silencing them. A harried, thin-faced man opposite them raised an objection. "Mr. Bingley isn't taking these charges seriously if he can't decide who his counsel is! And if said counsel brings a woman to the table!"

Lizzie kept her posture so impeccably straight that Mrs. Bennet would have been proud.

"Mr. Bennet," the judge said, "are you the barrister on Mr. Bingley's case?"

"I am," Mr. Bennet acknowledged, "although this position is rather a recent development, and I cannot claim full knowledge of the case."

"Then why are you in my courtroom?"

Mr. Bennet began to speak, as did Darcy, who rushed to say, "It's my fault, sir—"

"And you are?"

"Mr. Fitzwilliam Darcy, sir. I am the Bingley family's solicitor."

"Mr. Bingley, it's rare for me to find a solicitor from one firm and a barrister from a competitor at the same table—which one is in your employ?"

"Both?" Bingley answered.

The prosecutor was indignant. "Sir, I object—Mr. Bingley is making a mockery—"

"We take these charges very seriously, sir," Darcy began, flustered, just as Mr. Bennet cut in with a polite:

"If I may—"

The judge banged his gavel once more, until the only sound was a breathy, self-indulgent laugh. Lizzie didn't need to turn to know it was Collins. The judge looked to the witness bench and said, "I'm warning you, sir, you're very close to being held in contempt."

No one dared speak. Weatherford's irritation at this break

in decorum was palpable, and Lizzie forced herself to wait in silent agony. It was embarrassing to think that the court was looking to them with disgust, but their disorganization was due only to the fact that they'd been busy apprehending the *real* culprit.

Weatherford glowered at them. "It's been years since any-one has walked into my courtroom in such disarray, and I confess, Mr. Bingley, I'm of half a mind to remand you into custody and postpone your court appearance. Perhaps another three months in jail would give you sufficient time to confer with your counsel?"

Lizzie's heart plummeted. If the trial was postponed, that would mean they would be obligated to release Collins—and he would disappear, just as Lady Catherine had. She looked to Darcy and found him staring back. He seemed to wish to communicate wordlessly with her, except she had no idea what he was saying. Then, he mouthed one word.

Speak.

Lizzie turned back to the judge as he grumbled, "I have a full docket today, and I've already wasted enough time discovering who's who in this case, and still haven't learned the names of everyone at the defense table."

This was Lizzie's moment. With a hammering heart she stood, drawing everyone's attention. "I'm Miss Elizabeth Bennet, sir. My father is Mr. Bennet, and I've had the privilege of consulting on this case with Mr. Darcy. Please accept our sincerest apologies for our apparent disorganization—we've had a trying morning, but we are prepared to proceed, if you will allow."

The court didn't make a sound. Weatherford stared down at Lizzie, and she didn't falter. "How does a young lady come to address this court?"

She brought out her most polite society smile. "I'm afraid the story would rather detract from our purpose here, and as you have already pointed out, there have been enough delays as it is. But if you will allow me to proceed, I believe I can prove to you that we are indeed prepared, and furthermore, Mr. Bingley is innocent of all charges."

Talking in court was like a social call, Lizzie realized suddenly. Certain words were spoken in a certain order, the appropriate inquiries and responses must be made, and everything unfolded according to unspoken rules. She believed that her father's education had been preparing her for this moment, but she was surprised to learn that her mother had an equal hand in providing Lizzie the tools she needed for this day.

Weatherford considered Lizzie for a long moment, then said, "With your permission, Mr. Bennet, I will allow your daughter to continue."

"It is given," Mr. Bennet said, "for I believe that of all the people in this court, my daughter is the only one with a full understanding of the crime and its subsequent events."

The judge nodded. "Very well. Continue, Miss Bennet."

Lizzie took another steadying breath, but her words flowed smoothly. "Sir, the charges against Mr. Bingley are that he unlawfully entered the house of Mr. Hurst, then proceeded to stab him to death. However, I believe that if you question the butler, you will find that Mr. Bingley was admitted to the house when he brought Mr. Hurst home from his club, and the butler helped carry Mr. Hurst to bed. Then, Mr. Bingley left. By his own admission, he went straight home and retired, and did not leave until he went to the Hurst residence the following morning, where he was again let in by the butler. He grew impatient with Mr. Hurst and went straight to his bedchamber, where he discovered Mr. Hurst dead. Moments later, the valet walked in, and the Runners and coroner were called."

Lizzie paused, and when no one objected, she continued, "Mr. Hurst's butler and valet immediately cast suspicions on Mr. Bingley. However, they do not account for a length of time between Mr. Bingley's departure and his return, during which none of the household saw Hurst. A space of eight hours, which offered the murderer ample time to slip inside, find Mr. Hurst, and stab him to death. What I aim to prove before you today is that the murderer is *not* Mr. Bingley." She paused for effect. "But it is in fact Mr. William Collins."

The audience in the gallery gasped, as if they were at the theater. "Lies!" Collins spat out, and even the prosecutor joined in.

"Why are we letting a lady dictate the procedures of this court?" he bellowed. "We are a court of law, not a society tea."

The judge banged his gavel and returned his attention to Lizzie. "These are serious charges, Miss Bennet."

"I have evidence," Lizzie declared over the protests, "and I should hope that any court would respect truth above sex, so it should not matter who presents in this case."

"I'm inclined to agree with Miss Bennet," Weatherford declared. "Continue."

"Thank you, sir," Lizzie said. "First, may I ask that the penknife recovered from the scene of the murder be presented?"

The prosecutor shuffled his files, and there was a bit of grumbling under his breath, but he produced a muslin-wrapped object. The judge indicated that one of his bailiffs should take it, which he scurried to do. He unwrapped the bundle and presented it to the court. Lizzie inspected it and worked to keep triumph off of her face—but she was right! It was identical to the penknife that her father had given Mr. Collins. The silver blade was covered in dried blood that had smeared and dried over the mother-of-pearl inlay, and it looked rather morbid with the blade extended. Lizzie didn't jump to inform the court of this. Instead, she turned to the accused bench. "Mr. Bingley, do you recognize this penknife?"

Bingley glanced at it and went pale. "No, I do not."

"Do you recognize it as Mr. Hurst's?"

"No," Bingley said, and the prosecutor began to protest, but he was silenced by Weatherford.

Finding her stride, Lizzie asked, "Would you recognize Hurst's penknife if you saw it?"

"Yes," Bingley confirmed. "George carried an ivory knife with a stamp on the blade. It belonged to his father. My sister, Mrs. Hurst, can confirm this."

Lizzie turned abruptly to the witness bench. "Mr. Collins, do you recognize the blade?"

Collins glared at her with open fury. If he had not been restrained and flanked by the bailiffs, Lizzie might have felt real fear that he'd fly at her. "It's covered in blood," he spat. "How am I supposed to recognize anything in that state?"

Lizzie did not engage with him. Instead, she addressed her father. "Mr. Bennet, do you recognize the penknife that was recovered at the scene of the crime?"

"This is growing tedious!" the prosecutor declared, but the court shifted with curiosity.

Her father was grim faced as he stood and inclined his head. "I do. I gifted that penknife to Mr. Collins one year ago, when I named him my successor at Longbourn and Sons."

Now the gallery broke out into open whispers, gasps, and murmurs. Above the noise, Collins shouted, "How do you know it's the same penknife?! I'm being framed!"

The gavel banged, and Lord Weatherford cast a dour look

upon Lizzie, upset that she was causing such a ruckus in his orderly day. But he said, "Mr. Bennet, are you sure?"

"It's possible that a penknife identical to the one I bestowed upon Mr. Collins exists, but this one looks remarkably like it, down to the stamp of the lion."

"And Mr. Collins," Lord Weatherford continued, "can you produce the knife that Mr. Bennet gave you?"

Even though Lizzie was certain that it was the same knife, she still held her breath, fearful that Collins would find a way to wiggle out of this accusation. He shifted his gaze from the judge to her father, and finally to her, before admitting, "I no longer have it."

The court exploded then, and he shouted to be heard. "It was stolen! I'm being framed!"

The gavel came down once more, and Lizzie said, "Thank you, sir. May I continue?"

"You have more to present?" he asked with some surprise.

Lizzie flashed him the smile that Jane said made mothers underestimate her and charmed young men. "Yes, sir. I don't simply intend to prove that Mr. Collins's penknife killed Mr. Hurst—I intend to prove that he is guilty of premeditated murder."

Mr. Collins's shouting behind her did not distract her for a moment. Lord Weatherford raised a single bushy gray eyebrow and said, "Continue."

Lizzie then brought her own bit of evidence from her

pocket—the button recovered from Hurst's bedchamber. "I found this button caught in the window of Mr. Hurst's bedchamber three days after the murder. By the butler's own admission, no one had been allowed to clean the room after Hurst's body was discovered and disposed of. This button was behind the drapes, which provided a very good hiding spot for one to wait for Hurst to return home. Furthermore, the window was near a tree in the back garden—it would not have been impossible for someone to climb it, and then gain access through the window. May I ask, Mr. Collins—how many buttons are on your jacket?"

"I hardly see how that matters! Sir, I'm a gentleman and this young lady doesn't know what she is saying—"

"Mr. Collins, remove your jacket and allow my bailiff to inspect it!"

Lizzie could feel the onlookers' gazes now, heavy with anticipation and excitement as Mr. Collins removed his jacket and handed it over. This was the one piece she wasn't certain about—all she had was a distant memory of counting Collins's buttons that day she'd caught him flirting with Charlotte and coming up with an uneven number. She scarcely breathed as the bailiff inspected the jacket, counting aloud. "One, two, three, four. Five, six, seven . . . There are seven, sir, but a few stray threads and some puckering where an eighth ought to be."

Lizzie held out the button she'd recovered, and so complete was her satisfaction when it was matched with the bronze buttons on Collins's jacket that she struggled to contain her smile. Something so small, so seemingly insignificant, had placed Mr. Collins at the scene of the crime more neatly than anything else could.

"A button! You're going to indict me over a missing button? How many of you have missing or stray buttons? That button could have come from any haberdashery or sewing box!"

"Considering the amount of evidence that is up against you, I would advise you to hold your tongue, sir," Lord Weatherford warned. He looked to Lizzie. "I trust that you have more?"

"Just one more thing, sir." She turned and found Darcy holding out the false insurance policy. The look of open admiration on his face almost caused her to falter, but she pressed on. "Mr. Hurst was employed by Mr. Bingley at Netherfield Shipping. He was responsible for a number of inconsequential clerical duties. Witnesses will account for the fact that Hurst was a dismal employee, and Mr. Bingley limited his brother-in-law's power within the business. Yet upon his death, this insurance document was found among Hurst's belongings. I conferred with Mr. Bingley and Mr. Darcy, and they both informed me they had no knowledge of the document."

"I'd like to see it," the judge said, and Lizzie handed off the forgery to the bailiff. Weatherford examined it, his expression betraying nothing. "Go on."

"It's a falsification," Lizzie said bluntly. "Mr. Hurst was in serious financial trouble. Witnesses will account for his multiple debts, and Mr. Bingley has admitted to bailing him out in the past. However, knowing how he mismanaged and squandered money, Mr. Bingley would have never entrusted Mr. Hurst with a task as important as insuring the company."

Lizzie let that settle. "Piracy, as I am sure you are aware, sir, is quite a dire problem. Most merchants report a loss of thirty to forty percent of their goods due to piracy each year. Mr. Bingley, however, lost nearly eighty percent of his goods in the last year alone. No company wished to insure him. Except this one, a company no one has ever heard of, charging shockingly reasonable rates and containing no terms of cancellation."

"Indeed," Weatherford said, sounding curious. Lizzie had to keep from smiling.

"Which led me to suspect that it was a ruse, meant to mask the document's true purpose: extorting money from shipping companies in the form of false premiums in exchange for protection from pirate ships."

Again, the court gasped. But the judge did not reach for his gavel. "How did you come to this conclusion?"

"Because the mastermind behind this plot approached me herself," Lizzie told him pleasantly. "She's a woman going by the name of Lady Catherine de Bourgh, and she wished to recruit my help, although she didn't reveal her illegal dealings to me at the time. I declined, as I'm more than busy assisting my father, but her offer allowed me to connect a few important points about the nature of her work."

"This is nonsense—" the prosecutor attempted to say, but the judge banged his gavel without looking at him and gestured for Lizzie to continue.

"I examined the document, along with Mr. Darcy and my father. You'll notice, sir, that the wording is very precise, peculiar. It is of a particular style, one that I had seen many times while working for my father at his firm. The documents that shared a style with this one also shared a common author: Mr. Collins."

"She's a liar!" Mr. Collins shouted.

"Enough from you, sir! I am finding you in contempt. Take him into custody!"

Two bailiffs came forward with iron manacles. "Don't take him far," Lizzie requested, "for I'm certain you'll want to question him soon."

The bailiff gagged Mr. Collins, and Lizzie continued. "My suspicions were confirmed just this morning, when I consulted with Longbourn's legal secretary, Miss Lucas. She compared the handwriting on this forgery with a memo signed by Mr. Collins, and confirmed that they match. We invited Mr. Collins to call under the ruse of a social visit, and I inquired as to what his ambitions for the future were. He confessed to me that Lady Catherine de Bourgh was his benefactress, and that she had offered him land and an appointment to magistrate if he killed Hurst. Hurst was too much of a liability, getting drunk each night at his club, and I suspect Lady Catherine was concerned he wouldn't be able to keep a secret in such a state. By implicating Mr. Bingley in his murder, whoever succeeded him as head of Netherfield would be ignorant that the false insurance policy premiums were actually protection fees to pirates, and Lady Catherine would continue to profit."

"These are serious allegations," the judge said. "How did Mr. Collins answer to them?"

"By threatening my life and brandishing a penknife—and not the one my father gave him."

Lizzie removed the penknife, wrapped in her handkerchief, from her reticule and placed it on the table in front of her.

"Sir, I request that if this account matches witness statements, all charges against Mr. Bingley be dropped, and charges of unlawful entry and premeditated murder in the first degree be brought against Mr. Collins."

Lizzie knew that recommending charges was not the job of a defense counsel, but she couldn't resist—she felt authoritative and empowered, as if she could demand the crown jewels and her request might actually be considered. But, it was best not to get too carried away. She waited for the judge's response.

"Very well," Weatherford said. "You say that you are employed by your father?"

She glanced at Mr. Bennet, who beamed back at her in pride. "Yes, sir."

"Hmmph," the judge responded, then said, "If all legal firms employed young women such as you, Miss Bennet, I believe the number of hours I spend listening to cases would decrease drastically. You may stand down now; I have questions for the witnesses."

Lizzie didn't so much sit as sink into her seat. To her left, Darcy gave her a slight, encouraging smile that Lizzie barely managed to return. *I presented a case before the court*, she thought. Yesterday, it had seemed impossible. She was surprised to find that it had been not quite as shocking an experience as she'd once imagined. Surely, though, her father would not hesitate to hire her now? But she couldn't think about that now—Weatherford was calling forth witnesses, and Lizzie had to focus, writing down questions that were overlooked and redirects that she slipped to her father and Darcy.

Nearly an hour later, when all witnesses had been questioned, Collins was brought before the judge and his gag removed. He glowered at Lizzie as Weatherford asked, "Mr. Collins, what do you have to say in defense against the charges brought before you?"

"I only answer to Lady Catherine. She is the one who instructed me to take care of Hurst! He had no respect—"

The bailiff gagged Mr. Collins once more, on the judge's gesture. "I'm ordering Mr. Collins arrested and jailed until charges can be brought against him. I'm sure, thanks to his own admissions here and Miss Bennet's excellent evidence, that he will be found guilty of murder, at which time the appropriate sentence will be applied. Now, as to this case . . ."

Weatherford ordered Bingley to stand. Mr. Bennet, Mr. Darcy, and Lizzie stood with him. She wasn't certain if she would have the strength, but Darcy's hand found hers and gripped her tightly, lending his strength. Or, she thought as she glanced at his trembling arm, perhaps he was leaning on her for strength? She squeezed his hand once.

"I am granting Miss Bennet's request to dismiss all charges. Mr. Bingley, you have the court's apology. You are free to go."

The last words were drowned out in the rush of cheers that reverberated throughout the courtroom. Darcy released Lizzie's hand to go and hug his friend, who stumbled down from his bench in obvious shock. He shook Mr. Bennet's hand, then Lizzie's, as the gavel banged and banged, but the crowd did not quiet until Weatherford adjourned the court and the group spilled outside to mingle with the onlookers from the gallery.

Lizzie could scarcely keep track of everyone who hugged her—there was Jane, Charlotte, and her father. She supposed it was rather too much to expect a gesture of affection or even gratitude from Caroline, but Louisa shyly patted her on the back and Bingley exuberantly thanked her.

Then, Lizzie was preoccupied with a long line of well-wishers, mostly other clerks, solicitors, and barristers congratulating her on her first court case, a few offering unsolicited advice that she took with a polite smile. It was all wonderfully overwhelming, but as person after person passed by, she realized that she kept searching for Darcy's face in the wave of people.

She excused herself and looked about for Darcy but saw only Jane and Bingley making each other's acquaintance, Caroline complaining, her father conferring with a colleague . . .

"He's over there," Charlotte whispered, catching her eye and nodding to a corner at the opposite end of the courtyard where Darcy sat on a bench. "Go put him out of his misery."

"I don't know what to say," Lizzie admitted.

"That would be a first," Charlotte remarked, unsympathetic, and nudged Lizzie in his direction.

Not wanting to lose her nerve, Lizzie walked over to Darcy. He looked up at her as she approached, and Lizzie found herself unable to read his expression—hope? dismay? regret? Whatever it was, it made Lizzie panic and say without thinking, "Aren't you going to congratulate me?"

"Congratulations," Darcy said.

"Thank you," Lizzie replied, but found that she was back where she began, at a loss for words.

"How does it feel?" he asked.

"To have solved the case?"

"To have spoken in court! I've sat in court before, of course. But I've never spoken before the judge."

Lizzie laughed softly. Here she had spent so much time working to get ahead of Darcy, able to see only his advantages, and she had surpassed him in this way. But she considered the question. "It was a rush—and very intimidating. It feels good to clear an innocent man's name, but . . ."

Darcy was looking at her with something like longing. For her? *No, don't be preposterous, Lizzie.*

"You were wonderful," he said. "Measured and deliberate. I would have presented the button first, but you built your argument perfectly."

He was jealous, she realized. And far too much of a gentleman to admit it. He dreamed of wearing the robes and presenting cases one day, and she had beaten him to it. But—and this was almost as shocking to her—he wasn't bemoaning this fact. He was complimenting her on her success. A surge of generosity ran through her and she sat next to him and said, "You'll be doing the same and more before long. I'm sure you'll be brilliant at it."

"Really?"

"Oh yes," she said. "Just give the witnesses and magistrate your glower—yes, that's the one," she added as familiar irritation flickered across his face, "and they'll all fall in line for sure."

He looked away, and Lizzie laughed. "I'm only teasing you. You will be brilliant yourself. Besides . . . I couldn't have solved this case without you."

They exchanged smiles until Lizzie felt that perhaps their prolonged gaze was growing a bit indecent. But then Darcy looked away with a feigned cough and said, "You never mentioned Wickham."

"I know," she said. It had not been an altogether conscious

decision on her part, but as she stood before the judge, she went by instinct—pressing here, revealing there, taking a read of the room. "I suppose you must think me a hypocrite, going on about uncovering the truth. But if I had brought him up, it might have distracted the judge, and muddied our case—especially if we had to explain how you shot him. And then we would have gotten into Abigail, and . . . well, I suppose that you're right after all, the law doesn't care about true justice, it just—"

Darcy stopped her by taking hold of both her hands. "Elizabeth Bennet, we seem destined to misunderstand each other."

Lizzie looked up to see gratitude written across his face. "Thank you," he said, "for *not* bringing up Wickham. Evoking his name in court might have compelled me to lie in order to keep knowledge of what he did to my sister a secret. I won't have her reputation ruined over that man."

Not for the first time, Lizzie thought what a great injustice it was that a woman should pay dearly for a man's misdeeds, but she didn't bring that up now. She was instead reconsidering Darcy, letting go of all of her preconceived notions about him. She found that it was not exceptionally difficult. Her first impression of him was false, she could now see. He was determined, serious, and did not laugh easily. But he was loyal and willing to sacrifice his own reputation—even his own life—for the people he loved. She had greatly misjudged him.

"You're welcome," she said. "And I must apologize to you,

in turn. I misjudged you when we first met, and I held our first meetings against you. I'm sorry."

Darcy smiled and began to draw very distracting circles on her palm with his thumb. "I accept your apology, and offer one of my own—I apologize for dismissing you out of hand. I made some, ah, judgments about your character when we first met, and it led me to judge your abilities."

"I'll forgive you," Lizzie said, a teasing lilt to her voice, "if we can agree that I did not break into the Hursts' house."

Darcy rolled his eyes. "Miss Bennet, does it annoy you when I insist on accuracy in semantics?"

"It annoys me that you insist on switching back and forth between Miss Bennet and Elizabeth," she deflected.

"Does it now?" Darcy slid closer to her on the bench. "Which do you prefer I stick with?"

"Miss Bennet when we are discussing legal matters," she breathed, not daring to take her eyes off of him. "Elizabeth in front of my parents and our colleagues. But my friends and sisters call me Lizzie."

"Lizzie," Darcy breathed, and he closed the distance between them by brushing his lips against hers. Lizzie did not pull away, and he deepened the kiss. And Lizzie found out that she wasn't wrong just about Darcy, for she had not believed that there was a better feeling in the world than when the judge had dismissed Bingley's case. But kissing Darcy was just as good, albeit in a very different way.

When they broke apart, Darcy whispered, "Good work, Lizzie."

Lizzie glowed but could not think of an appropriate response, so all she said was, "Thank you. Although I'm not calling you *Fitz*."

Darcy broke into genuine laughter for the first time since they'd met, and Lizzie decided right then and there she would endeavor to make him laugh as much as she possibly could, for as long as their acquaintance continued.

EPILOGUE

In Which Lizzie Receives an
Offer She Cannot Refuse

A WEEK AFTER LIZZIE'S success in court, she was summoned to her father's office at Longbourn. This was not unusual, as Lizzie had been spending every day at the firm, working with her father to review all of Collins's old cases and redistribute his current workload. The fear that his crimes had blemished Longbourn & Sons' integrity was great, but thus far they'd worked to mitigate major disaster. Lizzie had not been surprised to find cut corners and sloppy legal work, though.

Charlotte's work in organizing and deciphering all of Collins's files had induced Mr. Bennet to call her the greatest legal secretary he'd ever had the honor of working with and mention privately to Lizzie that as soon as they could afford it, they ought to give her a raise so she wouldn't be tempted to leave them for another firm. Lizzie had agreed that while she would support Charlotte in all of her pursuits, even if they took her away from Longbourn, a raise was very much in order.

Luckily for them, Lizzie didn't think that it would be long before they might be able to afford it. Business seemed to be on the upswing, as was evident in the bustling atmosphere of the office as clerks hurried to and fro and the other solicitors worked at their desks rather than chatting. People were either curious, or inspired, or just in need of a solicitor, and, having recently heard of Longbourn, sought them out. Lizzie surveyed the office with a keen eye and tried not to let her imagination run wild. They had cases to attend to and clients who could pay, which was enough for now.

Mr. Bennet hadn't spoken a word about replacements or that Eton-educated young man he'd interviewed, and Lizzie hadn't brought it up. She thought often of the moment in court when Lord Weatherford had asked her father if she was employed by him. But they'd not spoken of it since, and Lizzie was too afraid to bring it up. Although she was happy to see her banishment at Longbourn lifted, Lizzie wanted the job. She wanted it to be official. And so she was half agonized, half hopeful as she headed to her father's office.

She knocked on her father's office door and he called, "Enter." When she stepped in, she noticed that he had, for once in his life, made an effort at cleaning up.

"Papa! Why, I had no idea your office even had a floor!"

"Very droll," he said. "Take a seat, my dear."

"I hope you didn't tidy on my account," she teased.

"What can I say? Your industriousness has inspired me."

He was teasing right back, but his words stirred up small twinges of guilt. Although she'd unraveled the mystery surrounding Mr. Hurst's death and cleared Mr. Bingley's name, she had disobeyed her father. Her wayward methods had resulted in Abigail's death, and although she didn't speak of it, Lizzie was still haunted by the sight of her body, pulled from the river.

"What's the matter?" her father asked. "You're frowning, and here I was expecting to discuss your achievements."

"That's just it," Lizzie said. "My achievements came at a cost, and I'm wondering if you think it was too great. The case didn't go as I expected, and it's left me questioning if there really is true justice."

"The matter of Wickham, and Miss Jenkins," her father said.

Lizzie nodded. "And not to mention Lady Catherine escaping in the night. I couldn't help but think that if I just hadn't—"

"No, no, my dear," her father said, waving his hand about to get her to stop. He leaned forward. "Do you know why I asked you to find your own case, and to convince me with logic?"

"To prove that I had what it takes to be a good solicitor?" she asked.

"Well, yes. But Lizzie, I already knew you have what it takes." His words warmed her but also took her aback. Then why the challenge? Mr. Bennet continued, "But I needed you to learn that some cases are complicated, and you can't always rewrite the rules to suit your needs. I certainly never expected this case to unfold the way it did, but I'm proud of how you handled it."

"Even though I broke *your* rules?" she asked, feeling as though she were a child waiting for a punishment or scolding.

"Yes," he said. "You have sharp instincts, my dear."

"How can you say that, Papa?" Lizzie asked with a fair amount of bitterness. "I'm clearly easily fooled—Wickham was likely tailing me for the better part of the week and informing Lady Catherine of my progress, and Abigail—"

"My dear, you're not responsible for the actions of evil men. In the moment of confrontation between Wickham and that poor girl, you weren't there. You didn't kill her. Wickham did."

His words brought Lizzie little comfort, even though she knew he was correct. Wickham was a person with his own mind and his own choices—choices that led to his death. "I'll endeavor to take your advice to heart," she told him.

"Good," he said. "Do you feel as though you have learned something from this experience?"

"Oh, yes," she said, embarrassed at the forcefulness of her answer. "Sometimes, I'm ashamed to think of my thoughts and attitudes a fortnight ago. I have instincts, but they've been proven false. I have wits, but they've been sorely tested. I can argue a case, but I wasn't able to argue well enough to prevent

Wickham's death. And . . ." Lizzie thought of the vindication of being proven correct. Of the firm's new business. But oh, the cost.

"What is it, my dear?"

"How can I have thought I was so clever?" she asked her father. "I've misjudged people. I've made mistakes."

"Hush," her father said. "You'll never be able to bring every criminal to justice. You must abandon that notion now, my dear, or it shall drive you mad. But your work has ensured one guilty man's imprisonment and one innocent man's freedom, not to mention you've exposed a very clever scheme. That's more than most of us can hope for. You must hold on to that success."

Lizzie didn't respond, so he added, "Do you think you can take all that you've learned and keep moving forward?"

She lifted her gaze from his desk, not daring to ask.

Her father smiled. "I shall need someone clear-eyed and determined to one day take on this firm."

Lizzie could scarcely breathe. "Papa?"

He looked down at his desk. "Your mother, as much as I love her, is frequently wrong, and she's wrong to keep you from the law. I would be honored to instate you in this firm and train you as a solicitor. And from there, we can discuss how you might become a barrister. I cannot guarantee that you shall ever be called to the bar, or that the magistrates and judges will be accommodating of a woman presenting a case, but you have more than earned a chance to convince others."

Lizzie sat very still, scarcely believing what she was hearing. It was everything that she had wanted . . . a week ago. She wasn't hesitating merely because she still felt guilt ridden over Abigail's death and likely always would feel that pang. It was more than that. The thought of one day ascending the ranks to be a robed barrister who got involved only when a solicitor had done the work and engaged her services . . . well, it was not quite as enticing as she had once believed.

Why had she aspired to be a barrister? Was it simply because it was a high position and Lizzie was nothing if not a high achiever? Or was it because she had dreamed of the credit and the thanks? Well, she had gotten much credit and thanks in the last week, but she didn't deserve all of it—Darcy, her father, Charlotte, Fred, even Mrs. Bennet and Caroline deserved a tiny bit of thanks for their parts in helping her unravel this mystery.

"Have I misunderstood your ambitions, my dear?" her father asked.

"No," Lizzie said, because Mr. Bennet was indeed giving her everything she'd ever asked for. But her mind kept sliding to all of the files in Collins's office, working with Fred, heading out to question witnesses . . .

"I should have known," her father said. "I waited too long. Mr. Darcy has asked you to work for him, hasn't he? Well, I wouldn't blame him. And I wouldn't blame you, either, for taking him up on it. I won't hold you back. I'm very proud of you, Lizzie."

It was the second time Lizzie heard him say those words recently, and it made her tear up. "But Papa, he hasn't. It's just that . . . what if I don't want to become a barrister?"

"You don't want the job?"

"I definitely do! I love this place more than anything in the world. And I want to work—but what if I don't want to become a barrister?"

Her father shook his head. "Don't tell me you've been put off by the idea after your ordeal in court. You handled Weatherford well, and I thought you had rather more mettle than that."

"This has nothing to do with Weatherford, Papa. But the experience with the Bingley case has given me a different perspective of things, I think. I took it on to prove myself, yes, but I kept with it because I sensed an injustice. In my investigations, I found even more instances of injustice beyond the case, and I think I'd be better suited to address them as a solicitor. Not a barrister."

Despite sounding unsure, Lizzie grew more confident in this decision once it had been made. She had so much to learn, and not just from her father or legal texts. From her clients and Charlotte and Fred and maybe, even, from Darcy. But would Mr. Bennet see it that way, or would he say she was indecisive? She waited for his reaction.

Her father absorbed this news and shook his head, chuckling to himself. "My daughters. Always full of surprises. Lizzie, if that's what you want, then I support you."

"Oh, Papa!" Lizzie launched herself out of her seat and hugged him. "Thank you! Then yes, a thousand times yes, I accept."

"Well, very good," he said, patting her back. "For I don't see that there's any reason why a solicitor could not one day take over this firm. After all, you know a very good barrister-in-training. And who knows—perhaps you could coax him to work for you."

Lizzie laughed. "Let's not get ahead of ourselves."

Mr. Bennet just smiled knowingly. "Well, I'm glad you accepted. In fact, I took the liberty of scheduling your first appointment."

Lizzie was not at all surprised to see a familiar figure with dark hair waiting in the empty office next to her father's. He stood when Lizzie entered, and her heart leapt at the sight of Darcy, who bowed slightly. "Hello," she said quietly.

"Lizzie," he said in return, and she was reminded of the warmth of their kiss. For a single moment she let herself imagine kissing him once more, then scrubbed the thought from her mind. This wasn't a social call!

"My father said you've business to discuss?" she asked, struggling to maintain a professional air.

Was that a hint of a smile? "I do," he confirmed.

Lizzie took a seat behind Collins's—no, her—desk. It felt

even better than the time she'd sat behind Darcy's desk and imagined this moment. "Let us see to it, then."

"Very well," he said. "I've just come from a meeting with a friend of my father's."

"Oh?" Lizzie repeated.

"He's an admiral," Darcy explained.

"*Of course* he is."

Darcy gave her a look, but Lizzie let him continue. "Last week I made a point of informing him of Lady Catherine's activities, but you can understand that the navy has more pressing concerns."

"The French," Lizzie agreed.

"Exactly. However, it turns out that the Admiralty has recently become aware of a privateer in league with the French. He didn't inform me how, but three days ago, the navy accosted and boarded a ship. It didn't appear to have a captain, but there was a lady aboard who claimed she'd been kidnapped."

Lizzie's professional air slipped as she became excited. "Lady Catherine?"

"My thought exactly. The admiral asked me to give a description of the lady, and I said I was unable to do so, never having gotten a close look at her. But she'll be returning to London in three days' time. The navy is making a big fuss about escorting her home. I suggested that you be among the welcoming party. If you're able to make a positive identification, she'll be arrested."

"Of course I can!" Lizzie leaned back in her chair, relieved at how this had turned out. Having prestigious connections could be awfully useful. "Thank you."

"You were the one who discovered her to be a criminal—but you're very welcome."

They held each other's gaze, and Lizzie felt the same stirring of emotion she'd had back at the courthouse, just before he'd kissed her. For once, Lizzie did not mind sharing credit with a man, not when he was so eager to give her credit for her own work.

"Come and work for Pemberley and Associates," he said suddenly.

"What?"

Darcy leaned forward, looking eager. "My father has promoted me to junior partner, and I shall begin studying to become a barrister this fall. He's allowed me the chance to hire whomever I want. I want you."

Lizzie couldn't believe that she'd gone from no offers of employment to two in one day! It was a marvel, but she laughed and said, "I'm sorry, but no."

Darcy's expression fell. "May I ask why not?"

"Because someone has already beaten you to it," she said, gesturing at the office they sat in.

"Your father?"

She nodded, pleased. "I know it isn't as fine as Pemberley, and maybe our cases won't be quite as exciting, but my father has already paved the way for women in this line of work by giving Charlotte a job, and I care about Longbourn."

Darcy nodded, and she was relieved to find that he didn't seem upset. "Congratulations, Lizzie. Your father is a smart man. And I hope that we may have reason to consult in the future. On business matters, that is."

She stood, and he followed suit. She held out her hand for him to shake, and feeling his hand in hers made her feel alive and excited, even if the idea of turning down a chance to work with Darcy every day was a little disappointing. "Yes," she agreed. "I'd like that very much."

She enjoyed Darcy's mind for legal matters, and once the proud veil had lifted, she could see his warm and loyal heart beneath his formal exterior. And yet, it wasn't just his legal mind she was interested in. She took a small chance and said, "But must we always see each other only about business matters?"

"I . . . suppose not?" Darcy looked flustered but hopeful. "What do you have in mind?"

"A counteroffer," she said. "Come to dinner. Mr. Bingley is calling this evening—I think he's taken a liking to Jane—and I was reading a text the other night that I'd like your opinion on. Just because we work for competing firms doesn't mean we must stop debating."

Darcy's sly grin made a gradual appearance. "Very well, I accept. Although I'm beginning to suspect you only value me for my legal opinions."

"I value you a great deal," Lizzie countered, and she stepped around the desk to be closer to him. "Your character, your manners, your sense of humor, and your generous nature. I look forward to consulting with you professionally in the future, but your legal opinions may be of the least consequence to me. Although . . . I shall always harbor great affection for your talents in that area."

"And why is that?" Darcy asked softly, closing the distance between them.

"Because," she said, eyes dancing as she drew her lips to his, "they brought us together."

FINIS.

AUTHOR'S NOTE

Readers with a passing interest in Regency-era England will recognize that I've taken a few liberties with what was and wasn't considered proper in this novel. While I tried to stay true to the etiquette and customs of the early nineteenth century, Lizzie's ambitions to become a barrister—or even a solicitor— would have been out of reach in 1813, the year that *Pride and Prejudice* was first published. In fact, the first woman to earn a degree in law in England wouldn't do so until 1878, and it wasn't until 1922 that the first four women successfully passed the Law Society examinations to become solicitors. As a young lady, Lizzie would never have been permitted to work outside of the house, and someone in Charlotte's position as a biracial young woman of social standing would have been limited to the role of lady's companion or governess, if lucky.

Nonetheless, when I set out to write *Pride and Premeditation*, I didn't want Lizzie to be controlled by the limitations of her era or stifled by drawing room etiquette. Inspired by my love of Jane Austen's sly and witty social commentary and Agatha Christie's classic twisting mysteries, I wanted to write a story that envisioned Elizabeth Bennet as a determined and highly capable amateur sleuth with ambition, grit, and a sense of justice—and so I fictionalized some details, while trying to stay true to the societal structures of the time period. Crime in Georgian and Regency-era England was not spoken of in polite society, and there would be no formal police force in London until 1829. As a result, criminals were often brought to court by their accusers, and there were no defense attorneys—for many poor souls, it really was a matter of guilty until proven innocent, and many cases were decided based on imperfect witness testimony. There was also no legal distinction between murder and premeditated murder, although the legal system did distinguish between murder and petty treason. In a society very preoccupied with social standing, murder was what happened when you killed someone who was your social equal or inferior, but petty treason was the betrayal of your social superior, and that "betrayal" was interpreted widely to include murder. You can read about the proceedings of London's Central Criminal Court, known as Old Bailey, at OldBaileyOnline.org, where transcripts of real cases from 1674–1913 are available for perusal. I built much of the novel's plot around court cases found on that website, and the descriptions of Newgate Prison as well as the courtroom scenes are taken from their articles about the history of Old Bailey.

Piracy was a very real threat to British ships in the 1700s, although it was mostly curtailed by the British Navy during

Jane Austen's lifetime. Nonetheless, piracy wasn't unheard of during the early 1800s—and who's to say that an exceptionally clever woman couldn't have found a way to outmaneuver the British Navy?

While most of the historical inaccuracies are intentional, some may be unintentional—in which case, those mistakes are completely my own. I hope Jane doesn't mind that I brought a modern, feminist sensibility to her time period and characters, although I can't possibly imagine what she would have thought about the murders.

ACKNOWLEDGMENTS

Thank you to my wonderful agent, Taylor Martindale Kean. Your excitement for this series has sustained me through the hard writing days, and your support over the years means the world. Thank you also to Stefanie Sanchez Von Borstel for stepping in when needed, and the entire Full Circle Literary team.

I'm so grateful to my editor Claudia Gabel for shepherding me through this process, and for all of the patience and hard work it took to help me polish off this novel. Thank you for your invaluable insight, sharp eye, and for always encouraging me to amp up the romantic tension! Thank you to Stephanie Guerdan for helping to keep me organized, your wonderful suggestions, and offering comments on early drafts that made me laugh. Many thanks to the entire HarperTeen team for helping bring *Pride and Premeditation* to life: Sona Vogel, Jessica Berg, Jess Phoenix, Filip Hodas, and Corina Lupp for such a gorgeous cover! And thanks to all of the people behind the scenes who I've not had the pleasure of interacting with directly who have worked hard to transform this story from a Word document to a real book.

I'd be nowhere without my writing community and dear

friends who keep me sane and inspire me to keep writing. Thank you to Monica Roe for always being ready and willing to read anything and talk through plot points, and thanks to Nora Shalaway Carpenter and Anna Drury Secino for a text chain full of entertaining GIFs and pep talks. Thank you to Kristin Sandoval, who is always enthusiastic and full of great advice. I'm so grateful to the entire Vermont College of Fine Arts MFA community, particularly my Craftographers, who made me feel like a real writer for the first time and who are some of the best people around. Thank you also to the 21ders debut group—it's a privilege to be on this journey with you.

Thank you to all the wonderful libraries and bookstores who connect books with readers! I'm so lucky to have worked with Miriam Andrus, Chris Cook, and Emalie Schuberg—and I'm glad my library family was present when I got the news that *Pride and Premeditation* would be published. Thanks to Jenny Kinne at Books & Mortar for your early support and excitement, and mountains of gratitude ought to be heaped upon my fellow Book Rioters for all they do to support me and books everywhere.

Thank you to my amazing family, especially my parents, who didn't seem overly concerned when I announced that I wanted to be a writer, and told me that if anyone could make it happen, it would be me. Thank you to my partner, Tab, who keeps me fed and watered and always makes sure my laptop is plugged in. You're simply the best.

And most importantly—thank you to Jane Austen for writing six wonderful novels that have brought so many people such enjoyment for over two hundred years. I'm sorry about all the murders.